To Barbara

Best wishes

Phil Turner

Aug '00

I AM
General Eaton

by
Philip Turner

ISBN #0-934745-26-9

Bar Harbor, Maine

To my in-laws, Julia and Louis Morse, whose money helped finance the production of this book, and their daughter, my wife of over fifty years, who aimed her arrows at my grammar and removed nearly all errors.

Books by Philip Turner

Affie,
A Story about the Aroostook Federation of Farmers.

Rooster, The Story of Aroostook County.

First John, King of the Mountain.

Dear Reader,

The 1950 movie *Tripoli* had so many obvious errors that I told Phil Turner to tell his story as close to the truth as humanly possible. I think he has done so, in this book about the first American hero to raise the Stars and Stripes over a captured foreign city. We all recognize that the absolute truth is known only by God, and we mortals must be prepared to accept man's best intentions. Although William H. Eaton was a well educated man, he made some errors in English grammar, as we all do in today's world.

Sincerely,
Winfred J. Martin,
President, 1994 -95
Caribou Historical Society
Caribou, Maine 04736

P.S. I should tell you that Phil Turner lives on a part of the Eaton Grant, which may explain why he wrote this different and interesting look at the man Eaton.

Acknowledgements

Many public and university librarians all over the United States were very helpful in my finding needed facts, as were persons in then-Senator William Cohen's office. My wife, Jean, and Avis Armstrong provide helpful criticism. Town record-keepers and librarians of Brimfield, Mass., Woodstock, Conn., and Sturbridge, Mass. took time to answer questions.

The front cover was designed and painted by my niece Lisa Turner of Seattle, Washington. Since 1983 she has had many exhibitions and her paintings hang in Europe as well as the U.S.

Gracious thanks go to the Brimfield Library for the use of the original photographs of the Eaton house and the General's gravestone, as well as the photo of the young Eaton.

The back cover painting of the *U.S.S Argus* is by Winfred J. Martin, a local teacher of art and a former President of the Caribou Historical Society. He also painted the cover for my previous book, F*irst John, King of the Mountain.*

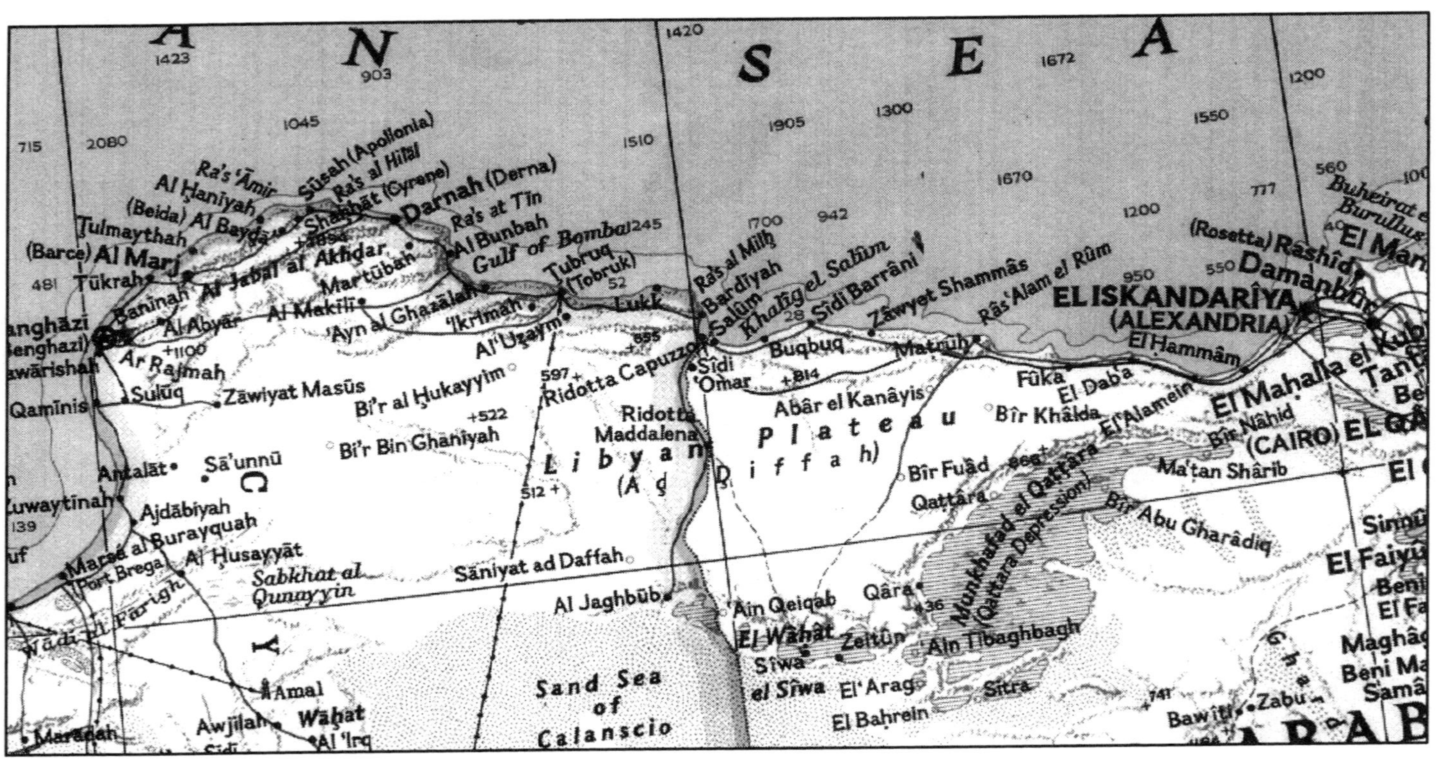

A
N
S
E
A
C
Y
EL ISKANDARÎYA
(ALEXANDRIA)
(Rosetta) Râshîd
Damanhûr
El Ḥammâm
El Daba
Fûka
Bîr Khâlda
El 'Alamein
Ra's 'Alam el Rûm
Zâwyet Shammâs
Sîdi Barrâni
El Sallûm
Bugbuq
Sîdi 'Omar
Abâr el Kanâyis
Plateau
(Diffah)
Bîr Fuâd
Qattâra
Munkhafad el Qaṭṭâra
(Qattara Depression)
Bîr Abu Gharâdiq
Ma'ṭan Shârib
'Aîn Tîbaghbagh
Sitra
Qâra
'Aîn Qeiqab
El Wâḥât
Sîwa
el Sîwa
El 'Arag
El Bahrein
Zeitûn
Bawîti
El Faiyûm
(CAIRO)
El Maḥalla el Kubra
Ra's al Milḥ
Bardîyah
Ridotta Capuzzo
Ridotta Maddalena
Libyan
Al Jaghbūb
Sand Sea of Calanscio
Ṣāniyat ad Daffah
Tubruq
(Tobruk)
Gulf of Bomba
Al Bunbah
Darnah (Derna)
Ra's at Tīn
Ra's al Hilal
Sūsah (Apollonia)
Shaḥḥāt (Cyrene)
Al Jabal al Akhdar
Marṭūbah
Al Makīlī
Ayn al Ghazālah
'Ikrimah
Al 'Udaym
Bi'r al Ḥukayyim
Bi'r Bin Ghanīyah
Zāwiyat Masūs
Ra's 'Āmir
Al Hanīyah
Al Bayḍā
(Beida)
Al Marj
(Barce)
Tulmaythah
Tūkrah
Al Abyār
Ar Rajmah
Sulūq
Qamīnis
Sā'unnū
Antalāt
Ajdābiyah
Al Ḥuṣayyāt
Buraygah
Sabkhat al Qunayyin
Marsá al Brega
Awjilah
Amal
Wāḥāt
Al 'Irq
Zuwaytinah
Marādah
Benghazi

In 1805, General William Eaton pushed his makeshift army, without a guide, through the trackless desert from Alexandria to Derne (Darnah on these maps), where they engaged in a short ferocious battle with the forces of the Dey of Tripoli. Eaton's men emerged victorious, and hoisted the American flag for the first time over a captured foreign city.

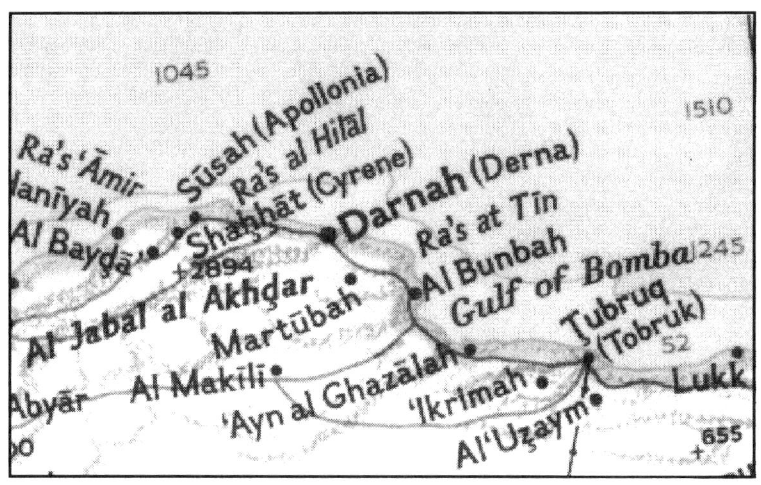

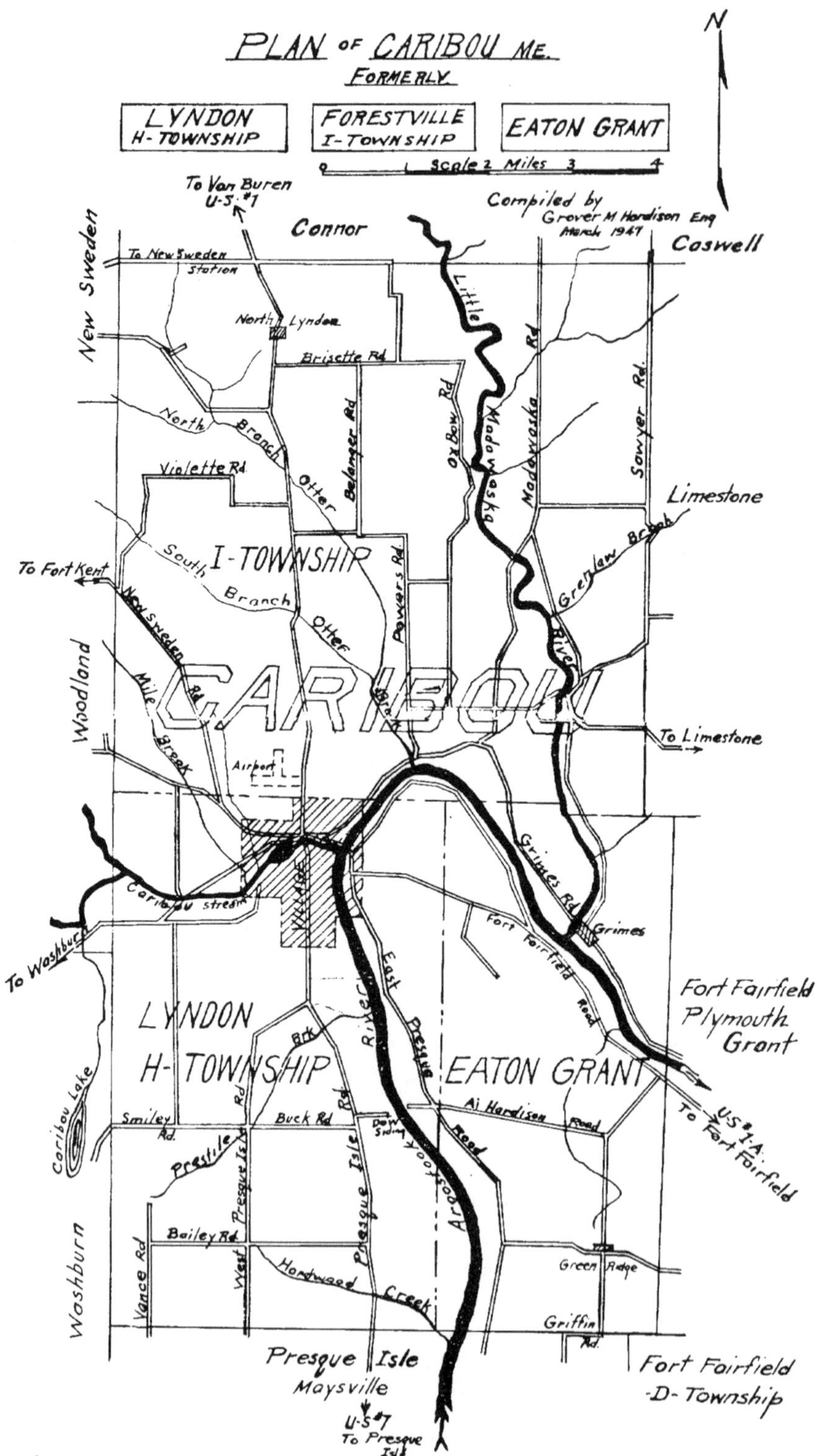
PLAN OF CARIBOU ME.
FORMERLY
LYNDON
H-TOWNSHIP
FORESTVILLE
I-TOWNSHIP
EATON GRANT
Scale 2 Miles
Compiled by
Grover M Hardison Eng
March 1947
N
To Van Buren
U.S. #1
Connor
Caswell
New Sweden
To New Sweden Station
North Lyndon
Brisette Rd
Little Madawaska River
Madawaska Rd
Sawyer Rd
Ox Bow Rd
Belanger Rd
North Branch Otter
Violette Rd
Limestone
Greenlaw Brook
I-TOWNSHIP
To Fort Kent
South Branch Otter
Powers Rd
New Sweden Rd
Woodland
Mile Creek
CARIBOU
To Limestone
Airport
Caribou stream
Grimes Rd
Grimes
Fort Fairfield Road
To Washburn
East Presque Road
Fort Fairfield
Plymouth
Grant
LYNDON
H-TOWNSHIP
Brk
EATON GRANT
Aroostook River
Caribou Lake
Smiley Rd.
Buck Rd
Dow Siding
Ai Hardison Road
U.S. #1-A
To Fort Fairfield
Prestile
West Presque Isle Rd
Presque Isle Rd
Bailey Rd
Vance Rd
Washburn
Hardwood Creek
Green Ridge
Griffin Rd.
Presque Isle
Maysville
U.S. #1
To Presque Isle
Fort Fairfield
-D-Township

Introduction

General William Eaton was a real military hero and in some ways larger than life. In the Barbary Wars of the early nineteenth century his exploits rivalled those of Lawrence of Arabia. He literally fought his way onto the world stage, only to be later discarded.

Nearly all the characters in this novel can be found in Eaton's biography, *The Life of the Late General Eaton,* and other historical sources. Most of the events depicted actually occurred; the dialogue and the setting of the story-telling at the Bunch of Grapes tavern are entirely my inventions. *I Am...General Eaton* is as truthful, and faithful to the historical record, as a novel can be written so long after the events.

The impetus for the writing of this book arose from the title search for my Caribou, Maine property, which is on a portion of the original Eaton Land Grant. In 1806, General Eaton was given a large tract of land in the Province of Maine, before it became a state, while it was still claimed by Massachusetts. The grant was a reward for his service to his country in the Barbary Wars. The Eaton and Plymouth grants involving Maine were both deeded on the same day by the Massachusetts Courts. That body gave away northern land then claimed by King George III — he was not consulted.

I included a brief episode about Eaton's journey to view his ten thousand acres in my previous book, *Rooster, The Story of Aroostook County*. I was finally motivated to search for the Barbary Truth by an old movie with Errol Flynn and Dorothy Lamore that told the Barbary story. Soon my friends were suggesting places that might help with the project. Then I was given *The Life of the Late General Eaton*, and became hooked. Visits to his birthplace in Woodstock, Connecticut, and to his hometown of Brimfield, Massachusetts soon led to research at many libraries in several states. The result you hold in your hands.

I hope you enjoy reading about the exploits of General William Eaton.

Phil Turner
Caribou, Maine

Inception

James placed the Flip on the table and said,

"I'm sorry to interrupt you, General. This drink is on the house if I kin hear the rest of that story y're tellin' my good reg'lar customers."

"Make a place for the owner, men!" and Eaton took a sip as he continued the tale.

"Well ...as I was sayin', I smelled, looked, and acted like an Arab on my white and black stallion, so when I entered Derne* through its outer gate, no one challenged me. So ... I took a slow tour of that city, notin' how their guns were placed and where the weak points might be. I did stop at the bazaar to test my lingua and haggle over a present for my step-son.

"I found the city was divided into three parts, two neighborhoods for the lawful ruler of Tripoli, Hamet, and one powerful section dominated by a bloody usurper.

"The next mornin' — I remember it was the 26th of April, 1805, I sent a flag of truce to the unlawful Governor with terms of amity. That same Governor had offered several thousands of dollars for my head. So when his laconic answer came, I laughed, for it said, 'My head or yours!' And, men, it sure wasn't my head. Now bring me another glass of that very well made Flip, Proprietor Vila."

As James Vila went to get a second drink for General Eaton, he mused, 'What if I could strike a deal with this story teller to entertain my regular patrons here at the Bunch of Grapes? Why just think! I'd have a lot more customers during the winter months, and my pockets would be filled with silver...'

*Present day Dernah in Libya.

William Eaton as a young man.
Courtesy of the Brimfield Public Library from the National Archives.

"Good evening and salutations, and please conduct me to my table. Bring a pitcher of your well-made Flip to soothe my vocal cords, for I am going to instruct my entourage in what made Eaton the General Eaton of the Barbary War. General Eaton is my title by my own works, for I led an army that planted the American flag over a city of Barbary. I shall often refer to myself as General Eaton, for so I am. I AM GENERAL WILLIAM EATON."

"Now, Mr. Vila, be quick, for this November weather is much like the Province of Maine, and I am in need of something to warm my cockles."

James Vila had recognized a good thing when he had overheard Eaton entertaining a few friends with stories of his adventures, and so he had sent a letter to Eaton asking if he would come and tell his tales at the Bunch of Grapes at the head of Boston's Long Wharf. He had also made a small bonus for the General by saying that he could eat at half price, but the liquor would remain at full price.

Eaton had responded by coming early the next morning to the tavern. Upon entering he had asked, "May I talk to the person who is in charge of your kitchen, Mr. Vila?"

"My wife is charge of cookin' and you ken."

The room was a large one and already smelled of the day's food in preparation. His nose picked out the smell of sage, thyme, onions and mace. Mutton was on the table along with some anchovies. Eaton surveyed the maids and the older Mrs. Vila busily cutting and cleaning the raw vegetables and meats. Vila spoke,

"Verna, my love, General Eaton."

"Good day, Mrs. Vila and will you take a moment to talk to me about cooking ... food that your husband has offered me for telling my life story to his many loyal customers?"

"I can spare a few minutes, Sir. Let's go into the eatin' area." Verna said as she escorted Eaton out of the kitchen.

After Eaton had spent some time with Mrs. Vila discussing the fine art of converting raw meats and vegetables into something that made your taste buds wish for more, Eaton left. As he was walking to his residence at 16 Ann Street, Eaton noticed the leaves falling from hardwood trees, and his mind raced back to his early youth when victuals were eaten only to satiate one's hunger. Mother had put on her table plain fare, and when he was in Ohio, it was Indian sustenance. Too much, then too little, with no thought to make it enjoyable. That had been his encounter with food until that lucky day he had recovered from seasickness on the coastal trip down to Georgia. That food had been served in three or four courses, each with its own wine. All of which had made one wish the eating could continue and continue.

Walking and musing, he found himself on Queen Street. When he noticed the publishing house of Eads and Gill, he remembered that during his last evening at the Adams' supper table he had heard about the publishing of Susannah Carter's book on cooking. Eaton stopped and bought *The Frugal Housewife* and had sent it off to Mrs. Vila.

When he returned to the Bunch of Grapes, General Eaton continued his narrative.

"Former members of our illustrious Continentals and even some from the Junior Service, you naval swabs. I will start at the beginning ...I am going to tell you about my early childhood. I was born in the State of Connecticut. It was cold that night in Woodstock when I arrived on the 23rd of February, 1764. My father had served as a Captain in the French and Indian Wars. Ottawas and Algonquins. Captain Nathan Eaton was a respected man, and I always looked up to him, as did his friends. They all took off their hats when they came into his house. One of my first memories of my father is when he caught my older brother Calvin and I (Me! Yes, and how many of today's Ph.D.s make similar mistakes?) stomping on ants that were devouring an old stump. It seems that he had heard one of us use the word pissermire. Don't laugh, but dear old father was in shock. God! he called us out with a sharp tongue lashing. He said, 'Now boys, the word you intended to use is pismire p-i-s-m-i-r-e, but a better one would be ant, a-n-t. And when you boys go to Harvard, they will tell you that these insects belong in the Formicidea family and are Monomorium minimum, that's the correct Latin name.' Then he ended by quoting the Bible at us...First Corinthians Chapter 13: verse 11...'When I was a child, I spake as a child. I understood as a child, I thought as a child: but when I became a man, I put away childish things.' Now, all my life I kept that saying of the Apostle Paul's in mind.

"On with the childhood of General Eaton, your entertainer and groit. Ah! yes, your very own story teller. My father moved our family many times. He was always in need of a teaching position to supplement our home grown food, always looking for a higher paying post. I had sisters older and younger who mended our well worn clothing and also an older brother Calvin who worked on local farms for some of our sustenance. Sometimes he brought home hard money, and that went for property and poll taxes. Hard money was a wanting item in New England at that time.

"I was an avid student, memorizing quickly. As I remember, I had completely mastered John Milton's *Paradise Lost* by the time I was seven. I have always had a good memory. I never let books, which I always have with me, gather dust. Father encouraged me in this learning. Mother, bless her, was usually more distant; she cooked and washed for the ten of us Eatons and was the last to bed. That might be said to have been her means of not having an increase in the family too soon."

Pausing to refill his glass, Eaton shouted, "Waiter, my God! This pitcher of Flip is dry. Please double the rum and bring also a bottle of good Madeira."

After he had sipped and wet his vocal cords, General Eaton continued, "I was addicted to Shakespeare and also had learned my Greek and Roman philosophy by very early manhood. I had become a confirmed Congregationalist and knew my Scriptures in completeness. I was instructed by some very fine scholars who were the religious leaders in whatever hamlet my father had found a well paying position. Ah, some of them were ...The Rev. James Cogswell , Yale...The Rev Samuel Nott, also Yale...and The Rev. Moses Welch, all from Yale divinity .

"Now I'll tell you about my first enlistment in the Continental Army. Yes, that's when I really was a soldier, not a general, but an eager young whippersnapper who knew he could win the war for General Washington. At the time I had reached my adult height of five feet nine inches, not so tall as General George but enough to see over the heads of my fellow patriots. I was then, as I was later in life, fully expecting that I would become a great hero, a man who commanded respect from his fellow travelers. Now let's get back to the War for Independence."

Eaton took a long draught from the mug of Flip. "Well, I'm sure of this because my memory is clear as a bell. Very dependable. It was in 1774 that Father moved to Mansfield, Connecticut and bought a fair sized farm . Yes...it was seventy-four, and he got the position of Head Master at the Academy with its financial rewards. Mansfield was a town of strong minded patriots. King George and that damnable Lord North would not have received many hurrahs in that town.

"Later when I was going on twelve, I was fully ready to take up arms for the Rights of Englishmen. Now Paul Revere had spread all over the state that our rights as loyal Englishmen was being removed from us by Lord North. Father kept me in check, but by the time news came to us about Bunker Hill and General Gage's atrocities on it—we, Dad and I, had already had a little disagreement about what college I would be going to—I for Yale but Father was for Harvard. So-o-o, that night with a full moon in the offing I borrowed —no took— my brother's musket and put a few eats and other necessities in a blanket and left for New Haven. I was going to join the militia but a fast talking recruiter for the Continentals needed to fill his quota. We trained in New Haven in our civilian clothes and nearly froze. God, now thinking back on it, it was almost like when I lived in that cold northern Province of Maine. When General Howe came down from Canada and landed in New York, I was put in Captain Reuben Marcy's company. It was part of Colonel John Chester's Regiment in the 6th Battalion. They were all part of General Jeremiah Wadsworth's Brigade.

It was quite a long march to New York, and before we got settled in camp at Flatbush we got routed. I think it was 'cause our own General Putnam was misled. It wasn't long before the whole British army was through the Jamaica pass and in our rear. So it was back to White Plains, and there we were beaten again. It was bitter cold, and I got a bad case of the ague. Captain Marcy said it was best for me to head home, so with discharge paper and no money I started. My head ached, my body was awash with sweat, but I remembered, 'Be a man,' from father's lecture . Soon I found some work in New Haven and saved a little. When I had what I thought was enough to see me home, I started for Mansfield. Then I got the damned ague again. This time I was in the country, not in a city, and I found a generous farmer who took me in and cared for me. Mr. Appleby had kindness in his heart and a daughter who was cut out of the same cloth—Sophie, a dear, dear little girl who stirred my young blood.

Colonel Pat Patrick, retired and an old comrade-in-arms, who was sitting at the General's table, interjected, "Now, General, you aren't going to tell us that this dear, dear little girl seduced YOU... the young innocent soldier?"

The veteran Continentals, who had had more than one refill of their mugs, all stopped their subdued chatter and listened. Every eye in the room turned on the General.

"I must say," the General said in a somewhat sarcastic tone, "that these fellow members of the fallen and forgotten heroes are most attentive whenever a story includes a female. Now, Pat, you know because you have heard this part of my lifetime again and again. If the patrons of this public house will be civilized, I will endeavor to tell the true love story of a smitten William Eaton when he was nursed back to health by the lovely, loved Sophie Appleby."

The crowd of listeners turned and faced the General with the knowledge that he would not leave out many of the better details , for most of them had been entertained by him previously. But tonight he was more poetic than graphic. His consumption from the bottle had been considerably curtailed.

The General continued, "Now she had blue eyes and long golden hair and a perfect visage. She was the finest model of feminine daintiness in all of the thirteen colonies. The care she gave this poor sick boy was just short of heaven. She bathed me; she washed my clothes; she fed me; and I was smitten. And even though I was indebted to that kind man, I fondled his daughter Sophie, and she became more free with her hands in washing me. As the weeks passed we dallied in the meadows, and, yes, we did what you are all thinking. Apple trees were in bloom when I deflowered my lovely Sophie. *'Le parfum aromatique des fleurs de pommier.'* I found that to be my aphrodisiac for the rest of my life. Later I wrote her letter after poetic letter from then on until.... Why, I may have sent her letters nearly all my life . Well I didn't send one today, but I might day after tomorrow.

"Yes, and years later she wrote me when she was married to some local pumpkin...no, bumpkin. Yes, he was a foolish dirt FARMER! Even so, I did stop to see the family a few times on my way from Washington to Brimfield. I would have married dear Sophie, but it was not to be.

"Patrick, have them bring us some of that supper I can smell and another bottle of Madeira. Now, as I recall, Solomon had words of love in his Song of Solomon, like this;

' O that you would kiss me with kisses of your mouth!
For your love is better than wine
your anointing oils are fragrant,
your name is Sophie poured out
therefore I love you.'

"And as Shakespeare said in *As You Like It,* my dear Sophie would have said these lines to me if she had had the burning — no...no...Learning! Now tongue, do it right!

'Come woo me, woo me;
for now I am in holyday humor,
and like enough to consent.'

"I think that's in the Fourth Act. And dear Sophie I did woo, but I became well. And she did consent. Where was I now - Yes , that is in the Fourth Act." Eaton had had enough to drink to make him a bit befuddled but he continued, "and Sophie I did woo, but I became well. Fourth act and now... I lost that paradise which brings to mind *Paradise Lost* by the Great Milton. It goes like this, 'Of man's First Disobedience, and the Fruit. Of that forbidden tree, whose mortal taste'... but who wants more of that?

"Now where was I in that life of mine?... Oh yes , I was leaving dear, dear Sophie for my home. I didn't stay long because my patriotic zeal swelled again, and I left after I had asked my father's help in enlisting in a better unit of the Continental Army. I'll tell that story at another sitting, for I can see that your eyes are glazed and your minds asleep.

Some of you did that changing of armies without so much as a by their leave, didn't you...?"

After eating, the General continued with his monologue, "I wrote poems of my devotion to lovely Sophie, the fair maid, for many years. I wonder how she fares? Better, I hope, than this unappreciated General of the Barbary Wars. God, my legs hurt from the frosting they got on that northern river called Aroostook. I always did like the warm climes. Even the desert without water is my preference.

"Now let's have one more serving of that very good Flip, and then I shall off to my lonely bed to be lulled by the god Morpheus. Waiter, I'll sign the bill for this night's entertainment."

As James Vila, owner, came and presented his bill, the General complained, "God, my leg still hurts from the cold of that winter I spent on the River Aroostook . . . Good night, to all."

Eaton stood and limped out of the King Street ale house for a weary and lonely walk to his less than elegant accommodations on Ann Street. The hangers-on felt no sympathy, for he had a bed, many of them did not.

That very night a tall, well-constructed man in his late years had been eating and drinking from his own purse. He had paid close attention to the groit telling his life story. Beauregard Smart, in his mind, verified Eaton's story and promised himself he would be present at all the recitations General Eaton would give to his hangers-on and that, if need be, he would set the record straight after the General had retired from the tavern.

When Eaton and Vila had picked the days that Eaton would entertain the patrons, Vila agreed to send broadsheets to the streets of Boston. These advertisements carried the news of General Eaton's story telling at The Bunch of Grapes. The starting time was to be just after eventide. Later broadsheets would give dates of further recitation.

Eaton was ready, and as we enter the Bunch of Grapes, we see the General standing in full spotless uniform, boots polished, not a hair out of place, and all his many medals tinkling and gleaming over his heart. The Barbary hero had begun the evening's tale. "... Now the next time Father was generous; he gave me some hard money, his own rifle, and a letter to a General Waterbury. Father had served under both Generals Waterbury and Danielson, and he had taught me the manual of arms. That's when I learned how important it is to have a sponsor. From then on I always found me some important man to help me on my way to fame and glory. A mentor. Yes, for even then I knew that I would make my mark in this world. It was during this time that I made a commitment not to drink much fermented spirits, if any alcohol, for I had seen the bad effects it had on much of the populace.

"I'm going to tell you how much a letter of introduction helped. With this letter to a commanding general of the Continentals and because many old soldiers were being let out and I was young and very aggressive, I soon got moved up to the rank of Sergeant Major. Captain Dana helped me on the way. Now when I look back ... I did have a lot of learning to do, and I was very much interested in helping General Washington beat the British.

Yet, I was one of the many who were left behind when General Washington moved the war to Yorktown and beat Lord Cornwallis. Captain Dana had taken sick, and thus we stayed in camp until he recovered. That's how it was done then!

"After Yorktown my duty was on the shore in Connecticut facing Long Island. This is where I acquired most of my military learning. I was nineteen when I left the Continentals in the spring of 1783 with some paper money in my pocket.

"Honorably discharged, I started for Mansfield, but first I had to see that fairest visage with the shiniest blonde curls. My blue-eyed Sophie, the very epitome of feminine daintiness, was calling me, in my dreams, to head for the Appleby's place. I wanted to tell my dear, dear Sophie that I was going to start making something of myself by attending college — any college. I told her, dear lovely Sophie, to wait for me 'cause I'd be back, and we would be married. I was sure I was to have dear Sophie for my life's mate.

The General broke off to address the proprietor. "Oh! Mr. Vila , would you tell your waiter to bring my meal with two bottles of your best Madeira." Then he went on.

"If I had been a little older, I might have won her, but, as I remember, I said, 'Now I don't want to be a learned professor nor a sober-sided minister, but I am looking to find some honorable profession from which we both can live a happy and comfortable life.' I said, 'Sophie, I don't need to be rich but I don't want to be always in need.'

"I was sure never to be as poor as my hard working father. No, I expected to be rich enough to never be in need. I should have wooed her to the altar or have swept her up in my arms and dashed to the nearest minister at that moment."

"On that visit lovely Sophie and I surely had many a good time in her father's orchard and haymow. It was spring and apples were in bloom. Yes , in full petal, when I retasted her fruit. And to tell the truth, a quick wedding could have happened. I wish now that pregnancy had taken place from our many romps but, as you all know, didn't. I can remember it all so dearly ... and clearly. But she married a real stupid dirt farmer... a pumpkin or surely a bumpkin, and my dear Sophie seldom answered my letters that I sent to her over the years. On this visit I kept her from the many suitors who where always pestering my lovely dear Sophie.

"Patrick, tell Mr. Vila to send in the forgotten food. I've had all the Flip I need. I am hoping to drink a couple bottles of Madeira if that waiter ever brings them. It will help my digestion of that lamb stew they are serving. I know it's lamb 'cause I can smell it, and I'm sure it will suit my palate better than some of the meat I et on the way to Derne. Thanks, Patrick."

"I'll tell this fine assemblage, as we eat and drink, about the few years I spent at that great college of learning, Dartmouth. Paper money they did not take, so I did tutoring while at the institution, and I even had to take time out to go teach in the local towns. Now I was a very good student and I studied. A very pleasing waitress, the red hot Sally St. Eam, was my only taste of life outside the walls of Dartmouth—yes, I'm sure that was her name. And she was good to taste and romp with. But never as good as my Sophie, Sophie of dreams and youth. She didn't often answer my many letters.

"Sally, the waitress, did what she could to help me forget that deep, deep wound in my heart put there by Sophie, who must have been forced into that union by her old scheming father. As often as she could, that waitress made trips into my bed, but my melancholy never, never left me.

"Patrick, will you seek out another bottle? I think they are cheating us, for these two bottles held about what one did a few years back.

"The story continues with my graduation in 1790, with honors, from Dartmouth. That was when John Wheelock, the son, was President of the university. As I have told you, I was an easy learner.

"We studied Guthrie's geography, Millot's history, read Locke's *Essay on the Human Understanding* and William Enfield's *History of Philosophy*. My great joy was in my complete mastery of both Latin and Greek, and I memorized Dr. Lowth's English book. I was in love with languages. Yes, I speak several quite well. Yes.

"I nearly forgot about an important episode of my life. I was not a diarist then, that came later in my life. The other day Israel Hatch met me on the street and asked me to come have the evening meal at the Sign of the Turk. It's on Newbury street next to Doctor Lamuel Hayward's home. Hatch owns the tavern, so I accepted. When I arrived a man of about my age was the waiter, and it wasn't long before I had the distinct feeling that we had met before. When he had brought me the second bottle of Madeira, I asked him, 'Have we met before ?'

"The waiter was dressed as a Turk and spoke in a Turkish accent. Then when he addressed me in his own voice, I knew him in a flash. He was Kaladi Wahab, my first teacher of Arabic when I was a Sergeant way back in the eighties. Now I'm going to tell you hangers-on his story, but first I'll have another Flip with a little extra rum, if you please, waiter! Kaladi, a name you'll not easily forget, had a strange story to tell me. We met one night in a tavern in New Haven. He came to my table and started to tell this story after I had bought him a draught of beer."

"Kaladi said," Eaton took on the Arab's accent and persona to tell the story. " 'I was born on the shore of the inland sea that you call the Mediterranean. My mother be English woman who was captured by the Sultan's ships. She was sold to my father, and I am the results of their union. My mother, she was one of my father's wives. Before I grew to a man, I was put aboard one of the Sultan's warships. When some gentlemens came from General Washington's army to buy some of our horses, I got a chance to go with them; it was known that I spoke English. I was a stablehand and was seasick on that long trip with very bad food. A big big wind came up, and the ship she hit a pile of sand, and the horses and men all fell into the raging sea. Big waves, big like the side of tall house. I was very good swimmer, so I swim to my favorite horse and together, we and a few other men and horses come to land. It was long way south in place called by you Cape Hatteras. It's too long a story, but we did make our way north with the saved horses, and we end up in New York City just when General Washington was leavin'.

'I knew some English my mother had secretly taught me. My English improves, and I survive by workin' very hard for any American who will let me work. Now, kind sir, if you buy me a small food, I will make your fondest wish come true.'

"I bought him a meal, and with that I asked him to teach me his language —my fondest wish. And so over the next few years we met, and I would buy him his evening meal and then spend the rest of the evening learning to read and speak Arabic. We had found some books in New Haven at the start of this experience. I wish now that I had started earlier with my diary.

"You can imagine my surprise upon meeting him at the Sign of the Turk, and I'm sure that I'll go back to see him in the days to come." Eaton rose from his seat and put on his hat saying,

"Now the food's gone, and I think I'll be finding my way back to my lodgings. So a hearty good night to all. I'm on my way. "

The elderly Mr. Smart, in his well-worn-thin coat, had been at the far side of the fire that night and had a touch of sore throat. He found Eaton's story to be close to the unvarnished truth.

A rare December thunder storm pelted Boston as the wet General Eaton rode his dappled grey Arabian horse into the stable behind the Bunch of Grapes. Mr. Vila met him at the door and, taking the General's outer coat, seated him in his accustomed place. A Flip ordered, Eaton surveyed the audience and said, "That downpour will wash and clean the streets of Boston. They might smell as good as Brimfield's with another rain of the same quantity. As I recall, I was starting to tell you about Dartmouth when the Kaladi story came to the forefront. Yes, it was true that some of my fellow students who did not measure up were rusticated, sent home in disgrace. Then I began seeking what I should now do to earn fame and some fortune, for I knew I was to become a person of substance. Yes and so... fortune smiled. It was the right time in the flow of history ....

"While visiting my sister, I found the Great State of Vermont was forming. But it first had to break from New Hampshire, New York, and Massachusetts and become The Green Mountain Commonwealth. I knew from the news that Governor Chittenden had denied the right of the U.S. Congress to interfere with the Liberty and Independence of Vermont and was dead opposed to its being divided up by other states, and these states were the common enemy.

I was made acquainted with the fact that in February 1780 Ira Allen and Stephen Bradley had been selected to go to Philadelphia as delegates to Congress. Congress had rejected them. I saw right away the possibilities.

"I bought a very good riding horse and made my way to the action. When I reached Windsor, Vermont, I discovered the capital had moved from Windsor to Bennington. So while in Windsor I stopped at a tannery and had my leather pants dyed green plus my hat, the horse and my frock, my saddle, my boots, and my hat...ALL GREEN. Even some of my light brown hair around my cap was green, from the sweat streaming down my fair ruddy face, by the time we got west to Bennington on that difficult road which became the Windham Turnpike.

"Pour me a drink, Pat, outa that bottle. I think they have sent a proper sized one, finally.

"Now back to the past, heroes. You all can draw that picture when I spurred my lathered horse up and down the streets of Bennington. Just as I do here in Boston when I've a mind to. In Bennington the populace went wild with cheering —"

Someone in the back of the room shouted, "They don't cheer him in Boston no more." Some recalled the Boston coppers tussling with the General when he had galloped his big Arabian stallion into a crowd at the market.

Eaton continued without pause, "— and soon I was talking to the most important man in town...SENATOR Stephen Bradley. He was a direct descendant of William Bradley, the first settler in New Haven, Connecticut. A great man and still my good friend. The Senator came out of his house and asked me to join him on his stoop.

"After we were acquainted he sent me to the best tavern for accommodation, the Catamount. I was delighted with their food, and they made Flip to perfection. It was October 1791 when I was appointed head clerk of the House of Delegates of Vermont, thanks to my patron Senator Bradley.

"My spectacular work there led to my appointment as head of all the pen and ink bureaucrats for The Green Mountain Commonwealth. That was a new learning. I was very busy and was very much absorbed in my work. Now when Vermont was admitted to the Union, the same advocator, the Senator, got me my Captaincy in March of 1792. I thanked him."

"General , Sir, may I speak?" A dark haired young man in a corporal's coat interrupted Eaton.

"Yes, Corporal ,you may."

"I was there the day ya rode inta town. You told it aright, and what a sight it were. I wuz only a boy then, and I never got to meet ya 'til we had that little tussle with them Indians down South. I was your corporal in that fight. 'Member that, General? "

"Yes, I do remember. You were in the South when I had that command. Send him the last of the bottle, Patrick, and then you might clear a path, for your General is in need. Flip and Madeira coming through." Eaton leaves and returns to his table.

"There! That's taken care of. I think... next ... I am going to tell you about the two year campaign against those treacherous and blood thirsty savages, the Miami tribe. Brigadier General Anthony Wayne had replaced that incompetent St. Clair. Wayne was the one who had raised the 4th Pennsylvania Battalion in '76. General Wayne and I got along without any major hitches, and that's saying quite a bit. As most every one knows, the General had a temper as big as all outdooors. Yes he did.

"Well... I suppose it's time to say that I married Eliza Sikes Danielson, daughter of Benjamin Sikes and widow of General Tim Danielson — a family friend — on the 21st of August ' 92 at Brimfield. She was twenty-four and I was in my twenty-seventh year. I blame this marriage on my brother Calvin who was living in Brimfield at the time. I visited him and there was Eliza, tall, handsome and ready for another trip to the altar. I thought she was very rich and that I had found my relief from hardscrabble. It was then I started to keep a diary. A little about our first night in General Danielson's bed ...she was no Sophie. It took me an hour just to get down to her skin. Eliza had enough night clothes on to keep her warm at the North Pole. No, warm even on that northern river called Aroostook away up in the Province of Maine. Yet she was cold and unresponsive. This unsuccessful first time to the General's bed was after I had spent three days in July taking the first three degrees of Freemasonry, and before going to the Miami Slaughterhouse. I took my leave of Eliza fifteen days into our marriage and I was glad to depart. Yes indeed, she had money but also a very sharp and untiring tongue."

"Before I tell about fighting the Miamis, I need to tell you about a little altercation I had on March 17th in '93. Now to be sure I got it right, I read my journal last night about this affair with Captain Butler.

"It was a Sunday in Springfield, and the Adjutant had ordered a General Review. Because of the deficiency of field officers —the high ranking ones had taken a leave to be with their wives— I was put in charge of the left column of the army. In the going to and fro of our maneuvers and after we had come to the point of having our troops return to their original positions, the Adjutant gave his orders to do so, and I so instructed my columns. Captain Butler countered my orders. I then gave my troops the right order for them to carry out the Adjutant's command. Butler again countered my commands and came on horseback towards me with his lifted sword. I met him with my "espontoon" raised (*a half-pike which served as a means of identifying an officer as well as a method of signaling troops*). We had a few hot words until General Wayne intervened and ordered the march to continue. I promptly obeyed. That evening I wrote the Captain a challenge as follows ; 'Sir,' I said, 'I am to understand... and am to be understood by Captain Butler.' And I signed it, Eaton. Now to all you uninformed, these words are those used to invite your adversary to a duel. Butler wrote me back a letter that in effect said he had company that prevented him from honoring me with a duel, but perhaps they, and possibly I, would take the opportunity of a general explanation in the presence of our gentlemen on Wayne's staff who had been in command, with the understanding that if this explanation proved not satisfactory I could name the place and have the duel.

"So the staff gentlemen met and, after questioning us, asked Butler and I to retire. When, after some time, they requested that we return, the spokesman said, 'The referees, to determine the difference between Captains Butler and Eaton, are of the opinion that however wrong Captain Eaton was, in the first instance, Captain Butler was equally if not more so in the second.... So it is incumbent on both to come forward and bury the matter in oblivion, by again renewing their former friendship.' We both gave our hand to each other. Butler never was a friend and I was glad to leave him.

"Leave? Yes, it's time I return to my quarters. My friend Aletti is expecting to go visit with his latest woman who may convert this bachelor to husband."

When the room had cleared of most of the patrons, the loquacious Mr. B. Smart was saying, for his clothes had not totally dried, "Yes Sir, we troopers all thought we were in for a real fancy duel between those two hot heads, Captin' Butler and Captin' Eaton ...."

Mr. Vila came into common room because the hands on the clock pointed to closure and cried,

"Time! Time!"

Late that December it was snowing — as it should be — in Boston. Winter was on its frosty way. Men with old worn clothing sought out taverns. The Bunch of Grapes offered companionship and warmth.

"With the Legion's (the name used for the U.S. Army at this time) battalions of New England I marched to Fort Pitt after my company had spent some time at Philadelphia, the nation's capital. I did find this most enjoyable." Eaton's voice was fully in the command mode, and he was standing tall in his over decorated General's uniform. All the lost and forgotten heroes' eyes and ears were on him.

"I was very attentive to the men who were at our seat of government. I especially favored Secretary of War Knox and the members of Congress. I knew it pays to have friends in high places.

"I early on took an interest in Lieutenant William Henry Harrison, General Wayne's aide-de-camp, who became helpful in my many nightly visits to General Wayne's evening meal. Harrison was a man that had the bearings of greatness.

"When we arrived at the savages' territory (in present day Ohio), General Wayne had us build several strong forts — one of which he called Fort Recovery. After we got them all to his liking, I got bored sitting around waiting for the red men to attack. I had learned the Miami tongue from a former scout, and so I suggested to General Wayne, as we were eating together one evening, that I be sent out to scout the Miamis. We were carrying on our conversation in the Miami tongue. He said it was not right to send a novice out to do a job at which even a well trained scout might not succeed and might very well get captured, tortured, and then killed. The General said, after taking a good draught of whisky, 'No , not you, tenderfoot.'

" Well, the next night I asked him again, and the next, and the next until he said, 'Damn it, Eaton, if you want to get yourself killed, why go! But write the letter that I will have to send to your wife on your demise.'

"I left the very next morning in old Indian clothes which some legionnaire had worn while building the Fort Recovery in order to save his uniform. Now this next part of the story never got into the official record."

Looking up, Eaton spotted a waiter and said, "Bring me another portion of that boiled beef, will you? Thanks." And continued without missing a word,

"I thought that the land was some of the best I had ever seen, and as I made my way along a well marked path, I came upon an abandoned Indian camp. While I was studying it and also looking for anything that might help me in the task I had set before myself, I discovered a nearly destroyed hut. As I got closer, out came a sobbing sound. It was emanating from the pile of rubble, and it was definitely a female sound . I rushed over, and, to my surprise, I uncovered a badly injured, yet very attractive, young squaw. I tried my Miami tongue and she responded. I recognized that she could be the means of finding out the tribe's intentions. I fed and nursed her, and soon we were able to travel. She took me to several of their encampments where I had the good fortune to be accepted as a Miami. I stayed with her for nearly a month and then made my way back to Fort Recovery with knowledge that astounded General Wayne. Oh yes! As I approached the fort, a damn Legionnaire sentry mistook me for a real Indian and fired one shot at me. Missed me, Thank God. But I informed the legionnaire he need to do some real practice before we started shooting red Indians.

"When General Wayne took out after those Miamis, I was ordered to stay at the Fort. Try as I might, I couldn't change the General's mind to let me be one of his scouts. But as you all know, it turned out just dandy.

"The Miami scouts watched General Wayne leave Fort Recovery with a large company of men. So in a very short time a thousand red warriors or more came at the Fort in wave after wave. First they wounded the...what's his name ....the Major on the initial attack, and I had him carried to a safe place. Then I organized the defense. The savages soon used flaming arrows, but we had water aplenty, for I had foreseen this, and we, therefore, put out all the small blazes as fast as they started. One of the reasons the savages didn't overwhelm us was that I had given firm instructions to hold the firing until it was certain to kill a red Indian. As each bunch of savages charged our line, we piled their dead bodies up at the base of the Fort. When the next wave of red skinned devils came screaming at us, I kept on confusing them with wrong signals in their native tongue. The super marksmanship of the Legionnaires and my deception finally caused those bloodthirsty Miamis to give up and run. They ran from the field with hair-raising yells. Then all my valiant Legionnaires stood upon the ramparts and cheered.

"Bring me an ale, will you? My voice box is starting to dry out." Eaton directed at a retreating waiter.

"Now you all know that General Wayne was quick to bring those savages to the peace table, and then he made sure that I got the medals and credit I truly deserved.

"My tour of duty in the West ended, and I was sent to New York City where I continued my career by finding important people to help me on my way to fame and fortune. Always my father's words, 'Be a man,' rang in my ears. While there I did write a few letters to dear lovely Sophie and had one in return. One to the wife also. I think I brought Sophie's letter, so I could read it to you fellow travelers tonight." Eaton pulled a well worn paper from his old journal and read the following letter as it was written;

" 'Mr. William Eaton.' She always addressed me thus. 'Papa sayes it will be a warm summer. I have gone for maney walkes, with my dog. A vistor who is a freind of Papa and Mama is now sleeping in the room that you sleeped in whilst you was here. I am Sir, your obt servant Sofie Appleby. '

"And, God, just now, I felt my heart twinge for that fair maid that I was so, so much in love with and who, despite my most earnest entreaties, married a stupid, no-good bumpkin farmer. Or was it lumpkin...? No... pumpkin. How I would enjoy a night like we had those many years ago. The smell of the apple blossoms comes to me now. Oh yes! Le parfum aromatique des fleurs de pommier, my aphrodisiac. God! its sensual. It's exquisite! I'm back in her arms. Forget these damn females of this modern age who have only the desire to lighten your pockets.

"Waiter, bring on the coffee while I go relieve myself of the Flip. I'll continue this narrative day after tomorrow. For I'll be at the Red String tomorrow. "

Leaving, General Eaton paid his night's bill to the owner, James Vila, while complaining of the pain the Aroostook winter had dealt his legs. Vila had heard that several times. Still, James got the date and time agreed to for the next broadsheet. Vila was pleased with the silver flowing into his purse on the nights that Eaton came to his Tavern and entertained.

In the cab taking Eaton to Ann Street he said to himself as he was jostled by the wheels running over the cobblestone, "Words said pass away. If I want to be a real man to those who come after me, why I'll have to put words about my life in a book that will be held in the best libraries of the world. Yes, I must look to organizing my journal and all those letters that fill three valises. Time I got started. I 'll start tonight. Yes, as soon as I get there I'll ask Aletti to get the pen and ink ready for my hand."

Back at the common room Mr. Beauregard Smart had been still about as long as he could, for he knew the husband and father of Sophie. As soon as the General's backside was out the tavern door, he started.

"Now I'll tell you all that husband of Sophie's was no downtrodden farmer. I myself saw that when he came into Hartford with the best looking coach and four you ever laid eyes on. Yes sir, he was loaded with money, and people said he owned mills and just acres and acres of land. Of course Eaton never met him. Now he's acting like any guy that lost his best girl to a better man. Yes sir...." Some of the men continued their drinking as another groit took up his story telling.

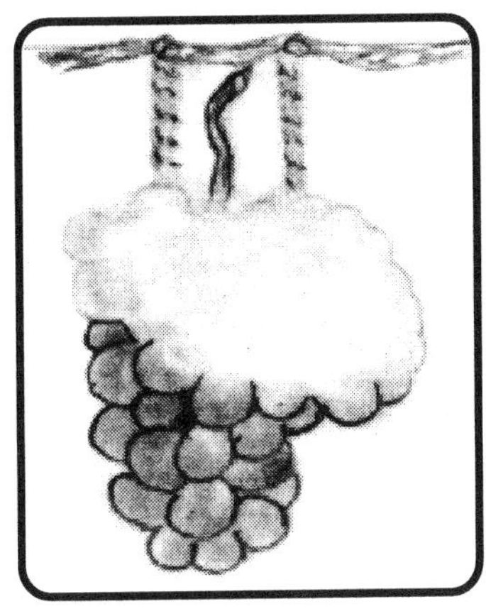

The General came into Boston's State Street late this cold night after a rather long, enervating (years ago it might have been more invigorating) visit at a better than average house of ill repute. Thus he was slightly less exuberant than usual. Pat Patrick had to help him to his table at the Bunch of Grapes, and the General did not respond to the waiting patrons until his plate was empty. Then, when the crowd of expectant listeners had filled all the available spaces, the General finished his drinking from a large mug of warmed rum and started the night's memoirs.

"Gentleman, and ladies, if there are any present, for last night as I remember I did say to a bevy of very pretty ladies that if they wished they might join me at my ashram here at this old tavern at the head of the Long Wharf. I just might be able to see some lovely faces if these lamps had been properly cleaned. Seeing none, I will continue my story of the Life of General William H. Eaton of Barbary fame if not of fortune. After the Ohio adventure came a journey to Georgia. But first, I spent a month visiting all the important people at Philadelphia and New York. I really enjoyed meeting with Secretary of State Timothy Pickering and others in his department. It was at many balls and parties that I was treated as a hero in the defense of

Fort Recovery and our victory at the battle of Fallen Timbers. I was thinking about my wife and that it was time I visited with her at Brimfield, so I packed my belongings and took the stage home. I was greeted without a kiss, and endured nights much like our first. Eliza's contentious unholy welcome at Brimfield caused me to ask Army headquarters in Boston for a quick posting to active duty.

"For the next few weeks I spent only weekends with my dear sour-puss Eliza. I went to Brimfield only because my stepson Eli was my pride and joy. Soon Eli and I were living together at the Springfield army camp. Orders came on the 16th of December 1794, and I left for the south just as soon as I had Eli properly installed at Dartmouth College. Eliza was opposed, but I paid the bill and so Eli was suitably educated. My company had already gone to Georgia, and I was to take command of them under Colonel Henry B. Gaither, who was soon to be my nemesis.

"I traveled toward Mansfield, Connecticut, visiting relatives along the way. I spent a few days at Woodstock with my sister who had married Major Amos Paine. I tarried in New Haven with the expectancy that dear Sophie and her dolt of a husband might invite me for a visit, for I had written her that I was going to stay at the Whale Tavern a few days in December. No letter came!

"In the capital I had very profitable visits with both the War Department and State. And some of the young females found that my time in their beds was quite zestful. Yet I still had a craving for that blonde-haired, blue-eyed dear Sophie. How quickly I would have responded to her slightest beck. Yes, just to feast on her heavenly countenance." Eaton sighed.

"And I had time to visit several book shops in Philadelphia where I purchased many Arabic books. I planned to expand my fluency in both verbal and written word while I was to be in the deep south. I had read the Koran and the

History of the Ottoman Empire in Fort Recovery. I now started planning the how of a visit to the lands of the Ottomans. It was Kismet for me to be in the Arabic region. The fate of God.

"The Creek Indians were threatening us, and the Spaniards in Florida were looking north with greedy eyes. And the very sly British secret agents were subsidizing the local war parties. My going to Georgia was serendipitous and at the time both *douceur* and sour, that is, *tournet au vinaigre,* to maintain my parallelism. Sweet, in that Georgia was made for this hero to become heroic. Sour, as my stomach found the seasickness. My first sea trip, and My God! I thought I would never take another. However, the coastal trip to Savannah was over too soon, for I did recover from *le mal de mer* and made *une decouverte* of the uncommonly good food. It was comfortably salubrious. Food that I found better than any of Boston's best eating places. Except here at Mr. Vila's, of course.

"On disembarking, I soon was introduced to the most *environs terribles* in all the states. Although it was a very poor area, a few rich gentry asked we Army officers to dine, Thank God! For the officers' mess was *affreux.* The people of Savannah were the friendliest I have ever met. They took us in and I was invited to all the best homes. My monthly pay of $42 was soon being saved. It was a social whirl, and I was the center piece.

"My commander, Colonel Gaither, a damned friend of my old nemesis, General Wilkinson, (you will hear more of them later in this story) sent us to St. Mary village near the Florida border to build a fort. We had work to do in preventing those agents of Spain and England from crossing into our country. Then I had to do it all over again since Gaither converted the first fort into a trading post. I built the next fort out of all that was available, mud and grass, on the edge of the St. Mary river. As soon as it was built, I started to scout the Creeks. This was better than staying at "the Monument of Mud," my name for the eleven-foot-high fort. The river water was muddy and so were all our uniforms. Yet on visiting the Creek people, mud and all, I was taken into the tribe as a blood brother. Seeing my need of a woman's care, they gave me a chief's daughter, Flower Eyes. Yes! A chief's. Well, I took Flower Eyes back to the fort, and she was very helpful in my controlling her tribe. I taught her English, and I learned Creek each night in her bed. For all the two years time I was in that area, no settler was molested by the Creek Indians. The Georgia legislative body voted me a prize of $500. I claim all of the credit for this inaction by the war-like Creeks.

"Now those few French words I've sprinkled in my tale are just left over from my very recent encounter with the most delectable French whore in all Boston - Desirée. I think I learned a few new ways from that one. She had fresh apple blossoms on the table to greet me. Ah... and it worked! To honor my Desirée, waiter, bring me a bottle of your very best French wine. It will also remind me of the food on the coastal ship *Doodilian.* The sweet part of this tour of duty was that I got into land speculation. George Washington did it, as well as most everyone with a little money. This venture of $200 yielded me in a few weeks just over sixty thousand dollars which I put into three separate banks. One of the bankers was William Phillips here on Beacon Street. The sour part was a court martial by Colonel Gaither in absente reo. His charge against me was that I was not working full time for the army. Who did for that pay? The fool! He had lost in a land deal doing the same as I had, buying in the hopes of selling at a big profit. I wrote his Honor, Secretary of State, Timothy Pickering, informing him I had named the fort in his honor and about the details of my argument with Gaither. I was never allowed to defend myself on Gaither's trumped up charges of mismanagement of my time. Gaither was sore because he had been in the land speculation game, and whereas I had won, he had lost his profit and as well as his first investment .

"The court-martial review board in Philadelphia reversed the findings of the 3rd Infantry Regiment on December 2,1796. My pay, honor and rank were restored. And best of all they rebuked Colonel Gaither. Gaither was now stuck at the Colonel's rank, and I was not going to receive any promotion from that enemy! So with the good news and seeing no future in the Army, I resigned! Those of you who want to hear the rest of this chronicle will be here — the broadsheet has — Pat, see if you can find one and tell this fine audience the date. Now I go and refresh myself with a visit to the head." (Because Eaton had been on so many naval ships crossing the seas he had put 'head' in his vocabulary for the word toilet.)

Eaton rode home in a cab and upon entering the house on 16 Ann Street he asked Aletti to bring him his ink and pen. *The Life Story of General William H. Eaton* had started to flow onto paper.

Back in the tavern Mr. Smart had taken Eaton's table and was telling about a few military men he knew who had done the forbidden act of speculating in frontier land. He informed the slowly dwindling crowd that he had once accumulated a fortune, but his very next buy had seen it blown away.

"**As I was telling you** all some evenings ago, from Georgia I took the fastest land travel available, the rented post horses. When I arrived on February 15, 1797 in Philadelphia, I was told, 'You will remain in the army for another six months. We have just changed the rules.'

"So what to do?

"I always carried a trunk of books with me and had been studying the Koran, and the Mohammedan lands. It was my intention to perfect my Arabic and visit or live in that land of the Ottomans. So continuing with those studies took up some of my time. I had new fashionable uniforms and civilian clothes made which would mark me a well groomed gentleman. Soon I got invited to revisit several accommodating ladies who had invited me to their beds at no out-of-pocket-money.

"I was still in the pay of the government and did as I was accustomed. I visited all my friends in high places which resulted in Pickering—yes, he did remember the Fort naming— at State asking the War Department for my services. I must say that most of the high government officials knew of my great service to the army in both Ohio and Georgia. While wasting a little time from my study of the Barbary problem, I had the urge to write to Sophie, so I composed and posted her this little line of words.

" 'To Sophie, my passion overflows for you who makes my yearning to mount into heavenly ecstasy.' I wrote and posted these lines of affection and love. Yes, and a few more to the love of my life, my dearest Sophie. Then in poetic form:

'Love is too young to know what conscience is,
Yet who knows not conscience is born of love ,
Then gentle cheater urge not my amiss,
Least guilty of my faults thy sweet self prove.
For thou betraying me, I do betray
My nobler part to my gross body's treason,
My soul doth tell my body that he may
Triumph in love, flesh stays no farther reason,
But rising at thy name doth point out thee,
As his triumphant prize, proud of this pride,
He is contented thy poor drudge to be
To stand in thy affairs, fall by thy side.
No want of conscience hold it that I call,
Her love, for whose dear love I rise and fall.'

"I recall that clearly. I wonder what Sophie made of it, she who had wounded me so deeply. Ah poetry! I wish thou had dwelt within me.

The heroes, forgotten and others, saw that the General was greatly affected by his remembrance of Sophie. After a short silence he took up his narrative.

"Secretary of State Pickering had a problem that needed to be handled in a most delicate manner. You all remember, I'm sure, that soon after we defeated old George the Third, France, England, and Spain had full intentions of grabbing some of our southern and western lands. They had secret agents, and Pickering knew the leader, a vile Dr. Romayne in New York City. Knowing my prodigious skill along these lines, the Secretary gave me a sizeable retainer to expose the dastardly intentions of this international cabal.

"Patrick, will you have them bring a small *morceau á manger* to me from the kitchen and another mug of ale?"

... and the story resumed.

"This Doctor Nicholas Romayne was a very prudent man and always covered his espionage work very carefully. I met him in New York. I put on my worst old faded clothes and rang the bell at the residence of the nefarious Doctor. I showed him the findings of Colonel Gaither's board. I also told him that I had lost all my profits in land speculation and the army had treated me very improperly. Then I said, 'Doctor Romayne, the Army court-martialed me in absentia and I want just revenge.' Then I turned my pockets inside out to show him that I was in need of some money. I said to him, 'I know the location of all the forts, their strength, and their plans for defense.' He gave me some money, and I found a cheap inn near Fort George at the lower end of Manhattan. God, was it a mean place, full of the ubiquitous bed bug and other vermin. I had to play this game for over a week, sleeping and eating in the manner of the damned.

"We both played the game for longer than Pickering wished, but fate would have it that Dr. Romayne went to a dinner party at the British embassy where he found it convenient to bring up Eaton's name. The brigadier general who was on our War Department's staff informed him that Eaton had been dismissed from the service and that the case was too painful for the general to discuss it any further.

"In a few days the Charge d'Affaires of the British legation, Dr. Nicholas Romayne, sent word for me to visit him at his clean and well appointed apartment at the British House. After having had a bit to eat, I informed him I had spent all of his money and needed some substance before we talked. I said to the foul Romayne, 'Sir, the Spanish legate has offered me a thousand dollars in gold for my information. I've never liked the Spanish, but for that kind of money and in my present situation I would and could tell him all the details of U.S. troop dispositions, locations of forts and their plans of defense. What do YOU offer, Sir? '

"He responded by matching the concocted proposition of the Spanish. Then I asked him to show me the money. When he opened his strongbox, I pulled out my pistol, and, whipping off my outer rags to show my Captaincy uniform, I arrested him. In his now open strong box I found papers which would show him to be a spy.

"With the help of a Captain John Gibbes and Sergeants Fox and Hill from Fort George, I had him taken to Philadelphia and placed in front of the Secretary of State with the secret papers I had taken. Quickly two French and two British military attachés took ship and left our fair country. And good riddance. Congressional members passed the word about me so that the new President of our great country had work for me soon after his inauguration on the 4th of March 1797.

"This President was Mr. John Adams whom I now have the pleasure to dine with. He gave me my next employment. As you all know we were under threat of war by both the British and the French. We were a young nation and without a suitable navy, so their warships were making the most of it.

"The presidential assignment had to wait. I needed to go Brimfield, for Eli was to be graduated from Dartmouth, and I wanted him to be with me on my next adventure. A very short joyless stay in Brimfield was offset by great happiness in seeing my grown son Eli, who looked like his illustrious father and carried himself in a military manner reminiscent of his father. Eli was a chip off the old block. Just like his father General Danielson. I knew that I would be exceedingly proud of him when I introduced him to all my friends at New York and Philadelphia — a praiseworthy son that fathers are proud of. He is in the Navy now.

"I think I'd better save the rest of this episode for another evening, for I am exhausted and need sleep.

"My dear Patrick, please be so kind as to see that I am returned into my servant Aletti's hands. A cab would suit me on this cold evening for the ride to Number Sixteen on Ann Street where cousin Joseph has rented me suitable accommodation.

"Patrick, will you tell the proprietor and the dear listeners that I shall return as Vila's advertisement says, at the same time to continue my story?" Eaton requested as he stepped heavily up into the cab with the help of Pat's strong right arm. Patrick quietly shut the door of the hack and returned to the tavern to tell the owner the General would keep his agreement and return to the Bunch of Grapes on the evening agreed upon.

"I was in a tavern with both Fox and Hill, and they said they was greeted like heroes when they turned that sneak spy Doctor over to the law. Yes Sir! Now they said..., "Our long-tongued Mr. Smart was spinning his tale to the crowd of noisy tipplers. The clock had not yet reached the hour when Mr. Vila would say in a loud commanding voice,

"Time, Gentlemen, Time!"

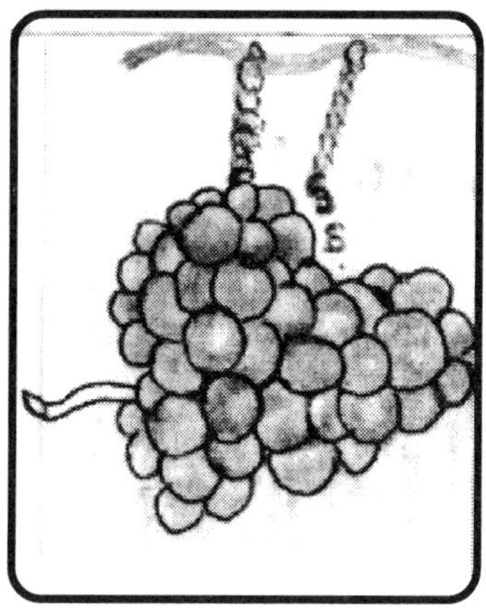

"**My God, man**! Look where you put down my soup! My journal nearly took a bath and would have been none the better for it. Now off to the kitchen and bring a new serving and be quick about it. Gentleman and dear friends, the beginning of my Barbary lesson will have to wait until I have satisfied my hunger and thirst. Patrick! I was better served in the deserts of Barbary. If this February weather keeps on its present course, we will have a very late spring ...."

The General continued his carping to all and to no one in particular. He and Pat Patrick ate in relative silence, for Pat knew this mood; he had encountered it many time in their long friendship. Best be still and Eaton would recover from his dark and unfathomable depression. They slowly spooned the soup followed by a main course of cod and boiled potatoes. Then finished with hot cakes smothered in honey. They both drank long draughts of their favorite wine throughout the meal. Then the lesson began.

"I should have given this talk first, but then, the composition of my audience kept changing. Now we seem to have wearied some of those who care not for the story I am relating. I hope not to be too long in the telling but rather to keep this short and yet include some insight into the Barbary. It all started with Mohammedan and his Jihad being answered by the Crusades. We Christians all know that story pretty well, so I will start with the Moslems' conquest of the Iberian peninsula. This began around 700 A.D. and lasted into the 1400s when Ferdinand and Isabella finished off the Kingdom of Granada, liberating hundreds of slaves. Yet this did not result in the total triumph of the Cross over the Crescent. No, the Berber inhabitants of the northern coast of Africa had a region suitable, in both terrain and prevailing winds, to the role of piracy. The wind and shore and even the shape and depth of their harbors were in their favor. From the Straits of Gibraltar to the shores of Tripoli the area abounded in sheltered small harbors seemingly made by Allah for those bloodthirsty scoundrels.

"The population was once made up of Phoenicians, Romans, Byzantines, and the local Berbers. Now, over time that population was improved upon by the many slaves who left their Christian faith and married into the local tribes. They all pursued ships in the Mediterranean and even raided as far as the coast of Iceland. They also had a go at all the natives of the many islands in their inland sea. Ransom was the main game, but they also sought more knowledge of ship building, cannonading, navigating, and many other western skills.

"Two of the most notorious of these pirates were the Barbarossa Khair al-Din and Dragut. Just for example, when Dragut raided the Gulf of Naples, he took so many prisoners that although their ships, the xebec and galliots, were full and over flowing, there still was a great number left on the shore. He, Dragut, ordered up a white flag, and the pirates invited the families and friends of the captives to ransom them forthwith. Some were, but some were not and were taken to work in the vineyards of Arab noblemen. Moslems, even with their strict rule against alcohol, had discovered the money-making potential of good wine.

"There are so many good stories about the endless captures and escapes that I hardly know which one to relate. I have read and been told about six or seven hundred tales. The most interesting adventures I wrote in my journal, but tonight I'll tell only two from that writing. The first is about John Fox of Woodbridge, Suffolk, England.

"Most of the attempts at mass escapes ended in failure. Failure usually resulted in the ring leader's being put to death. The methods were nefarious and intended to be as cruel as possible. Death by having wild asses pull you apart, death by slowly being roasted alive, death by having small bits of flesh slowly hacked from your body, death by being thrown to wild lions or dogs or being pushed off the parapet onto the sharpened stakes under the walls of the palace. Plus many, many more such diabolical means of killing so painful that there was, at various times in some of the black holes, a slave who would, if paid his fee, dispatch the victim by thrusting a long knife into his back.

"John Fox did not fail. John was a barber sold into Egypt. For fourteen long years in Alexandria he was a faithful and humble slave. He gave his various masters no reason to doubt his acquiescence to his lot in life. Yet all the while John was planning. He met a Spanish tavern keeper who had been a slave most of his life. In time John found him to be trustworthy and took him into his confidence. Foxy John procured files, and with these he and other trusted slaves made weapons. One night they executed John's plan and killed their head guard and all his subordinates. That former slave was a turncoat, so John felt a sin had not been perpetrated. They captured a galley and left the port under fire, reaching Crete after twenty-eight days and the loss of only eight men. Two hundred and fifty-eight men walked down the gang plank with hurrahs for John's courage and fortitude. The Dominican monks gave them all, and especially Fox, a hero's welcome. Fox gave the monks the very sword with which he had cut off the keeper's head. I saw it hanging in their monastery. The Pope at Rome gave him a Letter of Commendation when he received Fox very graciously. The King of Spain also offered him various honoraria, and finally he returned home to his much missed England. I find no achievement like his in all of the many escapes from Barbary. You see, that group of freed people had eleven different nationalities. A very remarkable feat.

"This next recital is about the adventures of Cervantes, the author of the Don Quixote stories. Miguel de Cervantes and his brother Rodrigo were captured on their homeward journey to Spain from Rome in the year 1575. Might I put to rest your doubts about my ability to remember so much about the Barbary peoples? I have read Baithwaite, Brooks, Busnot, D'Aranda, Navarro, Grammont, Haedo, Mouette, and many more. These pirates they wrote about have been and are even today a scourge of the sea. Cervantes was their prisoner. Miguel had no intentions of remaining a slave of those infidels. In the middle of the African winter he hired a Moorish guide to lead him to Oran, which was then held by the Spaniards. The guide deserted him, so without food or water Cervantes had to return to his master. Because he was a strong slave, the master put him in heavy fetters and had him more closely confined.

"Rodrigo and some high ranking Spaniards were ransomed in 1577 and .... Father Haedo says that Cervantes had enough courage, industry, and stratagems for the subjugation of all Algiers. Rodrigo's plan collapsed ...."

The endless drone of the General's story was not heard by most ears, because many of the loyal listeners had had a few too many to catch the full flow of words that came in a torrent from his lips.

"... a more modest plan by Cervantes....The Dey executed all .... Only Cervantes spared.... Cervantes considered valuable person...2,000 strokes ...bastinado....alive and planning his next attempt.....again placed below ground and securely shackled....

"Miguel concocted many escape schemes which came to naught, but often resulted in stricter imprisonment and beatings.

"My God! I've run on and on, and I'm dry as a cork leg. Waiter! Be quick and see that I have a fresh bottle of Madeira. As soon as I finish this Cervantes story, I'm off to my abode, so bring the charges now." Eaton was in the writing mood and wanted to return to pen and paper.

"Well, fate finally did free this Spanish story teller. The Moroccans had a great victory at Alcazarquivir, resulting in a large number of Spanish captives. The law of supply and demand resulted in the ransom price per captive becoming very small. Cervantes' friends and relatives sent the Dey's price, and Miguel was free to return to Spain to write for posterity. Thank God!" Eaton rose from his table.

"Adios, my dear faithful audience. That is all for this tale until another night."

The old gentleman with the unusual name of Beauregard Smart had eaten a frugal supper and beer. As he listened to the General's stories, sleep overcame him from the night's food and the warmth of the large glowing fire. When the raconteur caused a ruckus on leaving, B. Smart awoke and thought about that night's subject and then, considering his lack of knowledge in that field, left the tavern.

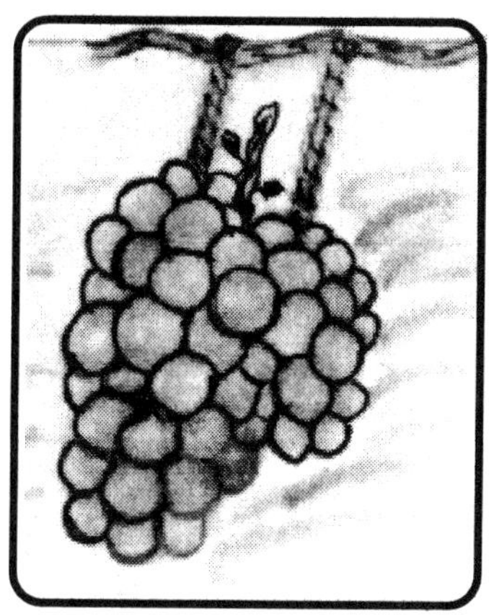

He was at home without an audience. Aletti was there to bring him his meals and other wants and necessities. The General was sick with a fever, aches, and a nose that would not stop running. In his bed and out, he didn't have enough energy to work on his *Life of General William Eaton.*

He mused, "Publishers, ah... the biggest...Yes, that's Isaiah Thomas. He's got a paper mill, a bookbindery, newspapers, and even the book stores. He could make my *Life* a great testament for the conqueror of Barbary. It would assure my place in history. Then there is Benjamin Franklin in Philadelphia — that's too far away at present. Yes, now there is Hugh Gaines, but I've never liked his books. It could be that the best procedure would be to find a good printing house.

"I'll have to be sure to save enough of the next money I receive from Maine. I should have more than enough if my solicitor is telling me the correct story. Maine, that was a dream. I thought a place like Knox built would have left the world knowing who General Eaton was. But that's not to be, so I must finish this book that will leave my honor and glory for all to see. I wonder if William Bently, that Unitarian, is still reading and translating Arabic. I should go visit with him. I'm sure he would be here in Boston if he's still alive. He was a great friend of Thomas Jefferson and sometimes a friend to me. He was my equal as a linguist. He did Chinese — I never did.

"Bently had a banquet, and I was there just after my return from Barbary. What food he put on the table and the drinks, mugs of hot flip, crackling roast piglets, cured hams, venison, and baked salmon. Glass after glass of that favorite of mine, Madeira wine. Fruits and nuts to mingle with the words flinging out of everyone's mouth to the enjoyment of all. Then too, we had tobacco but I never found smoking to my liking. I preferred a small candy with cinnamon and clove. You were more frequently kissed by fair maidens with that odor on your breath." Eaton paused in his remembrance to ask his servant,

"Aletti, do we have any cinnamon and cloves?"

"I'll go see. " Aletti said. Returning, he said that he had found the spices.

"Then will you make me a very hot drink with Madeira and a pinch of each of those spices? I think it might make this cold more agreeable."

The General, after he had finished the mug of wine, started a letter to his son Eli. Finally, he asked Aletti to fix the fire, crawled into his bed where he slept and dreamed the dreams of once again riding his black and white stallion into that nest of Barbary pirates. He was swinging his scimitar at many turbaned heads when he hit his arm. He awoke with a howl which caused Aletti to come running.

"Damn bed post! I've done it again, Aletti. I've hit the post with my arm, and every time I do, it always seems to be right where that Arabic bullet tore into and ruined my arm. Maybe we should wrap the damn post in a blanket to keep me from bashing my old war wound. What do you say to that?"

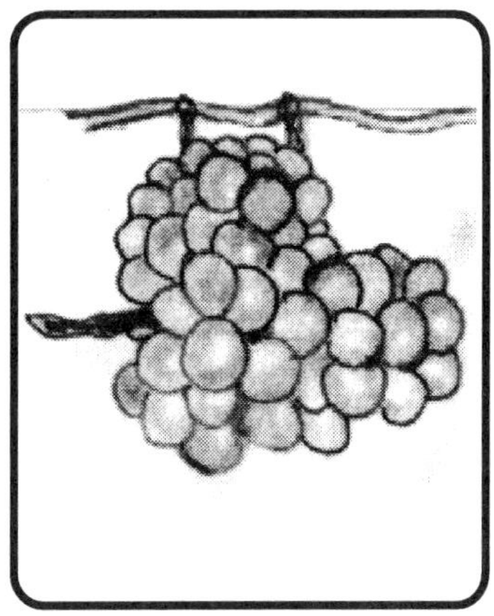

"**The memory of that great man** has never left my conscious mind. In all my travels he has been within my heart, that great Savior of our country. Washington was our leader. In this year of our Lord, one thousand eight hundred and nine on this eventide of February twenty-second here in the city of Boston at The Bunch of Grapes (pause for breath), all of you stand and be silent as we raise a glass of this good Madeira wine to our lips in honor of his birthday, and reverence for our President's memory." General Eaton commanded as he proudly stood in his immaculate, tailored, and slightly garish uniform. And they all, from all her wars, stood and saluted the most honored man of their new nation.

The General then gave them leave to sit and said,

"I was in the Barbary when I heard about the passing of our President Washington, so I took pen in hand and wrote this eulogy. I'll not burden you with all of it but just some of the most salient parts. " Clearing his throat he began reciting,

" 'Washington's Reception in Elysium

It was a glad morn when great Jove announced,
Our glorious Washington arrives today.
A thousand suns, to grace the arch of heaven,

Were lighted into lustre on the occasion;
And stars, that twinkled throughout the beams of day,
Were ranged to add a brilliance to the grandeur.
A barge, constructed of the deals of life,
Manned by eight heroes' spirits; ancient half,
Half modern; David, Israel's royal warrior;
Cyrus the Persian Conqueror; Philip's son;
And Rome's first Emperor, mighty Julius Caesar;
Alfred the Great; Louis the boast of France;
Peter the Czar, and Prusssia's deathless Frederick;
Drake at the helm; bore him across the Styx'

"And now I'll leave out some of my poetical elegance for if you need more you will find it printed in the wasted corner of the leading newspaper in the city of Philadelphia. I'll finish my expression of the man as soon as the waiter brings us another round of Washington's favorite drink, Madeira, that same wine he served most generously."

"Ah, I've never tasted better, and it does make my voice box more ready to praise the honored man. So to the poem—

'Weep not, Columbia, that thy Son and Soldier,
Ascends to glory unalloyed, eternal
Wouldst thou confine a soul like his to earth,
Where black ingratitude and envy reign
In half the hearts of men? Perhaps he still
Remains thy Guardian Genius and thy Friend,
Most sure I am heaven can bestow no gift,
No honors grant, confer no dignity,
So grateful half as this; reward so ample
For all his toils and virtues as a man,
And sure I am, there's no competitor,
In heaven or earth that can with him contest
the claim to this distinction and deposit.
Weep not, Columbia, WASHINGTON is still
Thy Guardian Genius thy immortal Guide.'

"From that writing you can plainly see I read Washington's '96 address to the citizens of the United States in full. I say it should be read in our holy places, and it should be bound about our necks and printed on our hearts. Amen!"

In the silence that followed the General's soliloquy, only the noise of the kitchen workers was heard. Then as the conversations started around each table, the deeply felt reverence seeped from the room, and the familiar mixture of men's voices in repartee overcame the tavern. After the General had eaten his meal, he stood and again commanded their attention.

"I never served with that great man, but I was very proud of my years in the Continentals. That was the start of my illustrious military career. I have read many memorials that were written about the Father of our great country. I'll just list a few that I know. Gladstone said, 'the purest figure in history.' Frederick the Great sent this along with his portrait, 'From the oldest general in Europe to the greatest general in the world.' If I had more of your attention I would relate further from Washington's many letters of veneration." Some patrons were speaking out of turn, from Eaton's point of view.

"Yes, Mr. Boberts, you wish to speak? Then do so."

"General and fellow hangers-on. I wish to say that when General Washington came into Philadelphia at the start of the War, I was there to help his servants, sell his old coach and four for a new coach with the finest of four horses I've ever seen, to bring him back to his home. I was also there when he come to kick the British Redcoats out of Boston. I was his stable servant then, and he was a man who was very fussy about the feedin' and care of his ridin' horses."

"Thank you, Boberts, and now Mr. Hewit, you too wish to speak to this illustrious group. Then stand and command their attention."

Mr. Hewitt hesitantly rose and stammered,

"General and friends all, m-m-my view of that great m-man was on the battlefield when he rode his horse past me as I were wounded on the ground at Trenton, yes that Christmas day in '76. The General pulled his big white horse to a quick stop, and he spoke to me, ' I'll send help. They will take you to a shelter where it will be warm. There a doctor will care for your wound.' And right away he wheeled and charged over to a d-d-distant bunch of soldiers and some of them c-came and saved m-my life. He took c-c-care of his men as well as his horses."

"General, Sir, if I may have a turn addressing this illustrious assembly of heroes, both Naval and Army. For I was here in this same tavern back in 1760 or near that time, and I'll tell you that John and Sam Adams along with Paul Revere came here most every night for a meeting of the Sons of Liberty in one of the small rooms that Mr. Vila has since made over into this much larger main room. We don't need to be out of any damn Redcoats' eyes any more. Now right here near the long wharf is where some of the men got together before they had that tea party right here in Boston."

And so the evening of drinking and story telling about the Father of the Country and some other notables continued until Vila said,

"Gentlemen, Gentlemen! Time, Time! Please!"

The evening of remembrances was finished and Mr. Smart in his area of the tavern had held his own with his tales about that great leader Washington.

"I was at Brandywine when the Hessians beat us, but my company held off the whole danged army of Redcoats. We were the ones who hid along the hedges by the side of the road and poured our fire at every officer that came down the road chasin' our brave boys who were out of gun powder and had to retreat so they could be ready to fight another day. Yessir, we made it danged hot for them Hessian officers. And...."

Having found an eating place a little more distant from the fire, Smart had stayed awake to enjoy the fellowship and had done his fair part in the story telling.

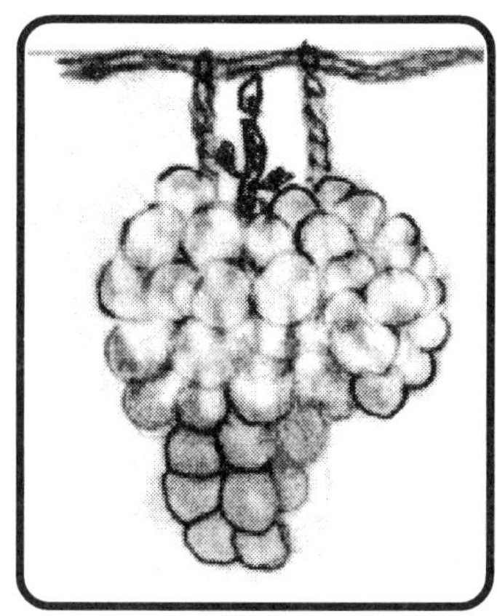

After digressions about Arabic culture and the birthday remembrance of George Washington, Eaton continued his recital of how he had saved his country one more time.

"My apology for being absent last week. John Adams had sent me an invitation to dine with him on the last day of February, and I had forgotten about it until Aletti instructed me. Now I will tell you how great a man is my friend John Adams. He performed many services for our glorious country and state. He became our country's President, a U.S. Senator for Massachusetts; he was our greatest Secretary of State, and the ambassador to Russia, Prussia, Holland, Sweden, Portugal, and France. John is a great man, and I am privileged to call him my friend.

"Well now, let's start the story again. After I had put to rout that dastardly British agent, Doctor Romayne, the word got around in the corridors of the capital. As soon as John Adams was installed as President, he gave me a very special assignment. This time it was the Spanish and their plans for grabbing all of Georgia and sending gunboats up the Mississippi River to prevent the westward flow of our sturdy American pioneers. I was invited to an intimate Presidential dinner party along with the Spanish legate. Now the legate, Don Diego, was very ambitious, and I could see right away that he was anxious to carry out his King's wishes. So I cultivated the tall dandy, and we spent many evenings conversing in old and new tongues, such as Latin, Greek, Spanish, Arabic, and the Creek I taught him. We were learning from each other. I was most grateful and in his debt. But remembering my task, I let it be known to him that I was soon to be discharged from the army. I conveyed to him that army powers had unfairly tried and convicted me, and worst of all, in absente reo. Now I want to say to you men that I was never found guilty of stealing time from my employer. I did my job and more every day. To the high-born Don Diego, I emphasized that I would soon be in dire need of money to send home to my dear wife Eliza and that my stepson Eli was in need of a new wardrobe, having recently graduated from Dartmouth. I informed him that I found myself financially embarrassed because I could not help this dear son. I also said I was looking to the future with much trepidation and disquietude. At one of our many evening dinners together I very confidentially spilled — no planted — the fact that I had been the chief military inspector of the border region. One night Eli joined us and told Don Diego of his myriad unpaid debts from his schooling. Eli then said, 'Either I or Dad will need to go home to Brimfield to help Mother with the great financial burden that she has incurred from our being absent so long.'

"At that point I could see I had him well hooked. Yes, all I needed now was to land him. Some days later he said to me, 'Sir, Mr. Eaton, if you could tell me more of what you know about the border forts and the plans of defense, I could offer you a very high position in our New Orleans government.' After suitable wavering I did tell the legate more than he ever had envisioned. He wrote it all down! We continued to play this game all of May, June and then into July.

"Finally, in late July 1797 Don Diego, who now thought

the baby country called the United States of America was as strong as England and thus not easy prey, called at the State Department and asked for a meeting to draw up a treaty of friendship with the United States. Ho! Ho! on him. All during the many evenings we had spent helping each other with learning languages, I had, with careful deliberation and very purposefully, fed him glowing and tall tales— all fabricated — about our forts and our well trained army on the border. I also mentioned many phantom forts and mountains of make-believe military supplies. When the Don offered me great opportunities in New Orleans and other improbable possibilities — even in Spain — I said that my love of country kept me from accepting his most generous offers and that I and Eli would do the honorable thing and make our own way. For the United States of America was a land which let all people who could, win fame and fortune, and I was to be one of them. I told him I would be acclaimed a hero for the past and also the future. We parted the best of friends with great regard for one another.

"After the treaty was signed, I visited Don Diego, telling him of my good fortune. I said, 'My friend, Don Diego, I've just recently been offered a new position with my own government, a foreign posting.' I pointed out that even my enemies in the army had not prevented the President from recognizing my worth. So now you listeners can understand that uncovering two dangerous agents made me a welcome guest at the Adams's Boston table. When President Adams invited me to dinner and asked what he could do for me, I called to his attention an opening at State for a legate to the Barbary Coast. Adams posted my name. Congress approved.

"Now, waiter, let's think of this night's repast. First I will have a good hot Flip, and I'll then have the soup of the day, some venison that my nose tells me about, well-done, to follow. If you hangers-on have eaten, wait until I complete my meal. Then I'll buy a round of beer, but you must be my attentive audience for the rest of this brief episode."

The food eaten and the wine brought, the General swiveled his chair so that the new patrons at the Bunch of Grapes fell within his gaze.

"I was going to the BARBARY STATES! In my head, mountains were climbed and oceans were crossed. As my dear father had said from the Bible, when you are a man, act like a man. I had done so up to this time in my young life, and I expected to continue for the rest of my life. I received my appointment in July of 1797. Eli and I went to Brimfield, where my short visit with Eliza seemed like an eternity. Eliza had plenty of money; she never asked me for any. It was just that she thought me a lesser man than Danielson and never stopped saying, 'If Tim was here he would do this and that', and she had such a cuttting speech which I had never heard when I was wooing her. God, it cut deep into a man's pride. And then too, she was very cold and totally impossible to have an enjoyable bedtime romp with. Best to go to Barbary! From my Barbary readings I expected to find a warm willing female that might just be as good in bed as my long, dear, lost Sophie. Lovely warm Sophie of my dreams.

"On my return to Philadelphia I met Mr. James L. Cathcart and wife. I was amazed to find that he and Mr. Richard O'Brien both had been captives of the Moslems. Mr. Cathcart had become the Dey's Chief Christian Secretary. I spent considerable time dining with these new friends. O'Brien left us on an early passage. It was months before Cathcart and I departed. I tried Brimfield a few times more and found Eliza in the same inhospitable state of mind. We set sail on December 22nd in the brig *Sophia* under the command of Captain Geddes. I had taken my stepson for my secretary as he had finished his studies at Dartmouth.

Fate would place me on a brig called *Sophia* and make me dream of that best love of my life. I wrote her a letter each Lord's Day after I had penned a letter of events to Eliza. We sailed with the overburdened Hero, a brig of 350 tons loaded with naval stores for the Dey. The *Hassan Baschaw*, a refitted brig of 275 tons, carrying eight six-pound cannon, the *Skjoldabrand*, a schooner of 250 tons which we had purchased from Sweden, sailed with us. She had sixteen four-pounders. Also *Le La Eisha*, a 150 ton schooner, mounting four four-pound cannon. These four ships were loaded with naval stores for this Barbary pirate.

"All this bounty for the Dey of Algiers! He whom we had paid and paid said, 'That tribute only covers the Mediterranean, not the Atlantic.' Just the good ship *Sophia* was to remain in our hands! It was part of the more than one million dollars the Dey of Algiers had blackmailed from our struggling United States. What a beginning — one of utter subjugation! We were not a happy crew. The winter storms delayed us, so we didn't land in Algiers until the 9th of February, 1799. I am never a good sailor and this trip was no exception. I spent most of my time retching and moaning. After a plague scare at Gibraltar, thank God, we soon made it to Algiers. Here the high hills come down to the sea. Their harbor is very small, but it was brim full of galleys on which we saw naked, chained slaves at the oars of those sleek, fast warships.

"We met Mr. Richard O'Brien, our Consul to Algiers, and as we walked among the people of Islam, I soon understood what they were saying about us. 'You dogs of infidels', they cursed us and made jokes about how the Dey would make them all rich by outsmarting these foolish Americans. Several days later we were taken to the Kasba to meet the Dey, and as I kissed his paw, I addressed him in his own tongue. He was much amazed, so were O'Brien and Cathcart, for I had kept my linguistic ability a secret up to this time. He was a huge man, sitting like a tailor on a low bench, with his dirty black hair hanging to his waist. I thought he reminded me of our black bears that sit and beg at some carnivals, except that they're cleaner.

"Now I enhanced the Moslems' regard for us by instructing all to hold the honey cake with their left hand and to lift the coffee cup also with the left hand. As you know, those people use the right hand only for unclean activities. On March 2, after a month's delay, the Dey allowed us, Cathcart and me, to sail for Tunis. Another storm — how sick you can be on these coastal voyages! We were spied on by two of their warships all the way to Tunis.

"Bad luck — as in Gibraltar where we had had to replace a mast. Now a large storm tore into us, forcing us to anchor at Bizerta. On 14 March we reached the old city of Carthage, now called Tunis.

"I was glad to set foot on land, where we were met by the Frenchman, Joseph Etienne Famin. He had been employed by our former legate, Joel Barlow, and had wrongly assumed the consulate's role when Barlow had gone home. The British Consular Agent told me to watch Famin carefully. I soon discovered what a slippery snake in the grass he was. Even though he offered to help, I quickly became aware of his intentions to sabotage us, and I trimmed his ears with a horsewhip in the street at the west gate. I gave him what was his just dessert. It was while I had him cowering in the street that a well-dressed naval officer addressed me, 'Sir, would you be Eaton, formerly of Woodstock ,Connecticut?'

"I knew the voice and answered, 'Charles...Charles Morris!' I put the whip away and walked over to give my childhood friend a hearty handshake. That night we all had the pleasure of Commodore Morris' tales at our dining table.

"Back to Famin; that Frenchman had earlier pushed his hired servants on me, but I soon sent them all packing.

That bunch was carrying tales to Famin. This was when I bought Aletti, a jewel only slightly tarnished. He was all that I needed. He had a knowledge of languages and had traveled in Europe and Barbary. In a short time I decided this man would be my paid servant as long as I could keep him.

"Aletti helped in my preparation for the first meeting with Dey Ahmed Pasha at his Kasba. I pushed a wheelbarrow with sacks which contained 10,000 silver dollars to the Dey's palace. The Satrap was very pleased with this and greeted me most kindly. He was as tall as I and much more slender than I am now. He was elegantly dressed and was well learned. We conversed in both Greek and Arabic. The Dey told me of Djama Zitouna and asked if I would like to visit that famous University. He gave me a pass and I spent many a happy hour at that great Islamic learning center.

"Eli was doing his job, and I didn't need to tend to all the small details, so I visited the market places, bargaining for our needs. I visited the countryside and learned the ways of the desert, always in the local clothing. Even then many mistook me for a native.

"At Tunis I was in day-to-day negotiations with the Dey Ahmed for the rewriting of certain articles that disgraceful Frenchman Famin had sent in the treaty for our Congress to approve. They had instructed us to rewrite them so that both sides would be treated the same. Dey Ahmed's insults in the bargaining were offset by his friendship at dinner meetings. Yet I was at times wishing I had a few fighting ships and a few Marines to give these pirates the taste of hot lead.

"I continued to talk and talk until the Dey Ahmed Pasha signed a new agreement, on April 26th. As we signed, three American ships came into the harbor with the promised ransom supplies. For this rewritten treaty, I was given an official commendation by the Congress and a letter of congratulation from President John Adams in November of 1800.

"I would like to point out to this audience that the Dey sent out only twenty cruisers that year, many less than years before. These pirate raids were mostly in the vicinity of Corsica, Sardinia, Sicily, the coast of Genoa, Tuscany, Naples, Calabria, and the mouth of the Adriatic Sea. Sometimes they went even to Venice. Their mode of attack was boarding. The long lattern yards were dropped on board the victim, affording a safe and easy passage for the pirates. With their curved knives grasped between their teeth and in their belts two loaded pistols, their hands free for scaling the gunnels or netting their enemy, they became very adept at this manner of capturing the poor undefended merchant ships. Even today they're still capturing all the crew, forcing them below, then sailing into a nearby Arab port to sell the prisoners and the booty. The money so earned makes them very rich and a little booty may be given to the slaves who were the power that made the capture possible. Of course the ruler also had his enormous share of the spoils. I've said enough for tonight."

Eaton was pleased with the night's recitation. But Vila said to him as he was pulling on his coat,

"General, if you like, I'll split that round of beer. And, General, don't think I've forgotten that missed meeting. You and I are going to have a little talk over your failure to appear as my widely distributed broadsheet told the whole town of Boston."

"As you like and please tell your pretty wife that her venison was good on my palate." His coat on, the General took a cab home and spent several hours with his journal and his papers, writing the *Life of William H. Eaton.*

This night found Mr. B. Smart at another tavern with some old friends, too hard of hearing to catch General Eaton's fast flowing words at the Bunch of Grapes.

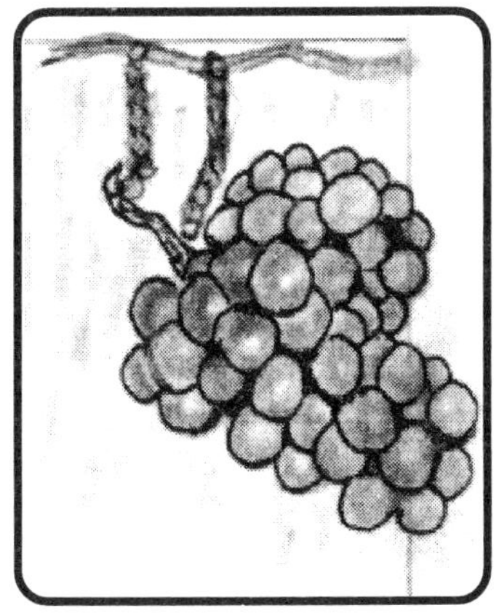

A few days later Mr. Vila was on his way to 16 Ann Street when he should have been at the market bargaining for groceries. As he had left, his wife had said, "Jim, just remember which side of your bread is buttered. The General has put a lot of hard money in our purse. So he missed once! Be calm; don't fly off the handle!"

'So this auctioneer cousin's home is the abode of our great story teller,' he thought as he knocked on the door with enough force to wake the sleeping dog.

"That will arouse them," James said under his breath as the door flew open and the cousin said in a loud semi-roar,

"Vila, I am sure you're not here to see me, so it must be the General. I'll take you to his rooms."

The General was still half asleep as he sat to talk with James Vila, but Aletti was making breakfast and offered a cup of coffee to the tavern keeper.

"I am not one to cry over spilled milk," Vila stated. "But I did expect the General to keep his appointments."

"Mr. Vila, you're right and...," Eaton offered.

"Mr. Vila," Aletti interrupted the General, "I was at fault for not reminding the General. Now if you and I can come to agreement on the days of the month that my General will be at the Bunch of Grapes, I will assure the good tavern keeper that the General will not miss any more commitments. For you see the General has relied on me now for many years to keep his calendar for him. I was even at Richmond when..."

"Give the man his coffee and bring me my breakfast, and let's all eat. I'm sure that Aletti and you, Mr. Vila, have all the problems solved." They ate and talked of politics and shipping. Before Mr. Vila left, he and Aletti had the calendar filled out 'til late August.

Three days later the General came into State Street where the Bunch of Grapes sign was swinging in a stiff March breeze off the water. Leaving his heavy outer-coat with Mr. Vila, Eaton did a military march parade in his very smart gold braided regalia. As he took his usual table, he was greeted with an exuberant cheer by the expectant peons. The owner also was gratified by his bargain with the General. Peons, Eaton had called them while consorting with a very different audience at the Red String recently .

That gourmand had a Flip and then onion soup, bread, roast beef and a bottle of Madeira wine. Turning, he said,

"I am feeling quite well, thank you. Last night's visit to the Red String got my essential juices flowin' again, much like a similar imbroglio that happened in Egypt a few years ago. I'll not jump ahead to that episode but take up where I left off. Now let me consider. That tall ,well-made Countess Bella Bellini just came vividly to my mind. I'll tell about that one after I finish the story I'm on. Yes. The year was 1800, and I was struggling in my effort of rewriting our commercial agreement with Dey Ahmed Pasha. I had had to bribe ($20,000) his principal minister, Sahibtappa, to get past his guards and then another bribe ($25,000) to turn the Pasha reasonable, and to continue the negotiations I had to bribe them both with more hard money. They were both, Ahmed and Sahibtappa, insulting to me and my country. I lost my temper and shouted at his Highness. The Dey, however, was calm in his reply, 'YOU consult your honor, I my interest.' I wrote and asked advice from Cathcart and O'Brien, and also wrote my personal feelings to our man in London, Rufus King.

"I said, and I quote from my diary, 'I have found my Kismet in Barbary, but I am not certain I like it. If I had my will here, I would use American arms to force the brigand kings to respect our nation. I am convinced that only gunshot and powder will compel the Beys and Deys of Barbary to treat us in a civilized manner.... ' I'll not read my whole letter, but it continues in the same vein .

"These long waits gave me the time to absorb the habits and the dialects of all the polyglot peoples of the area. I visited them in their tents, in their hovels, at the market and in their castles. I took on the appearance of an Arab. I think it was Eli who accused me of going native. I replied, 'I am like a lizard one sees in the garden. I change my colors to match those of the land. Once I was a Miami, then a Creek, and now I am an Arab.'

"The naval stores were very late in crossing the Atlantic that winter of 1799 -1800 and then landing at Leghorn, Italy instead of Tunis. The Dey was being persuaded by that dastardly minister Sahibtappa to send out his fighting ships to capture any of our ships. If they had naval stores, he would claim them as part of the America debt as stated in the treaty. I made it clear to Dey Ahmed Pasha the United States could not give naval stores to a nation that did not respect our flag. Thus they would not have the right to board our commercial ships at will. When he agreed to my terms, I had him send one of his ships to Leghorn and return with the naval goods. I sent Eli along in the Dey's ship to help in the projected transfer of cargo.

"While they were gone after the stores, the Dey and I negotiated and removed two very objectionable clauses from the old treaty. This was helped along by my promise of more naval booty, which came on the *Anna Maria* in late November in 1800. That was a very quick response, for we had only signed the new agreement on the 28th of April. For this treaty Congress voted me an official commendation which I received much later.

"Because of my good works I was asked by James Cathcart to come over to Tripoli and help him with the worst of the so-called Princes of the Barbary States, Yusef Karamanli. I left on the 28th of December, 1800 on the *Anna Maria.* The sea was at its worst. Yes, I was seasick as always, but I did write a letter to Eliza and also several to my lovely dearest chimera, Sophie. Yusef... ah- Joseph.... He is the one that some say may have put his father away and did murder his older brother, Hassan. He then usurped the power of his next older brother, Hamet, and had him sent off to Derne as his Governor. Yusef was puffed up to the extent that he thought himself equal to the Deys of Algiers and Tunis. Yusef, also called the Bashaw, had a renegade Scotsman by the name of Lisle, also known as Murad Reis, as his commander-in-chief of the Tripolitan navy. Lisle had a British price on his head and also one in Hamburg and Naples. The Bashaw had written a letter to President Adams, which arrived just as President Jefferson came to the office, so they both read this most demanding and insulting ransom epistle.

"I got to Tripoli in January, 1801, and found that, in truth, our relationship was near the breaking point. Lisle had captured three American merchant vessels and sold their cargo. Those two thieves denied it, even when we saw some of the goods in Yusef's palace. Oh, I must tell you that as poor as the city of Tripoli was, it did have on its eastern side one of the most beautiful oases in all Africa, the Oasis of Meshia, with over a hundred thousand palm trees. This oasis made me think of Milton's second book ...It starts like this ; 'High on a throne of Royal State, which far Outshone the wealth of Ormus and of Ind,— Or where the gorgeous East with richest hand Showers on her Kings Barbaric Pearl and Gold, Satan With Opal towers and Battlements adorn'd Of living Sapphire, once his native seat; And fast by hanging in a golden Chain This pendant world , in bigness as a ... mischievous revenge, Accurst, and in cursed hour he hies. ' That is from the second book of Milton's *Paradise Lost* that I put to memory so long ago. Yet I think I quote him rather well.

"Where was I in my tale of Tripoli?... I had just finished getting clean and was trying to rest when I was summoned by the Bashaw to his palace. What a beast...dirty, stinking, hulk of an animal. Slopped food covered his garments, and his nails were black, utterly disgusting, a bully and an evil man and one that I took a complete dislike to. He was my third ruler and the most nauseating of all. Upon being presented to his Highness, I was ignored. The Danish Consul, Mr. Nissen, tried again with the same result, so I addressed the Bashaw in Arabic. Whereupon the Bashaw told the Danish Consul that since the Americans would soon not need their flag pole and as wood was so scarce in Tripoli, he might send his troops to cut down the American pole and give it to the Swedes. Now I knew enough Arabic lore to recognize this, and so did all the other diplomats, that cutting down an embassy flag pole was equal to declaring a state of war. So he was threatening us, and all we diplomats were summarily dismissed. Then his man Lisle demanded fifty thousand dollars before he would open the door for us Americans to talk again.

"Lisle also threatened to make Mr. Cathcart a galley slave. That's when I intervened. I sought out that renegade. Oh! have I told you that this man was a Scotsman and a converted follower of Mohammedan, converted by money in his purse. When I caught him in a city street, I told him that I would personally pursue him even to the ends of the earth if such a dastardly treatment were ever carried out on such an important American. Then I informed him that when I found him I would treat him as I had that conniving Frenchman, Joseph Famin. He got my message when my well aimed shoe kicked his black ass down the street. In full view of his Muslim friends.

"We tried to reason with these Tripolitans but to no avail, so I left on the *Anna Maria* for Tunis and sent my report to Mr. O'Brien, in which I said we might never see Mr. Cathcart alive again and that all our efforts had been wasted. I also said war was imminent and would make our relations with the other two Barbary States much more difficult."

"What about that Countance?" came from the audience.

"No, I've not forgotten *Countess* Bella Bellini, but, waiter, bring me a new bottle of Madeira. While we wait for our drinks, comes the Bella story. So, Mr. Brown, my good friend, take leave and prepare my mount for the journey home.

"While Brown gets my mount ready I'll continue the story. Princess Bella Bellini, she came to mind when I used the Italian word back there in the start of the evening. This was no ordinary camp follower... she had two famous Venetian family ancestors... Gentile Bellini who taught the great painter Titian, and Giovanni Bellini, Gentile's brother, both sons of Jacopo Bellini, also a great painter.

"So, she had noble blood in her veins, and it was very evident. We met at the Swedish embassy where she had a group of eager expectant men surrounding her. She was dark of hair, cream of complexion, and about thirty in years. She had a very cultured voice, and it sent out honey to those around her.

"But first a little sip as my voice box needs lubrication and this fine wine will do." After a large swallow of wine, Eaton looked toward a few naval patrons who seemed to have lost interest in his tale, and he decided to prick their ears with a little overblown sex story.

"Bella and I soon were sharing our evenings and nights, and, yes, she was the most sought after female in all of Barbary. Bella would start cooing with her honey filled voice as she removed my clothing. Then as we lay naked on her soft silk sheets, she would start kissing my lips and then kiss my chest, my stomach, down, down to my navel and then just a little farther. When I had responded in like manner and was ready to finish by coming to the expected climax, my body was aching. Why? Because I knew after that first encounter —what came next. For when my penis penetrated her, it would turn her off, cold as my wife Liza. How many times did we excite each other and then a cold finish? Bella was eager and more than willing until that point. Well, some females are great to look at, but, my God, how unresponsive, and unwilling to learn the finer art of sexual performance was Bella. I was, at first, the envy of the embassies, but then I was the subject of their wagging tongues."

Eaton took another long sip of Madeira and paused as his mind wandered back to his many sexual trips to General Danielson's bed. Was his ghost the problem when he and Liza were having intercourse? Did she find him less a man than her former General? Did his spirit fill her as he — Eaton — tried to warm her sexual hunger? Sophie had never known another, and, yes, this Bella led you as Sophie had, and Eliza never had. A sudden crash as a waiter dropped a tray brought Eaton's mind back to the common room.

"She made me think of dear fair Sophie, but not in her performance. Some apple blossom fragrance on Bella may have made it last longer but then it wasn't me that was cold. My heart ached for those former romps in the orchard with my sweet, tantalizing, fulfilling Sophie.

"Soon I was sending a series of love letters to Mrs. Sophie Smith of New Britain, Connecticut. I wonder what her stupid pumpkin husband made of them?

"Yes, it was the smell of apple blossoms with Sophie. Yes, Patrick, I'm coming. You will help me mount. Good night all. I'll return— the date can be found in Vila's broadsheet, God willin'."

Beauregard Smart had heard it all and knew even more because, as he had said, he had sailed the seven seas meeting sailors and other wanderers. Old Beau said, after the General had gone,

"General Eaton was telling the truth about that Italian woman. I've heard it told a lot fancier, but the facts were the same. We will agree the story is mostly true.

"You have heard the General telling us he is welcome at Quincy House by the Adams family. I have been drivin' a gig in this town of Boston, and the other day I was driving the two Adamses back to Quincy House. They were atalkin' 'bout our General Eaton. Yes Sir! Them Adamses were asayin' how very polite and careful he was with his liquor, and they said he treated all their servants very respectful. President Adams said he thought the episode down in Richmond must a been a pack of lies or at least over exaggeration. Yes Sir! The Adamses, both of 'em, had great praises for our General Eaton. I had it right from their mouths..."

Soon the tavern was empty and Beau Smart was at the point of finding his boarding house, so he called for his bill and, paying, walked into the cutting March sleet toward Milk Street.

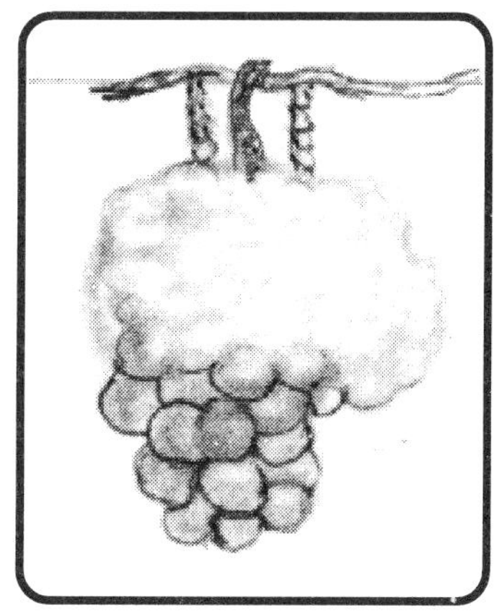

Eaton and his entourage were at the center of the taproom in Vila's Bunch of Grapes. In the blackened fireplace coals were glowing. The fire was being allowed to die down because the room was crowded with men anticipating an evening's amusement. The General and Colonel Pat had drunk and eaten their evening meal. The hangers-on had finished their food and drink and Eaton had started the storytelling.

" ... Yes, so it was the American flagpole. Cut down by Yusef's Tripolitan guards, and the word quickly spread to all the ports of the Mediterranean Sea. The United States of America's flag had been desecrated just as I had warned in letters to President Adams and Secretary Madison. Then the Deys of Algiers and also Tunis demanded a much larger annual tribute, just as I had predicted to the Secretary of State. The arrival of the frigate *George Washington* at Tripoli had saved Mr. Cathcart's skin but not the flagpole. That was given to the Swedish Consulate as Yusef had threatened. Thank God, the Danish Consul Nissen took James Cathcart in and gave him transportation to Leghorn. The Bashaw of Tripoli declared war on us on the fourteenth of May, 1801. We , all three of us (O'Brien, Cathcart, and I), had warned our government, and I had specifically asked for a thousand young and well-officered Marines to lead against the ammunition storage at Porto Farina. I pointed out in my letters that these brigands only understood the effect of hot lead and bayonets. I said I could assure my government that in a matter of a few months I would have these pirates bloody and suing for peace. Well, the government spent more money for our inept Navy. They should have got old John Barry to command it. I remember him when I walked the halls of Congress in Philadelphia. By God, he was a man who could lead a fight and win. Not all of them navy boys are old women, but just too many of their leaders were of that persuasion. Some of you swabs know that.

"Bring me a good bottle of Madeira and be quick, waiter. Yes and two clean glasses." A few quick sips and the General went on with the recitation while Colonel Pat was filling his glass.

"Now on my return to Tunis I found the Dey making demands I knew could not and would not be met by my government. The Dey Ahmed kept repeating that he wanted to hold our hand in eternal friendship, but I said that I could not see the difference between what he called friendship, and what most people called enmity. He blustered that I was insulting him, and I said he was an intelligent man and should know. That was the end of talk because I sent him a formal note saying I was done with negotiations on the new commercial agreement. I wrote a long detailed letter to our Secretary of State, Mr. Madison. I asked him and our government to consider an armed force of five thousand infantrymen and cavalrymen to be used by me to subdue these Barbary pirates who were in the habit of dictating their own terms for peace. Totally insufferable. Yet, whenever I met Ahmed that spring we had an exchange of words about the mutually hated Yusef of Tripoli. The Dey sent me a kettle of lamb and vegetable stew and later invited me to come to the palace for an evening meal. He did recognize a man when he met one. My father was tight! No..*right*! First Corinthians 13 verse 11. Right! I ate and talked and talked and ate with Ahmed at the palace. Because it was spring, I had found me a new woman, a redhead, who really knew what men enjoyed in bed.

"She was delectable and I was enjoying myself, in bed and out. Yes, she was the one whom I called Raska Ahmar for there were none like her in that country. She was a descendant of Peter Van der Mey, a Dutchman who in 1573 saved the city of Allkmar, Holland from being captured by Philip the 2nd's Spanish army. Smart Peter made sure that the Spanish General Don Frederick intercepted his false dispatches, detailing how the Duke of Orange was going to open the dykes and drown the Spanish Army. Heavy rains had made the ground under the surrounding army soggy, so Don Frederick ordered a retreat. Then the Duke of Orange became de facto King of Holland. I'm sure you all remember that tale. Was that Raska Ahmar a delight in and out of bed! I gave Aletti several gold pieces to purchase her from Ahmed's chief cook. She couldn't carry on much in Dutch, but she did help my Arabic greatly. Her Dutch name was Inger. She said it meant daughter of a hero. I set her free when I left to come back to America. I was true to my father's command, 'be a man.' Now Raska Ahmar's good medicine helped my thinking process, and it was then I came up with the great idea of collecting all the people of Barbary who hated the murderous Bashaw Yusef. I would general them and put his brother, Hamet Karamanli, the rightful monarch, on his throne.

"Hamet would be grateful, and we could make an honorable peace with Tripoli. The Deys of Tunis and Algiers would see my victorious army and decide that it would be in their interests to be reasonable and sue for peace. The cost would be small, and the results worth many millions of dollars to the government of America and also obviate the suffering of all those sailors who might otherwise be captured. I sent off a letter to Mr. Cathcart at Leghorn, and he liked my plan so much that he recovered from his melancholy over the cutting down of our flagpole and started for Tunis that summer. But his ship to Tunis was captured by Barbary pirates. Mr. Cathcart was stripped naked and all his valuables taken by men of the Tunisian navy. Ahmed wouldn't talk about this, and his naval captain, the one called Sahibtappa , joked about it all around the city. AND I found out that Joseph Famin, that damn treacherous Frenchman, who had worked for the United States Consul, was doing his best to get the Dey to set his Navy on all and every American merchant ship. Thank God they didn't keep him, Mr. Cathcart, in their filthy dungeons.

"It was July 17,1801. I remember it very well. I was at a scrumptious feast that Raska, my sweet Henna who always smelled of apple blossoms, had especially prepared for James Cathcart and Eli. We were all at table when Aletti came on the run into the dining room and exclaimed, 'American warships — many American warships — are entering the harbor.' We all left our food and ran to look at such a glorious sight. My God! One, Two, Three, Four, Five!

"We all counted them twice and then we cheered. And then we all cheered some more. Mr. Cathcart got all his valuables back, and the Bashaw at Tunis began treating us like the diplomats we were. Warships in the harbor make a consul feel great— it made us credible.

"I was mostly in good health, but around Christmas 1801 I must have had some food that upset my humors. It just happened that Captain Shaw had the *George Washington* at Tunis, and the ship's surgeon turned out to be my good old friend Doctor William Turner. William, after diagnosing me, offered to be the official representative at Tunis while I took ship with Captain Shaw for a health cruise to

Leghorn. I had, of course, to inform the Dey that this was to be for a short time and that I was not relinquishing my post. I had a very good trip on this passage. The winter storms, thank God, did not beat upon our sails. The food at Captain Shaw's table was to the liking of my stomach, and within a few days I felt my old self and wrote letters to all my superiors in Washington and to Eliza and to my dear, dearly loved Sophie. I told those in the capital about the desperate need for action by the navy and the great need of a secret means to help Sidi Mahomet Bashaw (Hamet), the rightful ruler of Tripoli. A land Army to work in joint action with the Navy was the plan I presented to both the State Department and to War. I also wrote to the President and certain members of Congress. Then I wrote to Sidi Mahomet and told him of my plans and also counseled him to be patient with the slowness of that new country called The United States of America. I emphasized the need to keep our plans secret and warned him his bloodthirsty brother would probably try to pour false oil on him and that he should not accept Yusef's words as his true meaning. That brother was a deceiver.

"There was a round of diplomatic parties at Leghorn, and I met a really fine young bed partner for the stay. She was not as dear as some, and Aletti had to spend only a few paltry dollars to afford me the pleasures of that young and amazing Egyptian. After those frolics I just had to send my still fervent love to my dear Sophie. I posted all my letters and attended all the required functions but still found lots of time to play at Antony and Cleopatra. What fun life can be!

"Too soon I had to depart for Tripoli since my small sick leave had come to an end — just as this evening's story telling is coming to an end. Those remembrances! So now I have a need to visit again the finest of Boston's houses, the Red String. I shall leave you late and early patrons to your own entertainment while I seek mine with some of the best performers in the business."

As Eaton went out the door he was saying loudly to Pat,

"Now I really think that Vila should have understood about that missed night back a few weeks ago, for I'm sure he would have gladly gone to sup with the Adams family if he had been invited."

As Mr. Vila was helping one of his very prestigious customers put on his frock, he said to the gentleman, "If that loudmouth braggart wasn't putting such a large amount of good hard cash in my pockets, why I would have thrown him out long ago. He has an overbearing way and commands no respect with his disreputable actions. Just the other day he charged his stallion into a crowd of people at the market, and even the Red String folks say he's no gentlemen at that place." Mr. Vila recognized the well dressed blue-blood, yet no name came to his mind.

The eminent gentleman responded, "Mr. Vila, most of the good people of Boston feel just as you do. You know that the legislators would have nothing to do with the General when he got himself elected from Brimfield. However, I did find him telling a most astounding tale tonight. When is he to be here next? I think I'll ask my renowned brother and some notable friends to come with me. When?"

The busy Mr. Vila handed the very distinguished gentleman a broadsheet.

Meanwhile the well versed Mr. Beauregard Smart finished the General's story by naming all of the merchant ships the bloodthirsty Bashaw of Tripoli had captured in that war. The aged Beau could do so for he had been among the captives. The beatings and starving he received from the pirates were magnified several fold by this groit. He finished with the information,

"That gentleman, who surely looked uppercrust, was none other than Admiral Dudley Saltonstall. It was his brother— or was it a cousin? —that piled up a fortune with the privateering *Minerva* during the war. You remember her that gathered up a kings ransom in British gold. Yes, it was the same bunch of blue-bloods who wore silk stockings...." That is what he told his ever decreasing audience.

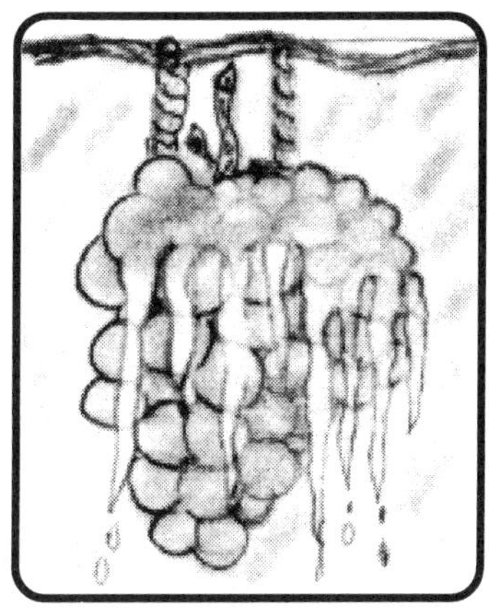

The General had come by carriage to the tavern. His gouty and frostbitten feet made this necessary. The late March weather had been unusual. The rain froze as it fell on the cobbled streets. Man and beast moved slowly, and so Eaton arrived well past his accustomed hour. Pat Patrick was pondering as he steered the General to his centrally located table. He thought it might be a good thing if he sent the General home early considering the weather and the fact that Aletti had let the General leave without proper clothing for March weather. It would be very cold tonight when he went back to his billet. When the waiter came, Patrick ordered two helpings of supper; wild duck with baked potatoes and two large bottles of Madeira and said,

"Please. Bring us a Flip while we wait. And, oh waiter, have them put in a little more nutmeg." Then to Eaton, Pat said,

"The minions are few tonight."

The General asked the small group to come closer as he had a slight head cold which was preventing him from speaking normally. The small company was waiting expectantly even though many of them already knew this story. It had been the talk of the new Nation, some of it at least. The General waved his hand and the room became quiet.

"The recitation for tonight will be about our new Navy and how they did and didn't do their duty. It's rather long, so I'll tell you some right now whilst we wait for dinner. Commodore Dale with his five mighty warships in the harbor quickly gained Cathcart and myself an audience with the Dey of Tunis, and we could see that he now looked upon the United States of America with different eyes. He wasn't demanding ransom, but instead he returned Cathcart's valuables and gave me a rather large purse filled with gold coins.

But then the Commodore sailed off to Tripoli, leaving the *Essex* to have some repairs. Soon after Dale had left, Carthcart and I wrote a proclamation which we sent to the Commodore for delivery to Yusef. Simply stated: 'Since you have declared war, then war exists between us and you.' In a separate letter we ordered the Commodore to go into Tripoli harbor with his guns booming to bring doom to that snake of a pirate Yusef. Later I found out that Commodore Dale had already made contact before he read our letter. Using the Danish Consul Nissen, Dale asked if Yusef intended to fight. Well, that renegade Scotsman Murad Reis would not fight after he saw Dale's warships, and so the Commodore commenced a passive blockade. God! Just a few quick blows by him would have brought them to an honorable peace treaty.

"Then Dale read my proclamation and lost his head, claiming that he should have signed it as the highest ranking official in the Mediterranean. Dale said—so it has been rumored — 'It's a deliberate slighting and embarrassment. And the perpetrators are Eaton and Cathcart.' I was the Naval Representative by Presidential order. He did, however, blockade the port, and when Murad Reis's Tripolitan sloop came out to run the blockade, why he let the *Enterprise* fight. And fight Captain Sterrett did! He captured the sloop and took off her guns and all her gear. Because we, the U.S.A., had not declared war on Tripoli—officially—he let the Barbary sloop sail back into the harbor with twenty dead and thirty wounded pirates. What a good show! But Dale chose not to follow up his advantage and left for Gibraltar and shore leave for his overexerted sailors! Humph! Another naval old woman who didn't know why she was there.

"I'll starve if they don't bring the food. Go and ask Mr. Vila if his good wife has quit, will you Pat? She does the work and he collects the money. And, Pat, order me a bottle of Madeira, too."

"Sir! General Eaton, sir. I'm from the Province uv' Maine, and I did serve with Capn' Morris. And even though I were jest a lowly seaman, I felt we shoulda given 'em bloody pirates a lot more hot shot in their backsides while we was there. Yes, Sir, I think a small body of Army and Marines coulda fixed 'em up so they wouldn' have been atakin' on America ever ag'in. And, Sir, if I might, Sir, I'd sure like to know when you 're gonna tell the next parta this story. Sir, I wanna be here ta hear it."

"Thank you for that testimonial about the Navy, Mr. Crafton. Thank you! While I still wait and wait for nourishment, I'll tell a bit of history that didn't get recorded. I found Commodore Dale, the Congregationalist, was not as lily white as he appeared in his overly embellished uniform. Aletti, my servant, found him abed with my redheaded Raska Ashmar, and she was giving him the same attention she gave me. Well, I never held it against her, for she had entered my bed from others. Aletti just made sure the Admiral didn't get to admire my Henna in the nude again. I did and she was one to remember. Yes, nearly as proficient in bed as my very much loved Sophie. The one I dreamt about every night, even when I was on my amazing march to Derne.

"Thank God the wine and food have arrived... I am famished. Let's eat now, Pat!" They both ate lustily without the usual banter.

"Now back to the story. Dale had sailed home, leaving the *Essex* and the *Philadelphia* under Captain Barron to protect all our merchantmen in the Mediterranean Sea. As the sails of our ships disappeared, Dey Ahmed, the Pasha of Tunis and his Commodore Shibtappa pressured me for cash, naval stores, grain, rifles, and gunpowder. I paid and paid until my own purse was nearly empty, for I had earlier run out of the federal money. And then Hamet, the rightful ruler of Tripoli, came and begged me for money. He had his three wives, their women, and their eleven children, plus thirty nobles, and their many wives, children and a whole tribe of servants in his entourage. I had determined that he was to be the ruler of Tripoli with our government's help. However, right then he needed dollars. I didn't want him to ask his bloodthirsty brother for alms.

"Fate came to my rescue —the Tunisians captured a Danish vessel which then came up for auction. Acting the man my father, God bless him, had always expected, I bought it for a small borrowed sum and hired an Italian as captain. With great difficulty I bought the cargo and engaged the crew. Thank God! In the end they made me a large pocket full of nice solid money. Now, trading in that inland sea was dangerous, and so the ship's master flew the American flag — or any other flag as was expedient—on my good ship *Gloria*. That was for the protection I needed. So what if I did overlook a few rules — filling my pockets so that I could pay the debts of my country — is that wrong? Those rules which my enemies have blown all out of proportions. I did the job! I gave Hamet his needed funds and repaid all my debts with a goodly sum left in my pockets. Why shouldn't my purse be refilled, for I had taken the heroic stance and with my self-determination I had succeeded. I had acted the man. Rules are guides, and when they need breaking, I will do it.

"I should tell you that the American flag was not disgraced by flying over the *Gloria,* and Captain Barron was fully informed of my undertakings. I reported all of these activities to the Secretary of State, Mr. Madison.

"The tale continues and in a most disastrous fashion. First, all of the ports surrounding the Mediterranean Sea got the word that a large new fleet of U.S. Naval warships was anchored at Gibraltar, with a new Commodore, that childhood friend from Woodstock, Charles Morris. What a reputation that man had! Tales were that he was the best of the best. It was reported that they had arrived in the middle of June and would soon be ready to sweep the Mediterranean Sea of those Barbary pirates. Murad Reis's navy had not got the word, for they came into the harbor at Tunis and asked Ahmed's leave to auction off the captured United States brig *Franklin.* I explained to the Dey of Tunis that if it happened, I would order the U.S. Naval Squadron at Gibraltar to come and bombard his city. I said it loud and very clear both in Arabic and English so all could hear. The Tripolitan navy abandoned the *Franklin* at Bizerta but left there with all its crew as captives. They actually sold some of those men into slavery in Tripoli. In vain I sent several official letters to Commodore Morris asking — no telling — him to go and rescue those poor unfortunate Americans.

"It was at this time that Hamet left his sanctuary at Malta and sailed to Derne. The arrival of the American naval fleet had made him think that the time had come for him to lead an uprising against his brother, the usurper Yusef. I sent several more letters of instructions to the Commodore. I wrote, 'In God's name, Sir, unlimber your cannon in the harbor of Tripoli, and we and Hamet will cause the pirates of Barbary to shake in their boots.' Then as time ran on and the fleet sat at Gibraltar, the Dey Ahmed became more demanding until, to satisfy the conditions of agreement between his government and mine, I handed over my *Gloria.* Then more and more of my money. I even gave up a very expensive present I was planning to give my red headed Henna; instead I gave her a small bottle of apple fragrance. Oh yes, *le parfum aromatique des fleurs de pommier,* that lovely aphrodisiac. Just the thought takes me back to Sophie." Lapsing into memory, the General stopped the story while he returned to those days of his youth when love was his dream and his heart bloomed with its every beat. Rousing himself, he continued,

"Finally the Commodore did sail to Tripoli. Now I began to understand the stupidity of this man, for he let the shore batteries and the Tripolitan gun boats have target practise — shooting at his warships. He slowly sailed back and forth by all the Arabic cannon and never fired back. Just like old man Dudley Saltonstall did when he was being driven up the Penobscot River by the British during our War of Independence. They court-martialled him, as I remember. Thank God those Arabs are the world's poorest gunners. They board and capture. Never or rarely do they use cannon. He never offered to return the fire but cruised the area for a few weeks and then went to Malta awaiting good weather. To what end, I don't know. With tonight's weather, I bet the Commodore would have starved in Boston rather than leave his comfortable quarters for a tavern. Now, that Captain Rodgers of the *Enterprise* was one who did fight. When he came upon a sloop of war with a Tripolitan flag , he captured and took the *Paulina* to Malta.

"It wasn't long before I got word that the Dey of Tunis had a claim. He said the *Paulina* was mostly his even though it was flying the Tripolitan flag. Then the final disaster— Morris came sailing into the Tunisian harbor on the 19th of February, 1803 after having arrived at Gibraltar nine months earlier— a very aggressive Commodore! Then

Cathcart and I wined and dined him just as State Department people are told to do. I spent long hours going over the plans that we diplomats had agreed might bring an end to the nefarious tribute payments to those Barbary pirates. Yet all for naught because this fool Morris, when presented to the Dey, was so insulting that Ahmed had three hundred soldiers blocking his path at the shore. Now, we who are diplomats know when to bow and when to bluster. This Commodore knew neither. It was only after he and all of us acquiesced about the *Paulina* and gave the Dey a purse of twenty-five-thousand dollars, which was really mine for replacement of personal money, that the Commodore was allowed back onto his warships. And I then made preparation to leave Tunis as I was now *persona non grata* to the Dey. Dr. Davis of the Navy took my place as legate at Tunis. I did not leave with Commodore Morris. I'd had more than a bellyful of him. Cathcart had also lost favor with Ahmed, so we left for Algiers with Rodgers on the *Enterprise*.

"I was sure my diplomatic life was over. And Hamet...well... he would have to make his own peace with that bloodthirsty brother of his, Yusef. I did what I could, but my future at that point did not look too bright. I sailed on the *John Adams* from Algiers. Before I left I found a Dutch captain to take Raska Ahmar, my Henna, back to Holland, for I had freed her. I had never considered her my slave even though I had paid good hard money for her. She earned her freedom for she had pleasured my bed in the same manner as my dear, dear much loved girl of my dreams .m-my m-my Sophie." Eaton was sick and tired. The many night's work of coming, orating, and going were draining him of his vigor. Pulling together his remaining strength, he announced to all the patrons,

"I've run out of the needed energy to continue this exposé, so call me a conveyance that will carry me home, dry if not warm."

After Eaton had departed, Mr. B. Smart scratched his head and held his chin in his hand and said, to all who would listen,

"The General made the Navy a little too unwilling to fight. I was on one of them naval store ships, and we had scant supplies. And you all gotta remember England and France was at war once again. We in the navy — I was then — were always athinkin' one of their ships of the line, a big one, would come asailin' up and demand to board us. They was know'd to take their more than fair share of any sailors they liked. Us sailors sure liked American admirals — saving supplies just in case we got into a shoot-out with one or the other of 'em. A French or English Man 0' War was not too friendly in those days.

It was coming spring, and the trees of Boston were preparing to bud, soon to send their aromas of the season into the nostrils of the winter-weary dwellers plodding the streets and alleys in their workaday exertions. In the big common room at Vila's we find General Eaton declaiming to a scattering of new faces and a few active duty men. He was warming up with an old story while waiting for his usual audience to drift into the tavern and for his supper.

"... Commodore Morris would not listen to logic nor to Cathcart's and my advice concerning the claim of Dey of Tunis on the *Paulina*. Damn him. He was too blunt and told the Dey that the ship was not his. The Dey, as you recall, put three hundred of his soldiers between us and the warships in the harbor. A complete standoff, and it cost us thirty thousand dollars of Morris's funds and the *Paulina*. I and Cathcart became *persona non grata* in Tunis, so I sailed with Captain Rodgers. I had refused to sail with that old woman Morris. When I landed at Philadelphia, I made haste to reach Washington City. There I reported to the State Department and soon had told my account to Jefferson and Madison, telling them the true state of affairs in Barbary, informing them how the Navy had failed in its duty. Jefferson was unstirred. When I look back on that meeting,

I now have concluded that both Madison and Jefferson were not thinking of Barbary but of the great French land purchase they were about to consummate with Bonaparte. Months later after many meetings at State with Mr. Madison and also Secretary of War, Mr. Smith, I was invited to have dinner with Madison and the President. Madison took sick and so just the President and I spent more than four hours talking. I pounded the dinner table to drive home that I promised I would thrash those bloody pirates, those damnable Barbary pirates, and the United States of America would never again ever be forced to pay tribute to them thieves. It was understood that if I failed I would take the blame and if I won then Jefferson would take all the credit. I left, planning on having just a few good Marines, two bags of gold coins worth $40,000, and a thousand rifles. What a day that was! In person I had made my plan clear to President Jefferson, and now I was on my way back to Barbary with no written orders. I was still on State's payroll but on loan to the Navy. I was now the United States Naval Agent for the Barbary Coast. Oh yes, I did make a misstatement the other night. I forgot I was legate not a naval agent when I was ordering Commodore Morris to unlimber his gun on Tripoli. Now, I was to sail with a fleet of warships strong enough to implement my design.

"The Navy had been instructed to provide me, Mr. Eaton, 'with such artillery as he may require for his purposes.' And I knew my purpose! Eli and I knew — now I could lead a land army with Hamet and put him back on his throne in Tripoli. But first I would need to find him — I had sent Eli to New York City that spring to buy us tents and cooking equipment. I gave him a voucher on my profit from the Georgia land speculation. He was to purchase me the best scimitar that could be made in that city. Eli also brought back to Washington City some $20,000 hard money from my Boston bank. I had said to him, 'Now go and visit your mother in Brimfield,' but I stayed in Washington City.

"That meeting with Jefferson had fulfilled the promise that Secretary of the Navy, Robert Smith, had made me back when I had returned from a unhappy and brief trip to Brimfield in the summer of 1803. God almighty!

"Where is the Madeira wine I ordered? Waiter, what do I have to do to get served in this tavern? Be quick now and bring the wine and my supper too.

"A small aside , my dear audience, just a brief story about another supper with Jefferson. He got to reminiscing about his father and the American Indians. Jefferson related how even as a youth he considered them the white man's equal. This led him to such phrases as these about slavery —'a shameful abuse of a power. I trusted that King George would right this evil, but he didn't. In America one half of the citizens trample the rights of the other half. This destroys the morals of the one part. Can liberty in America be secure in the minds of the people if they believe that liberty is a gift of God, then we must grant freedom to all.' He ended with these words, 'I tremble for my country when I reflect that God is a just God.'

"I then told him of my conversion when I saw our naval men as slaves to those bloody Barbary pirates. The day will come when all Americans will be FREE MEN.

"Now back to the story, the day we weighed anchor at Baltimore was the 4th of July 1804. We, that is, Commodore Barron, Colonel Lear, and my son Eli and I sailed on the *John Adams*. With us we had the other frigates: *President, Congress, Constellation,* and *Essex,* all hands yearning for a taste of Barbary blood. For word had come back to America of Prebles' and Bainbridge's good shooting on the Barbary coast. Favorable winds took us quickly to Cape Spartel on the northern coast of Morocco, but contrary winds made it a long trip to the Barbary coast. We in the *John Adams* continued to Malta where we heard the news from Stephen Decatur and Charles Morris about their battle at Tripoli. Our junior service had a good baptism of fire there and came off the victor. But the crew of the *Philadelphia* was still in Bashaw Yusef's dungeon, along with many other Christian slaves.

"Sir. General. Can I have a word?" intruded one of the navy men.

"Granted but be brief, for it is my tale that is being told," the General commanded as he wanted to tell his own story the minute he finished supper which had finally arrived with his bottles of wine.

"I was with Cap'n Decatur and joined 'em boardin' that Tripolitan ship, the one which run up a white flag and was commanded by that pirate who had killed Cap'n Decatur's brother. I'll tell this here gatherin' Captain Decatur was a wild'un, and when we board that enemy ship, he look and looked and he found that liar and went at him. All of us atryin' to protect him from them other Moslems who outnumbered us by ten ta one. But, my God, Cap'n Decatur was in a rage, and that fight was one that we nor them were askin' for any quarta. No prisoners! I kilt my share o' them pirates and so did my mates. Then I seen that Cap'n Decatur was astrugglin' and slippin' on the bloody deck. Him and that dastardly leader both of 'em tripped over a pile of dyin' Turks. They both fell. The Cap'n had broke his sword that is why he was tryin' to get that Turk under 'im. I seen that Turk pull out a dirk and try to stab Decatur. Then as they was arollin' on the deck, the Cap'n saw a pistol in the folds of the pirate's robe , an' he pulled it out and shot him dead right in the head. The Captain and I —we both was alaying under them dead bodies. The rest of our crew be still busy aslashin' and acuttin' up the rest a them pirates. But somehow one o' the Turks that I had split wide open got up and was about to chop off Cap'n Decatur's head. Both of us still be pinned under many dead scoundrels. I cou'n't struggle free, so I yelled a warnin'. Reuben James was ...was cut and hacked near dead. Both arms cut off at the shoulders, and his blood were aflowin' out like a stuck pig. He heard my yellin', and he, bless his soul, flung hisself under that down swingin' scimitar. The Cap'n turned the pistol up and shot that damned pirate full in the face. Good old Reuben! Noble Reuben! May his soul rest in heaven.

"Those we di'n't kill jumped into the sea, but we sailed over their strugglin' bodies as we made way to join the other ships outside the harbor."

"Enough, my fellow spiller of pirate's blood, but thanks anyway." Eaton interrupted. Eaton had given his supper his undivided attention and now the General was prepared to resume his oration.

"This is MY story not the Navy's. For with my eager young Marines and gold in my pockets I was chafing to start my plan to put Hamet, the rightful ruler of Tripoli, back on his throne. So the first step was to find Hamet Bashaw . My informers told me he was in Egypt. I knew it was a country in civil war and that bribes would be the only way to complete this part of my mission. Bribes and more bribes — enough to lighten your pocket very quickly. My son Eli helped me in this bribery business. It was distasteful to me. Oh! My God! What time is it? Eli is coming to Boston tonight on the stage, and I must meet him. He is to arrive at ten. "

"General, you have time if you go now. I will fetch a hack for you. Finish your glass of Madeira. Then you, Mr. Jounae, help the General to the door where I'll have a cab waiting for him." Spoken by Colonel Patrick Patrick in his usual commanding manner.

"Thanks Pat, and now I'll just say a few more words to you veterans and fallen heroes. My son Eli has been visiting Brimfield with his wife, the Secretary of War's daughter. I asked him to come have a visit with me for a few days before he returns to his naval life as a Lieutenant. He was with me in the Barbary affairs, and we were as brothers. ...If he had not been so in love with that Smith girl, I'm sure he would have asked to share, well at least a few of the bed partners I had. Some of them had his attention. And as I remember, several of the bed partners would have welcomed a younger performer when mine fell a bit short of the perfection I expected from them."

As the Barbary General was about to leave the tavern, he turned and shouted,

"I'll continue this tale here next week on Thursday. 'Tomorrow, Tomorrow creeps on this petty pace....' Anyway it's Thursday. Ah Shakespeare and his lines. I wish that I had his pen." Eaton had remembered the broadsheet and had taken a look upon entering the tavern that night.

Not too long after the General left, our old friend who must put every story aright, Beauregard Smart, took front and center at the Bunch of Grapes. But this night he verified how Eaton had convinced the reluctant Jefferson to grant him his wish for a few good Marines, bags of gold, and the armaments for a land battle against the usurper of the throne of Tripoli. Jefferson had agreed to this because Eaton had promised an end of paying tribute to the Barbary pirates. Mr. Smart said, "I know this was the truth because I heard the Secretaries of State and War conversing with Eaton in the hack I was driving that summer of '03. Both of them had been told this by the President, and they had said as much to Eaton after his session with Jefferson. Smith had said that Eaton had better win the war because he, Smith, would also get blamed if this action failed. Smith was a little nervous on that ride."

The streets of Boston were in bloom — flowers filled the air with their essence. As the two old and forgotten heroes walked this spring day to their rendezvous, Colonel Patrick asked Eaton,

"General, when you were telling your story, I noticed that you made little of your visit with President Jefferson and the bags of gold he gave you. Now with your permission, Sir, I'd like to tell these great listeners my version of that amazing event. Since I was in Washington with you at that time, I think I can do it justice."

"You were of help then, and I am still in your debt for it, so you're the raconteur for tonight," Eaton agreed, and they took places at the center table in the Bunch of Grapes. Colonel Patrick began.

"We all remember the *Philadelphia* loss to the Tripolitans. We had been doing darn well capturing their warships, but when Bainbridge lost her, we were all dismayed. You, General, were in Washington dreaming your dreams of an end to the arrogance of those pirates by using the Navy to bombard their cities while the rightful ruler, Hamet Bashaw, led a land army to force the capitulation of his brother Yusef. Then Yusef sent word that he would sign a peace treaty if Washington would send $500,000 immediately and

$500,000 in tribute every year in perpetuity. God! What brass! All the people, even the families of those in slavery to the pirate dogs, said, 'No more money for tribute.' Well, nearly everyone. The tightwad treasurer of our Country, Albert Gallatin, calculated that endless war would cost more than endless tribute. Some in the State Department and even the President vacillated. Most of the better newspapers were saying, 'Bash the Bashaw,' and others, 'Destroy Tripoli.' And you and I, General, agreed !"

A very young naval veteran of the Barbary prisons insistently broke in with,

"Colonel, Sir — Sir, may I have a few words? — You see, Sir, I war' one of 'em slaves aworkin' on the fortification in Tripoli harbor. We war' whipped, starved, and put in solitary for little or nuthin'. We spent months as slaves workin' for that damn bloody pirate Yusef. Sir, all us American seamen would 'ave order up the total destruction of Tripoli ev'n if our own deaths be its result. 'Cause we'da know'd that Yusef would've ben' kilt too. We hate him all our wakin' days. Thank you, Sir, I just wanted General Eaton to know that he was 'ppreciated by all us sailors, Sir. Yes, we know'd it when he captured Derne 'cause we got a lot better food and less beatin'. Yes, by God, they knew about that defeat at Derne. Thank you, Sir." Colonel Pat replied,

"We like heroes like you, so tell everyone that Eaton was the primary reason those bloody pirates released our starved and beaten sailors. Most people of the United States and the enlightened countries also recognized the General for his deed of causing the downfall of such evil men. Let's all stand and drink a toast to General Eaton. Now — you all, give a loud cheer — so loud that we can be heard in Dock Square. Alright! Hurrah for General Eaton — Hurrah — Hurrah — Hurrah!" Colonel Patrick led the acclamation and then went on with his story.

"Thank you all. Now let's see , concerning the last meeting you had with President Jefferson, as I recall, you said, 'When I asked for Marines to help take the rifles to Bashaw Hamet, the President nearly turned me down.' I wonder how he thought you could take all that gold and rifles plus powder along with the cannons to Hamet without some protection from the local pirates and thieves that infest the Barbary coast. Thank goodness Jefferson came to his senses. That's when you told him that you would carry out his orders, and if it failed, you would say the whole thing was a private affair. If it succeeded, then his Marines could have the glory of having carried out the orders of their Commander-in-Chief. Now I also remember that you told Jefferson you would perform this duty just as Washington had done as he led us to freedom; you asked only to have your expenses paid by the U.S. government. If the Barbary pirates had not captured the *Philadelphia,* Jefferson would not have given you any Marines or gold to set Hamet back on his throne. No, he would have done what his Treasurer said was least costly... send the millions and millions, year after year, to keep the pirates satisfied with the people's tax money and leave our fellow citizens in slavery."

"No money for Tribute! No money for pirates! No money for the Barbary slavers!" came the spontaneous cheer from the audience of loyal listeners.

"That's what the President should have had dinned into his ears, but as we all know he was of at least two minds. He sent Colonel Lear as Consul General and told him to buy the good will of the Barbary pirates. To our General Eaton, he gave the means to have Hamet retake his rightful throne. And now I propose another toast to the General, but first let the waiters pour us all a refill, for my mug is empty and my throat dry."

Colonel Pat stood and, saluting the General, he addressed the uplifted faces,

"May the memory of General Eaton stay in the minds

of the citizens of this great country for a thousand years and more. I am sure HISTORY will find a rightful place for our hero of Derne. May he be remembered for his amazing march across the Barbary desert."

They all yelled, "Hip, Hip...HOORAY!" Pat shouted,

"For he is our hero!" After the toast and some time of general conversation Eaton banged on his empty wine glass until the room of heroes ceased their chatter and turned their eyes and ears toward the center table.

"If you still have ears to listen with, I would like to read from my journal some of the words that I forced upon Jefferson and his cabinet members before they agreed to make me the Naval Agent and supply me with means to break the Barbary stranglehold on our commerce. While we and the Europeans continued paying tribute to those bloody pirates, I wrote, 'It would be indeed something astonishing that those pitiful hordes of sea robbers should have acquired such ascendancy over the small and even considerable states of Christendom, ...'

" 'Denmark and Sweden (and us) have gratuitously furnished almost all their materials for ship building and munitions of war. We have also given them valuable jewels and large sums of money. We are continually paying into their hands for their forbearance and for the occasional ransom of captives.'

" 'Holland and Spain bring them cash, naval constructors, engineers, and workmen for their dock yards. They would sink under their own ignorance and thus want the means for their mischievous acts. (If we had not helped) Why do we furnish them the means to cut our own throats?'

" 'And from the principle of commercial rivalship among the tributaries, which aims to supplant each other in friendship of these chiefs by the preponderance of bribes: a principle , however, which ultimately defeats its own object: — for the Deys, like apostate lawyers, take fees on both sides, and by a rule of inversion, turn their arguments against the client who has the heaviest purse.'

" 'Immense quantities of that essential life article (wheat for bread) are annually shipped from both those Regencies (Tunis and Algiers) to ports of Spain and Italy, and occasionally to other ports of Christendom in that sea. We of the United States of America are their rivals in this commerce. In Algiers and the others as well (wheat) is farmed by the Jew House of Bocri and Busnah, well known to have influence on that government.'

" 'I believe...my motive...to be a man, to gain the honor due a hero and the ardent zeal to serve my country by chastising an enemy, which richly merits chastisement, in ways economical, effectual and honorable.'

" 'I can remember, can you? All those naval ships we turned over to the Dey of Algiers, the *Hero*, the *Hassan Bashaw*, the *Skjoldabrand*, and the *Le la Eisha* — all ready to fight our very own, and other Christian, seamen and put them in slavery. God, that's why I had to find a way for my country to stop this great sin of giving them Barbary Pirates the means to cause all that sorrow. A small army well led, I knew, could right these great injustices. That is why I never gave up the idea of putting Hamet back on his rightful throne.' " Eaton straightened and rubbed his eyes.

"Enough from my journal. The light in here is not too good for reading, so I'll have another serving of that good old Naval rum that I smell. Also, waiter, bring me a small repast before I take this aching body off to dreams of honor and glory."

Mr. Smart was a no show this night because he had sprained an ankle and wasn't walking.

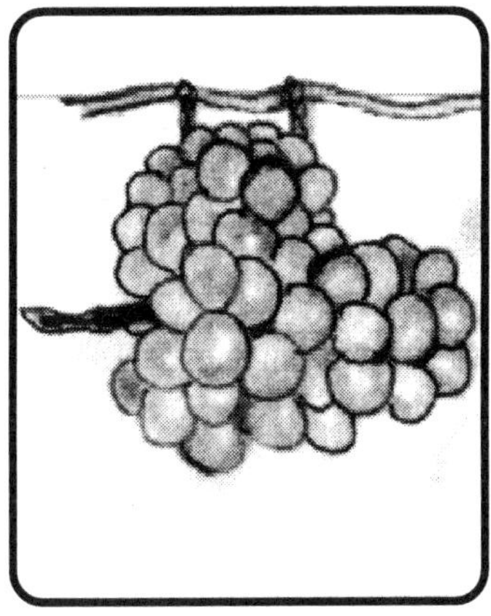

The Bunch of Grapes was short on patrons the next night Eaton was scheduled to return. Eaton and Colonel Pat finished the evening meal with relish as they drank one bottle each of Madeira. The main dish of roasted spring-run salmon was not new to them, but Mrs. Vila had not done the usual thing with herbs so it was a thrill to their taste buds. Eaton said ,

"Pat, too bad we didn't have those herbs for that dead camel we et on the way to Derne. It sure would have gone down with a lot more ease."

"Yes, my General, I'm sure it would have gone down better, and you would have had a larger serving of roast camel. But General, you have to keep in mind that **I** was not on that long walk across the sands of Barbary. We did our marching together in those wars against the Indians."

"Well, some of the wild game we shot for meat then would have made holiday feed with Mrs. Vila's herbs. Pat, make sure I visit the kitchen before we leave and give that lady her due."

The waiter cleared the table, bringing a new bottle of wine and fresh glasses. After a few sips Eaton addressed the small gathering .

"Gentlemen," Eaton said because when he had looked

at this night's audience he had seen some of the high nabobs of Boston,

"I now have remembered that I needed to say some few words about Tobias Lear. We were good friends until the end of the Barbary War. We were, after all, both former Army officers and had dined many, many times together. Colonel Lear was a very moderate drinker, well read in the Greek classics, and we discussed them at length because we had *oceans* of time while crossing the Atlantic. You see, Commodore Samuel Barron picked the smallest vessel for his crossing, the *John Adams*, and invited us, including Eli, to accompany him. So we got to share a damned small cabin for a long trip to the shores of Barbary.

"Before we all sailed we did get the astounding news that Captain Decatur had burnt our *Philadelphia*, which the pirates had captured in Tripoli harbor, right under their noses. A ship of the line that would not then be out on the high seas capturing more of our merchant ships.

"We sailed with five of the most powerful frigates in the U.S. Navy to join our fleet already in the Mediterranean sea. With this and my Marines, gold, and promised cannon I was sure Yusef's days as Bashaw of Tripoli were coming to a quick end and that I soon would have Hamet Bashaw on his rightful throne. Best of all, the prisoners in Tripoli would be free to return to their families and homes. Now I had had a disagreement with the Commodore's brother, Captain John, but Commodore Samuel Barron and I stayed on good terms until the very end of the Barbary affair. Although my guns and other supplies were on the larger *Constellation,* I remained on the small sloop *John Adams* from Gibraltar to the blockading U.S. Navy fleet at Tripoli. The sloop made a quick journey to Commodore Preble, and he was soon informed of my arrival.

On the evening of August 9th in '04 I was invited to dine on the *Constitution* (now sitting in Boston harbor) with

Commodore Preble. I told him that Commodore Barron would soon be at Tripoli. Preble told me that he had sunk and captured many of Yusef's ships that had attempted to run his blockade. The naval losses had been light, somewhat less than fifty officers and men killed or wounded. He was sure that the naval blockade had so harmed Yusef that he would be willing to sign a treaty. I didn't think that this was possible, having dealt with this pirate more than once. However, to keep Preble happy and to do my duty, I asked him to put me ashore under a flag of truce. He set me ashore in the gig, escorted by two gun boats. As I walked with Eli over the Tripolitan stone wharf, I could see the many American sailors working on the Dey's fortifications. A small crowd gathered around us, causing the prisoners to look and some of them soon recognized me. A ragged cheer went up. As more prisoners recognized who was on the quay, the cheer rang out loud and strong, and it rolled out to our ships in the harbor.

"Then them dastardly overseers laid their whips on the backs of our poor, ragged, starved, American seamen. Seamen from the *Philadelphia*. But they only cheered louder, and that cheer went out to the ears of American sailors in the harbor. As I walked up into the town, I was met by my old friend the Swedish Consul Nissen. I talked to him in a very loud voice so the American sailors that were near could hear me. I said, 'Be of good faith men. All America stands with you. You will be saved.' Nissen got me an audience with Yusef after I met with prisoner Captain Bainbridge from the *Philadelphia* in Nissen's house. I promised Bainbridge that I would do everything in my power to help him and all the prisoners. After this brief freedom Bainbridge was returned to the dank, dark prison. Murad Reis, that damned turncoat, was at the palace and wanted to be our interpreter but I said to the Bashaw, 'You know, and I know, that I, Eaton, need no help from that renegade Murad Reis to communicate with your Highness.' Yusef Bashaw said to him, 'You leave us.'

"Then Yusef said to me, 'I , the Bashaw of Tripoli, am still on my throne and you, Eaton, have not yet been able to put my stupid brother Hamet even in the city of Tripoli. Eaton, you haven't found that small minnow yet.' It seems that words travel fast in the desert. I did not react to his taunting but told him that I was instructed by my President to deal with his latest claims of tribute. I said, 'I am authorized by President Jefferson to negotiate a new treaty.' After many words spent in this fashion Yusef finally came down off that foolish half a million dollar demand and now asked for a more —Hrumph! Yes, he *thought* a more reasonable ransom. He asked for only the pittance of $150,000 and annual tribute of $250,000. If I could pay this he would release all the men of the *Philadelphia*." Eaton paused a moment to address the waiter.

"Will you fill our mugs and offer some to our patient audience? Then tally up the bill because I should be getting back home before Aletti sends out a search party. But I need just a bit more time to finish up tonight's discourse.

"I told the big, dirty, ugly brute he was asking for far more money than we were willing to pay. And I also told him that my countrymen could be freed by hot lead and not gold. At this point he threw one of his famous temper fits and yelled so loudly that his palace guards came into the throne room with drawn scimitars. Now under normal circumstances I should have groveled at his feet, but this was not a normal meeting. I told the Bashaw that if he carried out his threat of killing all the men of the *Philadelphia*, which he had just uttered in his madness, I would order Commodore Preble to hang him, the Bashaw of Tripoli, from the yardarm of the U.S. Warship *Constitution*. I stated this in a loud and commanding voice, and the Bashaw got my message. Then he said to his wild Arabs swinging their scimitars that he was in a mind to have my head on a platter before the sun set.

"That's when I told this thieving cutthroat about the four largest warships from America that would, in a very few days, be sailing into his harbor with the full intent of leveling his city by high explosives from their big guns. I made this announcement very slowly and with much emphasis, naming the ships and their respective armaments. His bodyguards released me from their bonds.

"Then the Bashaw ordered me back to my ship, and when I was on the street leading to the quay, I met Nissen again and told him the state of our affairs with Yusef. I spoke in French because Murad Reis was in the group of people escorting me back to my ship.

"Later at supper I got to tell Commodore Preble that because of the day's confrontation I would venture the Navy could not bring about the defeat of Bashaw Yusef with a naval blockade. He was very polite, as he always is, but I think he was not listening to the naval agent, William Eaton.

"Bring the bill now! I'll sign it and be on my way. Pat, do you wish to join me in the hack?"

Beauregard had been in another tavern, but finding that one nearly empty of people, he had come late to the Bunch of Grapes. After Colonel Pat and General Eaton left, Mr. Smart started his story of the day he had rowed Eaton to the quay at Tripoli. He said the sailors working on that fort sure looked like they needed a good meal and since the mention of food caused his stomach to remember that he had not eaten since early morning, Beauregard ordered his evening meal.

Back at his rooms Eaton was again thinking about his heroic life. His mind was reviewing the scenes of time spent in Richmond during the Burr trial. Eaton mused, 'If that Dutch woman had stayed in Holland or if I had sold that redhead in Barbary, then maybe the newspapers would not have been full of my ...well that act might never happened. Now then it might be that those nabobs of Boston and those legislators would have at least treated me as an equal. Well that's spilled...went down the drain, as Mr. Vila said. The only way I'm going to remain in my rightful place in history is this book I'm writing. General, you had better get to work on your book, *The Life of William Eaton* and stop looking back on things that cannot be changed. Time — how much do I have?'

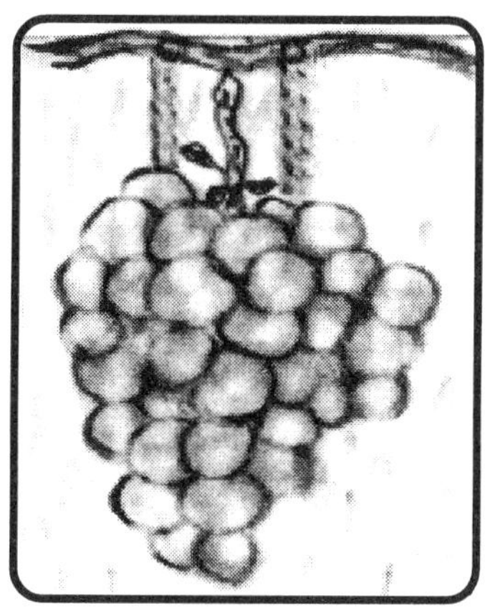

"**I have the distinct pleasure** of reading to you from my diary. I want this part of my revelation, about my astounding march to Derne, to have no embroideries as some hagiologists are wont to present. No magnifying glass of legend, for I shall read you the facts as I recorded them in my journal. I will not read every word because that would be taxing your ability to sit and listen. Since you beer swiggers, or 'grognards' as one of my former erudite professors would have called you, are expecting a good story, I'll do my best to make it entertaining. On that sea-crossing we all had become better acquainted since we shared one small cabin. Commodore Samuel Barron was so sick that he had to go ashore when we stopped for provisions at Atlantic islands. We all thought it was too bad that such an elderly man had been given this sea command.

"Now, good waiter, be quick and bring me my Flip and my bottle of Madeira to wash down this evening's repast. Bring a light so I'll not strain my eyes." The General turned the pages in his journal as the waiters in the Bunch of Grapes brought several tall candles to the center table.

"September 2 , 1804 at 6 P.M. — arrived at Sardinia.

September 5th Quarantined by the port authority at Malta because of plague in the area.

September 5th Mr. O'Brien said he had been to Tripoli and Tunis, by authority. To the Dey of Tunis he had offered an annual tribute of eight thousand dollars to take the place of a frigate that he had demanded and that State had acquiesced to.

"He had also offered one hundred and ten thousand dollars to the false Dey of Tripoli for a peace treaty and freedom for our noble captives. Those thieves rejected our terms.

"You can see what difficult people we had to deal with in that conflict," Eaton said as an aside. Then continued,

"Let's start the search for Hamet Bashaw. I had been told by my friend, Mr. Pulis, that Hamet was under the Dey of Egypt's protection.

"November 10,1804 — I removed my baggage to the *Argus* which was under the command of Lieutenant Isaac Hull in preparation for the expedition. Captain Rogers took the *Constitution* and Captain Decatur the *Congress*.

"Nov. 14 we set sail with Hull from Malta toward Alexandria. A British Man of War sails with us to keep us safe. We left in the port of Syracuse the frigates *Constitution, Congress, Essex,* and the *John Adams*. The frigate *President* has gone off to help blockade the port of Tripoli. Commodore Barron is sick ashore.

"Nov. 25 We arrived in Alexandria. On the 28 of November saw the local officials. They gave us suitable food and entertainment."

Eaton held up the story to speak to Colonel Pat. Pointing at a very elderly man in the back of the tavern, Eaton said,

"I think we have a famous man with us. Look right to the left of the naval cadet. Isn't that our famous Paul Revere?"

"Yes, I do believe that you are right, General."

"Pat, go to the head and then stop by and ask the man,

if you determine that he is Revere, whether he would like us to introduce him to Vilas' patrons."

On his return Pat said, "Yes, it is Revere, and yes, he said you may introduce him." General Eaton stood and said in a very loud and commanding voice,

"ATTENTION! I ... We have the honor of having among us tonight one of Boston most famous personages, the silversmith, the patriot par excellence, the gifted artist Paul Revere. Will you stand, Mr. Revere, as I ask all here to applaud you?"

Many eyes turned toward the elderly Revere. The patrons raised their hands in a round of clapping. Revere bowed, resumed his seat and said in a tremolo voice,

"Continue."

Eaton turned a page and started the journey.

"It was the 28th before we left for Grand Cairo via Rosetta. With me are Lieutenant Blake , Navy; Lieutenant O'Bannon, Marines; Midshipman Mann and my stepson Eli Danielson; Mr. Farquhar and Seid Seli. Alli, and a drogoman (a boat handler), and six other servants.

"Dec. 1st, We enter the Nile where we soon met an English barge with Dr. Mendrici. Landing we were met by the British Resident of Grand Cairo, Major Misse. He was at Rosetta because of the war between the Turks and Mamelukes that was raging in the vicinity.

"Dec. 2nd, the religious chief Skiak, seized all our boats as it was the beginning of Ramadan.

"Dec. 3rd. We found boats and helpers. They call the boats *marche*. We bought food and left for Cairo. Captain Vincent and Doctor Mendrici joined us while Lt. Blake returned to Alexandria. Now we have eighteen able bodied men who are well armed and provisioned. Vincent flies the British flag, we fly the American.

"On the 5th, after having a late meal amongst the local villagers, I took a rifle and for their amusement, fired three shots at three oranges, splitting two at the distance of thirty -two yards. The natives all have a universal prayer that England would return and put order in the countryside. We land in Cairo in a melée caused by my servant and the drogoman, Alli, firing muskets. I explained the mix-up and the Turks were appeased.

"On Dec. 8th, I enter Cairo on horseback with a few Turkish officials and a horde of people of all ages and sexes, all curious to see an American.

"Doctor Mendrici arranged for our meeting with the Viceroy by telling him that an American General - a pasha - accompanied by several young gentlemen of the Navy came to gratify their curiosity and wish to pay our respect.

It was on the 21st of December when I engaged a German engineer, a Colonel from the Tyrol Battery by the name of Eugene. I call him Leitensdorfer. I advanced him fifty dollars.

"Dec 22nd, We all visit a house of Almee, dancing women. They were haggard prostitutes, disgusting, obscene monsters, who exhibit savage nature in gestures of studied and practised depravity; like the Spanish Balario." Eaton looked from reading.

"I should add that I've seen many dancing women, and these were the worst. Now I shall skip the travelogue as the important work was to find Hamet. I found Hamet's secretary of State and two ex-governors. They were destitute of everything but resentment. Even hope had abandoned them. From them I learned that Hamet was with the Mamelukes and he had very few Tripolitan and Arab auxiliaries in the village of Miniet in Upper Egypt. I made haste in preparation for the journey to meet Hamet in Miniet."

Just then Eli entered the large taproom and came to the General's table. Eaton greeted him, saying,

"Let me introduce to this great listening audience my dear son and companion Eli Danielson. I'm sure some of you remember his blood father that good General Tim Danielson of the war we had with the French. He is a chip off that old block, much like, well really a near copy of his famous father. I had this young Major do all my paper work as we crossed those hot sands of Barbary. He was my right hand and more. I found that he had courage and a keen ability in solving many military problems. Eli, would you like to say a few words to these, my nightly companions?"

"General, as you are well acquainted with me, you know that I did the planning and paper work of the army. I'm not the speech giver, yet I might like this once to tell your friends about a little known episode that took place on the desert of Barbary. I'll be brief and leave out how the wind blew, how the cold nights made one long for the Franklin stove, how the lack of food made vivid dreams of the farmers' markets here in Boston, how the drinking water at times made me hold my nose to get it to stay in my stomach. No, I'll not elaborate about those minor difficulties, but... I'll tell you how the General, on one occasion got that army of thieves and opportunists, downright lacking in manliness, to keep marching in the direction of Derne. Manliness —-that's what the General always stressed.

"He would counsel all us Christians with those words from the Bible that say something like this 'when I was a child I acted a child, but now that I am a man I act like a man.' Well I'm not a Bible scholar but that's the meaning. Now to the event. As I remember, it was about in the thirtieth day of our forty day sojourn that we ran out of rice which had been our money for buying the local foods, such as olives and dates. Oh yes! and meat, goats and poultry. Now without the local food, we were down to naval hard bread; so hard that a cup of water took almost a whole hour to make it soft enough to bite without breaking a tooth. Half of the Arabs were for returning to Alexandria. The other half were going to steal all the remaining supply of naval hard bread. Well, the General got wind of this and had the Marines under O'Bannon placed so they could defend the food stores. When the Arabs tried to sneak into the tent, the Marines let in the ring leaders and then closed the trap. With loaded rifles they took the culprits to Eaton's marquee. He picked out two of the most troublesome of these cowards and had them trussed up. They were the same two men the General had reprieved from the Turks who had found them guilty of murder and were going to remove their heads. The Turks had given them into General Eaton's care, thinking no doubt, that his whole army was going to perish on the sands of Barbary.

"In the morning, General Eaton ordered all the troops to parade in front of his tent. When they had assembled, he led the two troublemakers out, and as the sounds of a drum roll crested, he whipped out his scimitar. The same one he had paid a great sum of money for to a New York ironmonger. Oh! with a mighty swing the General whipped off two heads, and they rolled down a small hill toward the troops all standing at attention. Two heads, spurting blood all the way, stopped at the assembled warriors' feet.

"The disgruntled Arabs were impressed with the General's strength and vigor. They cheered and promised to obey his orders. We started for Derne, leaving the naked bodies of those renegades for the circling birds of prey. I think it was that very day we came to a desert watering spot and found a multitude of local peoples with food for sale. We discovered the brass buttons on our Marines' coats could be used for gold. We had a few good meals paid for by those Marines of Lieutenant O'Bannon."

"Sir, Major Danielson, sir, may I ask a question of the General?" An unkempt sailor asked in a rather feminine voice. The same funny one who had been at many other evening meetings.

"Ask him yourself; he can hear you," Eli said.

"General, Sir, I've heard said that when you was in those Barbary lands you kilt a LION. Sir, when will you tell that story 'cause I wanta hear it?"

"Well, it will not be tomorrow because I've a dinner engagement with the Adamses." Eaton then looked at a copy of Vilas' broadsheet that had been given to him as he entered the tavern.

"Let's say... I'll tell that story the next night after my supper with the Adamses, right here at the Bunch of Grapes."

"I'll be here to hear it, and I'll bring all my Navy friends too," the queerest sailor present stated.

When the waiters began pouring ale into the empty expectant mugs sitting on the wooden tables, including one for Major Danielson, the room was filled with the sound of many voices, in less than normal decibels, conversing privately.

When the large walnut-encased clock indicated the hour of closing, the General raised his voice and said,

"Now if James Vila will present his bill for this night, I will pay, for I just received a little more money on my very frigid land in the far north Province of Maine."

Pat said as Eaton was about to leave,

"General, the last time we were here you said, 'Remind me to say some good words to Mrs. Vila about those herbs on the salmon.' I'll ask Mr. Vila to get her." Pat went to the kitchen and came back with the smiling cook .

"Your salmon was delicious and you certainly had the herbs in just the right amount, Mrs. Vila. Now I think you're old enough for a Gentleman to kiss." And the General bussed the lady on her check and then her lips fell on his. A spark struck, and he responded with a full sexually pressed kiss on her expectant mouth. Mr. Vila had stayed in the kitchen and was not in sight. The flustered and warmed Verna Vila slipped her arms away and quickly ducked through the nearby kitchen door. Eli exclaimed,

"Dad, you sure told the cook what you thought of her cooking but probably not in a way Mr. Vila would applaud! The cab's waiting, so let's go."

The April day's shower made the cobbles wet and slippery so Eli helped the General into a cab which soon had them at Eaton's rooms. Visiting continued far into the wee hours of the morning.

The tavern's official critiquer, B. Smart, had been at the far corner of the tavern and had enjoyed the story. He didn't think the time was right to correct some of the small errors Eaton and Danielson had made in their tales.

The Bunch of Grapes had a full house since Vila's broadsheet had told the people of Boston that heroic General Eaton would tell about his AFRICAN LION HUNT. Even with Colonel Pat's help it was difficult for the General to pass through the crowded patrons to his assigned table. Eaton had come to the tavern in his best civil suit, cut in the latest style. It made him appear to belong to the silk stocking society. The room was full and running over with naval, marine, and army veterans of all ages, and a few who were still in the country's service. Each one was expectant of a very good tale. The waiters were running to and fro, but as soon as the General sat, Vila sent his best servant to Eaton's table.

"I'll have a Flip while I wait for the evening viands. Please bring two bottles of Madeira with our food." Potatoes, squash, peas, venison, and a large cut of maple walnut pie were brought to the General's table.

When Eaton and Pat had finished their food, the audience became quiet.

"I looked in my journal and found that this Lion Hunt took place in Tunis in the second week of November 1800 just before Cathcart asked me to come to Tripoli. The Dey of Tunis was well pleased with my handling of the naval stores that he had been expecting. So his Highness said to me soon after their arrival, 'As a small reward for your service, Mr. Eaton, I will allow you to accompany me on my annual Lion hunt.'

"When these pirates go hunting its a major operation, camel about twenty and a mounted escort of fine Arabian horses, slaves with wagons carrying tents. I think my journal said I counted a full one hundred and fifty-three persons in the Dey's retinue.

"The hunt took place after we had traveled for two days into the mountains where the Dey set up his tents near a Bedouin encampment. These nomads informed the Dey the lions had a cave on the other side of the mountain and that if we wished, they would lead us to them. The following day we set off with much expectation. After a morning of riding and no sign of lions, we took a small rest under tents that had been brought by the Dey's people. Soon I was restless and left the sleeping Dey to explore for myself the cave we had passed that morning. I rode up to it and after thorough examination decided it was a cave long abandoned by lions. Looking around at the landscape, I became curious about an outcropping I could detect a mile to the southeast of this cave. Even though the temperature was extremely high, I rode over to investigate its geology. This ride was much longer than I had calculated. There were many ravines, called wadis, and sand hills which slowed my progress. The sun was nearing the 3 o'clock position before I arrived at this unusual exposed rock. I took samples and then mounted to return to the Bedouin camp.

"I adjusted my horse's speed so that the distance to camp would be gained by the time the sun set. Yet the sand was soft, the ravines deep, and the sun was sinking quickly. In nearly the very last rays of sun my eyes made out a large male lion watching me from a clump of camel brush on my left. Slowly, very slowly, I edged my horse downwind of the animal and got my firing piece ready to shoot. The lion watched but evidently did not smell us, for it made no effort to attack or to leave. Keeping a wary eye on the "King of Beasts," I approached the camel brush. When I was about fifty feet from it, the large male lion sprang up and swung its head in my direction. I pulled the trigger. The bullet sped to its mark and I came into the Bedouin camp with a trophy for my mantel in Brimfield.

"The Dey was pleased that I had killed my first lion, and the camp had a really wild celebration that night. First we had roast camel. I'm sure some of Mrs. Vila's well blended herbs would have vastly improved its going down. Also roasted squash, fruits of many kinds, nuts. We washed it down with hot tea. All during the feasting some servants played their unusual musical instruments for our entertainment.

"Then the men sang while the women brought more food. To delight our eyes the chief had to show off one of his too many daughters to the Dey of Tunis. She was a lovely lithe young thing just in her middle teens. The more she danced, looking very provocatively at his highness, the more the Dey's eyes undressed her. I knew that the local chief was expecting some arrangements might be made. Some gold was exchanged, and the fresh young girl now was the Dey's property and his to deflower. This is how it is done in Barbary.

"I never got to keep that lionskin and head, for when the time came to help Cathcart, it was at a Tunis shop being made ready. I returned for it weeks later, but the shop was closed, and my lionskin and head had been sold to the highest bidder, I am sure. Although the Dey sent some officials to look for my property, I knew it was a lost cause."

The loyal listeners all stood and gave the General a thunderous applause. Colonel Pat helped the sore-footed General to his feet, escorted him to the head, and went to call a cab. Leaving the toilet the General met the owner's wife at the door, and she quickly handed him a small sheet of paper and said softly,

"General, please read it later." Verna had seen that James Vila was about to leave the common room for the kitchen, and so she joined him there. Then Pat and Eaton left for John Woort's Sign of the Dragon on Union Street. John was a friend of Colonel Pat's.

It was an almost impossible situation for our well traveled Mr. Smart. He nearly burst with his story but did wait for the General to exit the tavern.

"In my youth I was in Tunis, and that very Dey's father let me, an infidel, accompany him on a lion hunt. We didn't get just one lion as Eaton did but after ...I think it was three days of hunting... we had bagged and skun about... no, I remember now — it was twenty-one large male lions. I was allowed to shoot one, but the Dey kept the head and skin. Yes, all we did was find caves and... and more caves and then shoot and shoot. The Barbary desert was full of lions then ...."

Later, much later, that May night Eaton read the note from Verna Vila. He read '*He goes to market at five*' and smiled lasciviously.

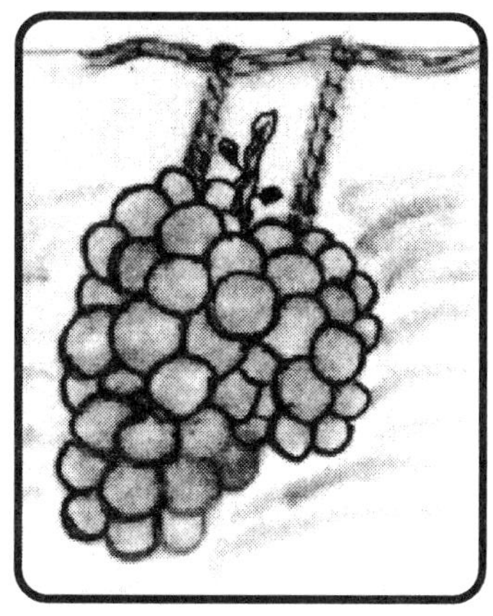

The General was in his flowing Barbary robe. He had ridden his white and black stallion to the head of the Long Wharf and stabled him. Striding in a military manner with his scimitar swinging by his side, the General made an entrance that spoke loud and clear to the assembled listeners. I AM GENERAL WILLIAM H. EATON; I AM COMING TO MY TABLE. MAKE WAY! With all the appropriate flourishes he took command and ordered up his food and drink. We now can hear the General speaking to the eager audience in the well-crowded taproom; he has already started.

"...could understand my consternation when I discovered that Hamet was with the Mamelukes in upper Egypt. Those Mamelukes and the Turkish Army regulars were having a voracious civil war in the Egyptian countryside. I was invited to visit the Turkish Viceroy and what a sumptuous palace! Sitting on his right, I answered query after query about world news and about my new country. After we had coffee and sherbet, the hookahs were brought in just as the Viceroy was dismissing his retinue. As we smoked, he turned to me and asked in French, 'You have more than idle curiosity, monsieur, to travel into my land at this critical and dangerous time?' This opened the occasion, so I told him in French that we were there to find the rightful ruler of

Tripoli, Hamet Bashaw. He understood me and responded that he indeed knew his Highness, Hamet Karamanli, Bashaw of Tripoli, telling me that he had furnished Hamet supplies and money. The Viceroy continued in French that he would do all in his power to help us in our plan of action.

"Upon my preparation for leaving, his Honor the Viceroy offered me a letter of amnesty for Hamet so that he might be unmolested in passing the sentry posts of the Turkish Army. So all I had to do then was detach Hamet from the Mamelukes — a very delicate operation. They might think he was changing sides and subject him to the law for deserters. I spent several coins before I found trustworthy agents to carry my letters to Hamet.

"My God! Where are the waiters? Will they not come and receive my order?" Eaton spoke very loudly, so Colonel Patrick got up from their table and went to the kitchen. After the Colonel's return, and the General's being assured that a waiter would soon arrive at his table, Eaton continued the recitation. "I should say that I had previously sent several letters by secret means to Hamet. I sent the Viceroy's letter of amnesty off on the 15th of January in quadruplicate by four different conveyances to Hamet Bashaw. As of then, I had not any direct word from him since before my going home."

A waiter came to the table , did a slight bow, and asked,

"How can I serve the General?"

"So! Waiter, you have finished your meal in the kitchen and have now deemed it time to serve your master's customers? I've waited too too long for my first drink. Now be quick, *tout suite*! And bring me a pitcher of ale and the food.

"Colonel Patrick , thank you for bringing the waiter. And as the waiter has deemed it wise to leave his meal in the kitchen and sally into the common room, he will take your request first," Eaton declared. The two old army companions of the Ohio and Georgia campaigns ate and drank their fill while the main storytelling waited and then began again.

"I shouldn't leave —" the General was interrupted by an elderly farrier.

"Sir. General Eaton, Sir. I found the tavern on King — Sorry! I knowed they has changed the name to State Street now, but when I wuz here in Boston in '76 it was King. Sir, I'd like to ask about yerr Arabian stallion....the one you brings back from the Barbary coast. Sir, I'm not goin' to be in Boston after taday. I'm goin' home ta the province of Maine ta shoe hosses in the big woods."

"It's my story, but since you have rudely interjected yourself, what is your question?"

"Sir, your pardon. My question is — Be he the hoss that you ride inta town ta night, and be he the same hoss that 'tis said comes when you call even at a mile 'n' half? I heerd that in Springfield. Thank you, SIR."

"Yes, it is my white and black Arabian that I rode into Boston today and, the same that comes at my command. I bought him in Tunis, and I've also put him out to stud in Brimfield. He is a very remarkable stallion." Eaton stopped to yell,

"Waiter ...Waiter...WAITER!" and from the kitchen the waiter came on the run, for Mr. Vila was in the tavern.

"Pour this interloper a whiskey and bring Pat and me a — no, two bottles of your best wine.

"I now will tell the assemblage this little tidbit about a Mr. Drouette, a French Consul who was , I found out later, a friend of that damnable Famin, the one I horse-whipped in Tunis. This Drouette insinuated to the Turkish Viceroy that we were British spies and had come to deliver a credit subsidy to the Mamelukes. I found the means to prove that he lied. Now with time on my hands, awaiting word from Hamet, I sought out former Tripolitan emigres to test their loyalty to Hamet. Loyal ones I recruited into his service. In one case I interrogated a Turk by the name Arnaut who had been in Tripoli in the service of Joseph Bashaw, that dastardly usurper. He, Arnaut, was present when the American Navy had bombarded Tripoli city. He said, 'Tripoli lost many men during the different attacks by the Americans last summer. The city was much damaged, and the inhabitants are in such a state of consternation that nobody sleeps inside the city walls. Nor is any business done inside the walls of the city.' He wept as he told me about the fireship that American Captain Somers had blown up in Tripoli harbor, smashing many of Yusef's ships and killing many of his defenders. I continued my questioning and found that many of the Tripolitan people where wishing that Yusef would be overthrown. But he knew it would not be by Hamet because he said to me Hamet was dead by Yusef's assassins. This was, I deduced, believed by Yusef because his hired murderers reported that they had successfully poisoned his brother, thus collecting their reward.

"In a few days I received a letter from Hamet which had been sent before he had received the Viceroy's pass. Hamet wrote that he would be taking up lodgings at the house of Ab'd'el gavir el be Kourchi and would await me there.

"I had gone to Alexandria, so I left for that Arab's home, taking with me Lieutenant Blake, Midshipman Mann, and an escort of twenty-three men armed and mounted. When I had gone about seventy or eighty miles, I was detained by a large detachment of Ottoman or also called Turkish troops. The headman, by the name of Kerchief, was bribed and cajoled until he sent for a young higher ranking chief from the tribe called Ou ad Allis, who knew Hamet Bashaw and verified my story to Kerchief. We then were allowed to eat and drink.

"Drink — Yes, the results being you soon need relief, for your kidneys have done their job and your bladder is full. I'm off and the story can wait."

After the General's urine had been expelled, he returned and took a long draught on the Madeira wine. Then as the clatter and chatter abated, attentive eyes and ears were again aimed at General Eaton.

"Contrary to expectations, I met up with Hamet in Alexandria because messages told me that he was there. On February 23, 1805 we both signed a convention composed of fourteen articles concerning the duties of the United States of America and his Highness, Hamet Karamanli, the Bashaw of Tripoli. I had Lieutenant P.N. O'Bannon, Dr. Francisco Mendrici, and Pascal Paoli Peck sign as witnesses. I had this document published and distributed to all loyal Tripolitans and sent copies to Commodore Samuel Barron. A secret article had been added to the copies sent to Barron and to my and Hamet's copies. It concerned the Bashaw of Tripoli, his family, and Peter Lisle. That turncoat! We, Hamet and I, put it in the addendum and we did expect and hoped to send all these criminals to the United States for safe keeping.

"Then as we tried to leave the city of Alexandria, the Turkish guards arrested the men in Hamet's baggage train, and our provisions, which were on a boat in the harbor were kept from us. I laid all this to that damn French Consul Drouette, and I found out later that I was right. Well, a little money here and a little more somewhere else spread around by Eli got the supplies freed. With some additional help from the British consul, Hamet's train was on its way to the Arab's Tower some thirty miles west of Alexandria. I planned to meet Hamet there on Sunday with my Marines as well as my Christian and Moslem recruits. Arriving at the meeting place, I found that my commissary and quartermaster department head, Mr. Farquhar, had embezzled all of the 1,350 gold dollars I had given him. I discharged him and took over that work. On the 4th of March

I was visited by Dr. Mendrici who had helped buy Hamet's supplies and some of mine. I paid him $16,500 and Captain Hull had paid him $4,000. Balance still due the Doctor was $12,500, or so he informed me!

"Now we needed camels to cross the desert, so on the 5th of March, according to my Journal — it says here —I got 190 of the beasts from Chiek il Taiib for eleven dollars per camel. He wanted more but I pacified him with promises of plunder at Derne. It took until the 10th before all the difficulties over the camels were settled. The Chiek insinuated that we Christians would defraud him, and he demanded money and more money for services not yet carried out. So I ordered all the Christians under arms to march back to Alexandria. The chance to pillage was over for the recruited thieves. My motley army seemed to be disintegrating." Eaton stopped and yawned.

"I have need for some time with the God Morpheus. So, Pat , tend the details while I summon the energy to ride my stallion to my lodging. Good even' to all a-a-and I'll return as — the Vila broadsheet — told you."

The General's tongue missed a little because he was tired, and his physical decline was becoming more evident. As he prepared to open the outer door, he was given an envelope by one of the waiters.

Beau Smart missed this night's talk because he was trying to frolic at a lower class house than the Red String.

On this night at the Bunch of Grapes, the narrator had eaten early on — May run salmon, potatoes, peas, and beans. After he finished a large strawberry pie and a bottle of the tavern's best wine, the story began.

" ... my stepson Eli told...no, ordered...that collection of riffraff and Marines not to leave. Thus the first of many threatened mutinies was avoided, and we marched twelve miles into the desert toward the port of Bomba where the Navy was to meet us with food and armaments. My maps were sketchy, but I think I had measured it to be about 400 miles. Now ...I'll read from my Journal a few lines for each day. But before I go to my journal let me tell you about a typical day on the march to Derna.

"Morning would start with reveille and food and personal chores done by the time the sun was an hour on its orbit. We had developed an order to our march, and I had the Marines enforcing the rules. We placed outriders to prevent a sneak attack and a sizeable force to watch our rear. We marched until we would find a suitable watering place and grass for our animals. Making camp quickly, we ate and then practised our arts of war — rifle men with their weapons and artillery with our two small cannon. Some evenings the Greeks were wont not to put their hearts into the practice. When that happened I harangued them fiercely.

March 11th Eleven miles today.

March 12th Marched twenty-one miles.

March 13th We covered twenty -five miles. An informer came into camp and told the Bashaw Hamet that the Governor of Derne had armed the province to help him overthrow his brother Yusef. The Arabs celebrated with a *feu de joie*. The Bashaw's soldiers, who were in the rear, came running up to help in the defence of the Bashaw , for they had heard the rifle firing during the *feu de joie*. Deep wells and good water at this campground near the sea.

March 14th Twenty-six miles. Camp on the border of Egypt and Tripoli on a barren plain. Cistern of excellent water which I had led them to. The hired guides were lost in this wilderness.

March 15th Marched twenty-five miles. Cold and rainy. An Arab stole a musket, bayonet, cartouche box, cartridges, and all of our cheese. I hope he dies of thirst in this sand.

March 16 Rain and more Rain. Thunder and cold high winds. We moved at 3 pm to higher ground to avoid the flood of water coming down the ravine we had camped in.

March 17 Morning rain. We had to again promise the Arabs plunder at Derne to get them to march. We marched 12 miles, camped in a ravine with lots of rain water to drink. Days are scorching hot and nights are bitter cold.

March 18th Arrived at castle called Masroscah on an extensive valley. Completed 15 miles to this place. Viewing many vestiges of ancient gardens, houses, and forts. Now I find that Bashaw Hamet has contracted with the freight handlers to this point, and they have been paid no money. They would not go to Bomba, nor would they wait our going there and returning with the money. I agreed to pay them if they would but go two days more. They agreed. I borrowed money from the Christians, and Hamet did the same among his Arabs.

"March 19 God Damn! Hamet Bashaw paid off his caravan, and now they, all forty of them, have left. They who had promised to march two more days!

"March 20th The remaining camels and handlers apparently left us in the night. A rumor swirls about the camp that a force of eight hundred cavalry and many footmen are on the march from Tripoli to defend Derne and are already past Bengazi.

"To me this was precedent for haste. But the Bashaw's chiefs typically wanted a council and more council. I was not consulted. They decided to remain, those damnable lying Arabs. Yes, on the spot until a runner could go to Bomba and return with the truth. I shut off their rations and planned to fortify myself and the Christians in the castle to await intelligence from our naval force. And, if need be, leave these Moslems to their own subsistence and safety. I was sure that they would be lost in that vast desert. My great desire was the liberation of three hundred Americans from the chains of Barbarism." Eaton looked up from his journal.

"I'll have a bottle of wine. Waiter! Are you hard of hearing? Go and bring two clean glasses. (*Author's Note: Not very many people ordered up clean glasses in those days, but as you remember Eaton had spent some time on a ship going to Georgia. The Captain of that ship was a connoisseur of good food and he insisted that it be served in the right manner. Clean glass and shined plates with each course.*)

"Now, back to the journal.

"March 21st Last night's ultimatum took effect. Fifty camels with Arabs aboard are now marching with us. We covered 13 miles where we found good water in cisterns. I lead, for the paid guides are still in a strange land.

"March 22nd Marched 12-1/2 miles. Stopped at 3 pm at a place called Oak korar ke barre, amidst camps of three

Arab tribes. All together 3 to 4 thousand souls. They viewed us with curiosity — their first Christians. Our rice was traded for dates and many rare foods. In need of grain for our horses, I dispatched a courier with that request of Captain Hull at Bomba.

"March 23rd Stayed in camp. Great news — eighty mounted warriors joined our Bashaw. Provisions reduced to hard bread and rice. Cash, we find, is the only deity of the Arabs as well as the Turks. From Alexandria to this place there is not a living stream, nor rivulet, nor spring of water.

"Water — just saying the word makes me thirsty." Eaton closed his journal and continued relating his adventures.

"I should have told you more about the composition of our little army. First we had nine Americans, including Lieutenant O'Bannon and his six Marines, Midshipman Pascoe Peck from the Navy, and one other, a strange Marine they called Private X, I think. I hired in Alexandria Selem the Janissary, a former officer in the elite Turkish Army. He was a total drunk but a good and loyal soldier. Then I found Captain Lucas Ulovic, a Macedonian turned into a excellent thief — sometimes needed in this type of army. He recovered many lost items for General Eaton. And to my delight I hired a big, tall, dark, athletic Greek, Lieutenant Constantine, strong as an ox. Next was the charming dapper Frenchman who spoke and read French so beautifully but in times of distress reverted to Spanish, his native language. This most entertaining young man was named Chevalier Davis who spun the most astounding tales around our nightly camps. And then the man of hate — he would have liked to cut all the heads off those Moslems, the sons of Allah — Lieutenant Conant, English sometimes, American other times, but he was truly from the West Indies. Our medical fates were in the hands of Doctor Mendrici who had done his previous work on the livestock of the region. Now he was going to practice on us.

"Next we come to the Farquhar brothers — one a thief, the other a most loyal servant. Percival as Quartermaster and the other, Richard. He claimed a captaincy in the British Army, but that was questioned by both Eli and my servant Aletti. My greatest find was Leitensdorfer whom I made my adjutant and leader of the Christian side of General Eaton's ragamuffin army. Now I have said many things about this man, all proclaiming his worth. Dorfer's paramount help in my guiding that caravan army on its way over the dry and hot land of the bloodthirsty pirates to Derne is to be rewarded by our government. Oh, and I might add that will happen only after I and my mentor, the Hon. Stephen Bradley of Vermont, work the halls of Congress valiantly.

"The only propellant for that motley entourage was the hope of plunder at Derne. But MY hope was the freedom of all those captives in the infidel's prison at Tripoli.

"That's all for the reading tonight, faithful vassals. Now, will someone see that the waiter comes and pours me a portion of that Navy drink, good old dark rum?"

After some pause and local banter, Eaton turned and said to some of the old cronies,

"It's still in the shank of the evenin' so let's drink and talk and then drink some more, but let's do it at the Red String and ...."

Mr. B. Smart was in the Bunch of Grapes. After Eaton departed he took the center stage and began,

"Well if you were paying attention tonight you can surmise that the two Farquhar brothers are not like two peas in a pod. One was a thief and one a loyal soldier. I've asked the General which was which, and he would never come right out and point the finger. Well, after hearing his story tonight I'm sure that the thief is Richard, 'cause I think I find Percival later in the story." Beau continued rerunning parts of the Generals story until the noise level rebuked him. He paid his bill and left.

The next morning while the General was eating his breakfast, he had put into his hand by Aletti a letter folded in the shape of a envelope. On it were the words, in large scripted letters, *General Eaton.* After the food and coffee were finished, Eaton opened the envelope, and out fell a woman's pink garter. Fishing into the envelope, he removed a small scrap of paper. It read, *'You could remove the other one. V.'*

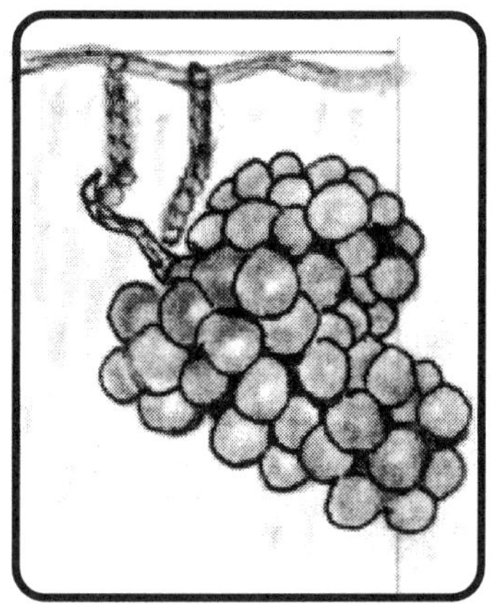

"**Tonight** — this third day of May, the first Wednesday of the month and in the year of our Lord one thousand eight hundred and nine, I'm goin' to paraphrase from my journal just for the sake of making the story quick and pointed. Now, WAITER!" Eaton hollered, "if I could have my meat du jour and potatoes with a full bottle of Madeira. Make sure it's not one from which you have poured some into your glass. Be quick now so I can take care of my growling stomach. Then I'll relate the trials and tribulations of leading my army of the very best thieves, murderers, and other riffraff ever put together in the Near Eastern world. After I clean my plate, I'll give you all my full attention."

Having the table alone for supper — the soup, the main dish, and the apple pie along with coffee — the General was quickly revived.

"Well, the first among my officers ... (Yes, the General did start the story he had told previously.) ...did me a favor by slicin' the head off a Tripolitan tribesman who was threatening to desert. That got the other Tripolitans' attention. Also that of the Farquhar brothers, Richard, and Percival, one a thief, the other a loyal leader in the march to Derne. And my good Doctor of Medicine, Mendrici, who had done his practising on pigs and goats and then on my army —

"Ah! I'll now read from my journal. I'll start with the 25th of March 1805. Forty-seven tents of Arabs join us with their families and movables. A hundred and fifty new warriors on foot. The Arabs like our bread. We use it and rice for money. Rice, we thought, had all been consumed but more appeared. Likewise the bread. An Arab woman offered her fourteen-year-old daughter to one of my officers. She was a well proportioned, handsome brunette, with expressive hazel eyes, perfect teeth, well formed lips, rather voluptuous. I forbade it, much to the Arab mother's annoyance. I had, from the beginning, forbidden all my Christians from having sexual intercourse with the many offerings from most of the Arab families.

"March 26. Intelligence comes to the moving army that five hundred of Yusef Bashaw's cavalry plus a great number of foot Arabs are within a few days march of Derne. The forward movement of my army stops. The camel drivers fled, and I shut off the food again. A council was held. At eleven I learn that the trouble maker, Chiek il Taiib, had resolved to stay at this camp until he could know for certain that our vessels were at Bomba awaiting us. I told him he lacked both courage and fidelity, that I regretted having made his acquaintance and that he could be off to Egypt as long as he did not interfere with the disposition of the other Arab chiefs. In a rage, he left. When the Bashaw Hamet wanted to send an officer to pacify and bring him back, I would not allow it. So the Bashaw also left temporarily.

"March 27. I ordered the march to start at 7 am. after telling the Bashaw that I liked an open enemy better than a treacherous friend. By 10 o'clock the Chiek il Taiib sent word that he was going to Behara. We continued our march, the Bashaw bringing up the rear. Chiek il Taiib sent word that he will join us when we halt. The Bashaw asked if we can camp. We do so at twelve thirty. Within an hour and a half the wayward Chiek came to my markee with visible chagrin on his countenance. We made only five miles that day!

"March 28. Yusef Bashaw has seized all of Hamet's nerves. He took away the horses he had given my men to ride and drew off with his loyal Mahometans and was very reluctant to order them to join us in our forward march. I met this with demands and reproachment. Hot words flowed. I ordered the march. The Bashaw caught up with us two hours later. We marched 12 miles and camped at Shemees at one in the afternoon. Hamet Gurgies was sent after the body of Arabs who had joined us on the 25th and then left. The Chiek il Taiib was behind this desertion, I find.

"March 29. Waited in camp for Gurgies to return. Local Arabs brought lots of cattle, sheep, butter, fowls, eggs, and dates. We barter rice for them and also the Marines' coat buttons.

"We continue to find more rice in storage! The land is enchanting, capable of cultivation, good well water, fig and palm trees. War has put a ruinous aspect on the land. At four in the afternoon, Gurgies came into camp with the Arabs who had deserted us several days ago.

"Bring me a pitcher of ale, and, waiter, if this attentive crowd of old war veterans need refills, I'll take a breather." Eaton commanded in a loud carrying voice. After a few large swigs and some small talk with some new members of the audience, the General was ready to continue the reading.

"March 30. Resumed march at 6 A.M. At the start the Chiek il Taiib and Chiek Mahamet got into a dispute about money which they both had received from the Bashaw. Then all the other Chieks took sides, and it looked like we would have us a little war right then. They retrograded. They started back to Egypt. Gurgies was sent off to recover the malcontents. We march 15 miles but then retreated 3 so we could have good water.

"Eli and I said that if we ever got to Bomba, we just might have those malcontents all strung from the yardarm of one our frigates. By this time I was burnt to an ebony color, and some of my good neighbors in Brimfield would have thought me a darky just like one of their servants. Let's get back to the journal.

"March 31. Remain in camp. Rain and more rain." Looking up, Eaton said as an aside, "Did I ever tell you the desert is wet and dry? You have to hunt for water to drink, and that same night it runs down your neck in torrents. Back to my Journal.

"From Alexandria to this place we have had continual altercations and delays by the Arabs. They have no sense of patriotism, truth, nor honor. They also have no attachment where they have no prospect of gain, except in religion to which they are enthusiasts. Poverty makes them thieves, and practice renders them adroit in stealing. Wait for Gurgies, and wait. The Bashaw is absent.

"April 1. At my markee the Chiek il Taiib with three others makes demands for more rations. I gave him and them a dressing down, saying he, il Taiib, was the cause of all our problems. He had boasted, in a promise to me, that he would bring us to Bomba in fourteen days. We have marched for twenty-five days and have gained only half the distance. He said he could not subsist on rice alone but needed bread. I asked him if he could compel it, and he answered, 'I am a greater man here than either you or the Bashaw.' I said, 'Leave my tent — and if I find a mutiny in camp I will put you to death instantly.' He left.

"At two the Chiek il Taiib returned and said he regretted that he had lost my confidence and that he was devoted to me. At five he came AGAIN TO PROFESS ETERNAL OBLIGATION.

"At six P.M. the Bashaw has not returned , but the Chiek il Taiib came and offered his hand with promises and oaths.

The day has been rainy, blowing ,and chilly.

"April 2. Last night I visited an Arab tent, and they showed off one of their daughters. I complimented her elegant proportions and symmetry. She seemed elated with the visit. Gurgies and all those who had separated themselves from us have returned. Even the Bashaw is with us. I ordered a meeting in my markee at seven that evening. I exhorted them to union and perseverance. I said that only together could we have the means of insuring our success of this important enterprise. They all gave pledges of faith and honor. We now have about six or seven hundred fighting men with us. Many Beduoin families and other followers, young and old. In total about twelve hundred souls.

"April 3. Marched ten miles, and then the caravan stopped for the Arabs to go and get dates at a place called Seewauk in a valley upon a vast elevated plain. Cistern water here, but I ordered the column forward; they refused. I threaten to leave with the Christians for Bomba where there is food. They say we do not command the sea and that they will seek dates. I consented. That afternoon we witness an Arab wedding— an endless *feu de joie*. The bride, I discover, is a girl of thirteen.

"April 4th..." Eaton stopped to rub his eyes. "Well, let's call it a night. My eyes are going blind in this flickering light. I'll be back day after tomorrow. Same place and same time but not so long in the recitation."

The General then turned and, looking at the kitchen door, he said,

"Bring me the cost, will you? Now ...Good night to all." Colonel Pat had gone to Springfield to attend some business, so the General had to manage his way from his table to the door. There he was met with the bill in the hands of Verna Vila. James was off visiting some friends. The bill was held tightly in her hand as she reached up around the

General's neck and pulled him down to be kissed. Kisses that said "take me! " Verna said in a whisper,
"My other garter is for the taking."

Eaton responded to the kiss but not to the temptation of removing the garter, for he was well aware that he had made a hero into a fool at a tavern in Richmond. He was excited and eager, but this was where he was telling his story to see how it would play out in his planned book on The Life of General William Eaton. Yes, Yes. Verna might be fun to bed but this is the wrong place and not the right time to spoil the deal he had made with her husband.

Yet his hand found a way to rub her breast and his lips pressed with urgency on hers as she let her arm fall onto his covered erect and awaiting penis just as he pulled away from her grasp.

Eaton left. In the kitchen Verna tossed his bill into the fire with a few choice words as it flamed and vanished up the chimney.

When the entrance door to the Bunch of Grapes had opened, the eyes of the late-arriving B. Smart was accosted with the scene of two bodies rejecting their blatant attraction. He stored the picture for future tales at other times.

Invigorating spring weather, with the sky clear and blue, motivated Eaton to slowly walk, without his outer coat, to the Tavern. After jollying with some of the many familiar patrons, he said in a strident and commanding tone,

"Good evening to all. Now! Good waiter, bring my soup and pour the wine. I'll do my reading after I've taken care of my bodily needs."

"Ya," was the response from Hans, the new waiter.

The General was in a mild mood; as the weather in Boston had been on the sunny side all day long. The temperature was on the mend. Soon the flowers along the Commons would spring forth. Eaton had never had a love affair with cold. He craved the warmth of the desert, and the icy blast of Boston winters continually reminded him of that winter in his cabin on the Aroostook River, an adventure he wished had never happened. He still suffered most of his waking hours from the pain of frosted feet and also from gout. But now spring was just about to blossom, and that made his body feel years younger. He had said, 'They should have left that north land for the Indians; civilized man would not, nor could not abide there.'

Turning his body in the chair after the waiter had

cleared the remainder of his meal and had brought another bottle of wine to his table, the General cleared his throat.

"I'll use my journal as a guide to keep me on the path of truth, starting with the 4th of April, 1805.

"We stopped at four in the afternoon after having marched eighteen miles. Captain Selem chased down a wild-cat, height two feet and length about five. It was cooked, and it ate very well. The wells...one ninety feet and the other one hundred feet into solid rock. Very good water.

"Now on the next day, the 5th, I see that we marched 12 miles and were only seven leagues, that is about 21 miles, from the sea, where there loomed a large stone castle one hundred eighty feet square. Large cistern with lots of good water. Our guides fix this nearby port as Tobruk; one hundred and fifty miles from Derne. Truly I was never sure of their calculations. On the morning of the 6th we found that a band of wild Arabs had stolen nine of the Bashaw's horses. We sent a detachment after them. On the march that morning one of our horses fell into a seventy foot well, killing it. We didn't have the time nor the desire to remove the dead horse. Anyway the water was putrid and saline. Continued our march for fourteen miles. Camped at Salaum, on French maps called Cap Luco. Ninety miles from our food at Bomba. No water. The next day we march in mountainous area for eighteen miles. No water but good grass. The 8th of April, we were descending the west side of the mountains. Found a cistern with good water at nine in the morning, and while the troops were refreshing themselves, I took a small party to reconnoiter the country, intending to resume the march. When I returned, I found the Bashaw ordered them to pitch their tents. He said the army needed one day of repose. I pointed out to him that we had only six more days of rice rations, no meat nor bread. This, I said, was reason enough to continue our march. I had to order the rations withheld because I had discovered that it was again the intentions of our Arabs to steal them. I beat the call to arms. My Christians formed a line in front of the magazine tent.

"The Arabs faced us, and we faced them. Then the Bashaw ordered the Arabs to take down his markee. This might have ended the tumult if I had not ordered the Christian troops to perform manual of arms. This is what we were accustomed to do, just as routine as our artillery practise, but the Arabs took alarm and, remounting, shouted 'The Christians are preparing to fire on us.' Then the Bashaw jumped upon his horse and put himself in front of his troops. Two hundred mounted Arabs came on in a full charge sweeping, the Bashaw with them . They swung their scimitars in the air and yelled an Arabic shout which means 'death to the infidel'. About half of them had their hands on the triggers and the barrels pointed at us Christians. Some of their officers cried , 'Fire', but some of the Bashaw's officers cried, ' For Allah's sake do not fire! These Christians are our friends.' O'Bannon, Peck, and Farquhar stood firmly by me. Captain Selem, his lieutenants, and the two Greek officers remained steadfast also. The others abandoned us. I rode amidst the turmoil to the Bashaw and, taking him by the arm, halted him. I waved my arm and in a loud voice — not full of fear but with authority — I demanded their attention. At that critical moment some of the Bashaw's officers — royal... no loyal, to General Eaton — rode between the opposing lines with drawn sabres. This repelled the mutineers. Then I had the Bashaw calling me his friend and protector. I said that I would give orders to issue rice rations if he would promise to march tomorrow morning at reveille. He promised. That night the Bashaw called Lieutenant O' Bannon his brave American.

"During the mutiny one of the Arabs pushed a pistol at Farquhar's breast and pulled the trigger. Thank the good Lord, Thank God, it didn't fire; otherwise that one small pop would have been answered with a mighty roar from our trained Marines' muskets. A bloody disaster averted by poor powder.

"April 9th. Ten miles to good water and good feed for the horses. The 10th, we marched ten miles and camped at noon in a beautiful valley. Excellent cistern water. And finally the detachment that had left us to seek the Bashaw's horses returned without having recovered them. Rice and water at half rations. The Bashaw tells me he is fearful that we Americans will give him up to his brother Yusef in order to have peace, for he has been deceived twice by Christians. Another council of war. The Arabs want to wait on intelligence that our ships are indeed at Bomba. At seven I am informed that the Greek cannoneers are demanding full rations. I order them to be told that rations would remain at half options. If they were still mutinous, I cautioned them, mutiny would result in their untimely death. I called O'Bannon and told him of the unrest. A courier arrived from Bomba with the good news that American vessels are there. Hamet Bashaw was sick with attacks of vomiting all night. On the 11th we made only five miles because the Bashaw's sickness made him remain in his tent until late in the day. I see that we again sold brass buttons from our uniforms; they are swapped for dates. By six p.m., the Bashaw has recovered. We marched twenty-five miles the next day. No water nor fuel. Dry rice eaten. On the 14th we covered fifteen miles, arriving at water and feed for our horses. Only dry rice for us to eat because there was no fuel to cook it with.

"The next day found us searching for roots. We ate wild fennel and sorrel. My army was a mob, starved and desperately looking for water. We struggled into Bomba at seven p.m. Bomba is desolate —— no water, no humans, and no vessels. All was in turmoil, and so I took my Christians up a high mountain where my Aletti and others stayed up all night carrying wood that had washed up from the sea for the fire which we all hoped would be seen far at sea if indeed our ships were out there." General Eaton stopped to drain his wine glass and said,

"Now this night's entertainment must end. I have an early morning appointment with President Adams. I am going to walk to my abode, for this mild weather calls my strength back into command."

B. Smart had spent this night trying again to frolic with one of the new girls that had just come off a ship from Sweden. The next morning, all the young active girls had a good laugh at old Beau's antics.

As the hot sun of approaching summer was first shining into the town of Boston, a letter with the same hand writing was given to Eaton by Aletti. After the General had eaten, he opened the envelope and read, *'My garter is waiting to be removed by you. V.'*

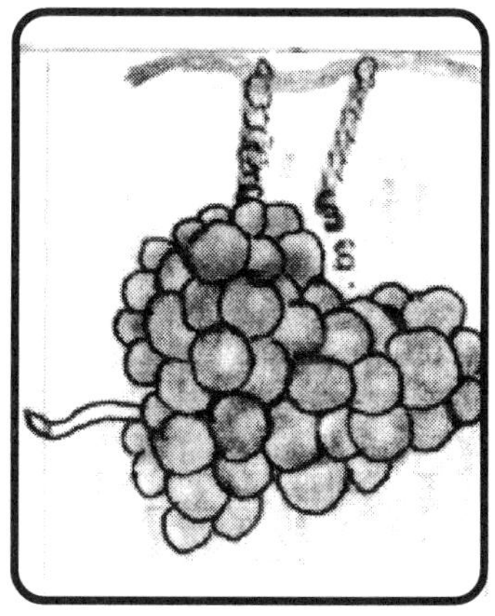

The tavern at the head of the Long Wharf in Boston was nearly empty when a tall middle aged man with a sailor's walk came in and ordered a meal and rum. After he had satisfied his hunger, he asked the waiter,

"Is this not the tavern that General Eaton often comes to and recites his life story?"

"Ya, and he be here dem nights what our broadsheet tells public. You can't tell about him, das est sur." Hans, the new waiter from Germany, replied.

"Is it too late for him to make an unpublished appearance here this night?"

"Ya, you can never be sur das General him come here anytime."

"Then bring a large bottle of Madeira wine for me while I wait on the General."

The tavern soon filled with the old and young heroes of the new nation. The Midshipman from Annapolis was at the table where Eaton was wont to give his recitals, so a few of the less restrained members of the forgotten and old lost heroes said,

"Sir, we thought General Eaton jest might come by here but it seems he stopped at the Red String or maybe the Turk. Then, sir, seein' that youse are sittin' at the table where the General sits, why, Sir, if you should wanta we would like to hear your story."

"I came to visit with Eaton, but well...yes, I do have a yarn or two to tell here in Boston town. First you must be still, and I'll start by telling you who I am.

"I am John Mann, born in Annapolis, Maryland and a Midshipman on leave. I came to hear Eaton's tale of the Barbary war. I was with him when he captured the African city in Tripoli. Lieutenant Hull of the Argus was my superior. I was with Eaton so that messages could be sent back and forth with our flags. I'll not relate to you Bostonians any of the land battle since I think from what I heard before I arrived that Eaton has or will elaborate about that battle sufficiently. I will give in few words what I learned from my naval companions concerning their action in that capture of Derne. Sailors from the *Hornet, Nautilus,* and the *Argus* were somewhat resentful over the great hero worship that Eaton and those few Marines got. Not that they didn't deserve a lot of credit, but I assure you the city would never have fallen without the naval guns which hammered the defences into ruble.

"Our well-trained gunners sponged their guns, loaded the cannon with linen bags of powder and solid shot, ran out the guns, pricked the touchholes, and were standing by ready to fire the next round into the infidels' nest long before the captains had time to suck in the needed air to yell loud and strong so all could hear, 'FIRE!'"

This shout of *Fire!* caused Mrs. Vila to rush into the common room and look wildly about, exclaiming,

"FIRE!! Where is the fire? I don't smell any thing but pipe tobacco!" All the windows were open this warm evening, and Mrs. Vila surely didn't want that inept fire company to come galloping down the street with their axes and water. What a mess the Bunch of Grapes would be. James would blame her — for he had always done so whenever a small catastrophe happened.

"So sorry Ma'am, I just got carried away by my story telling. I beg your pardon. I'll be more careful in my telling."

"Please control yourself, or I'll have to ask you to leave. Those words can cause a riot here by the Long Wharf."

The Midshipman continued in lower case.

"If he had waited for our gun boats to come up the coast and fire with us, why that city would have been flying our old glory before noon that day. Yes, we did have a few injured sailors, mostly some wood splinters into naval flesh, but all recovered.

"Now I was with O'Bannon on land, and I helped him rip that dirty green flag down, and together we raised our Stars and Stripes over Derne. And only two dead Marines. Eaton was lucky that he had Hull with two other ships manned by very well trained crews. Commodore Barron was concerned that either the French or British Navy might attack us. Therefore he ordered dry firing and actual firing nearly every day while crossing the Atlantic. Bad weather or not."

The night was warm and Eaton had been wandering the streets of Boston. His steps followed a path to the head of the Long Wharf. Entering the Tavern he ambled to the center table and after inspecting the night's groit, reached out his hand and clasped the hand of Mr. Mann.

"My God! Look who is in Boston — Mann. I'll buy you another bottle of Madeira, and let's drink it while you tell me what you have been about for the last few years."

The two men spent the rest of the evening pointing out the many tragedies that had occurred from their government's faulty handling of the Barbary and the impressed seamen problems. Eaton said,

"When I was touring the western part of our country, many times after I had addressed the crowd and while we were at supper, some influential person would say to me, 'For the good of our country we need to send a force, a mighty army and once and for all bring Canada into the Union. Combined we could be a force in world affairs.' Now when I was in the southern part of our great country other well placed men would fill my ear with the need to push the Spaniards out of Florida and some also added all the Texas lands west of Louisiana.

"I kept my tongue still on these subjects, for I didn't want to join any political party. I was also a New Englander, and my two most helpful mentors were of the firm opinion that trade was to be maintained at all cost, well nearly all cost. I well knew that New England citizens depended on their merchant ships to fill their wants and needs. I had fought my battle with Barbary but was not permitted to finish conquering that pirate state of Tripoli. No, Lear made a most damaging peace with those Barbary extortioners. The politicos of Washington City are still sending cash and military supplies to those bloodsuckers."

The other patrons had lost interest, and Mr. Mann was left alone to hear Eaton lecture on and on about the evils that State and War had perpetrated on this great country called the United States of America.

The tavern owner had taken the stage to Portland, Maine because his Grandfather on his mother's side had left him an inheritance — of several hundred acres of forest. Vila would be gone for a few days as it was his intent to sell this land as soon as he could. The Bunch of Grapes could use some modern fixtures and a new coat of paint.

Mrs. Vila was the one who came into the common room to put an end to the General's monologue. She came and said, "Time! "

On the walk home, Eaton resolved that his life story would have to be printed by one of the best printers and that he would speed up his bringing together the many letters and his journal so that an excellent book could be put on the market... not that he wanted it published before he was in his grave. After his death, he reflected, would be soon enough. The book would also be something that would live on. Maybe his alma mater would have a special section of the library for the collections of General Eaton. Maybe he should have some friend suggest that to the trustees. Now his Life ... It would have to be his monument for all those brave men who had tramped ,cold and hungry, across the sands of Barbary to help set our navy prisoners free. He would finish it ...soon.

Verna had locked the Tavern and quickly ran to a waiting cab. She said to the driver,

"Please follow that gentleman, for I must see that he arrives at his lodgings." The gig slowly progressed to Ann Street. When it pulled up and stopped, getting down, she paid the driver and said,

"Thank you, now you may leave."

A clean, soft, comforting breeze was blowing the city odors away that night. Two shadowy figures, one a male who had been contemplating a different kind of evening's work and the other a female who had been imagining a sensuous encounter with the hero of Barbary, were seen going into the dwelling at 16 Ann Street.

The General speedily found that he could not refuse to remove the other garter from the proffered well shaped leg of Verna Vila.

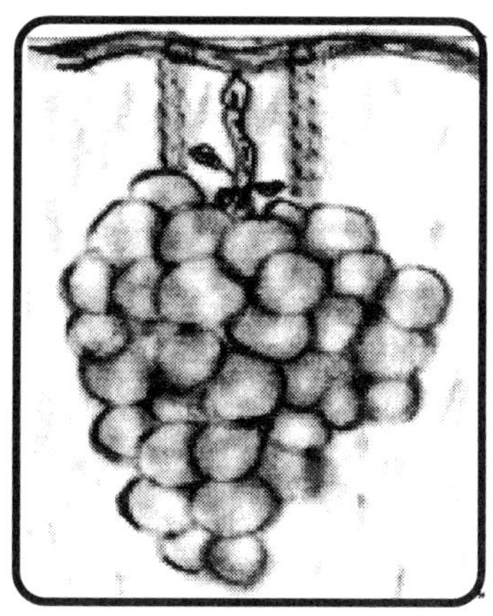

"General, you've had the pleasure of talking to these very good listeners now for a couple of months. I'm your stepson, and I want your permission to have the speaker's platform all by myself tonight."

"I'll give it up to you, Eli, if you let me pay," the General acquiesced. "Now let's have our dinner while you plan your address."

The table cleared — Colonel Eli Danielson (Mr. Eaton conferred rank on his co-adventurers at his discretion) stood and faced the eyes of Vila's customers.

"I beg to have the pleasure of telling you about one of the most remarkable men that I or General Eaton have ever known. I will do so in as few words as I can. He was born Gervasio Prodasio Santuari in a village near Trent in Tyrol in western Austria on the twenty-first of October, 1772. He studied for the priesthood in the Romish Church, but not liking that life, he got married. This occupation was also not to his liking, so he joined the Austrian army on its way to Belgrade when Joseph the Second sent them on expedition against the Turks. He fought in the siege of Mantua under General Wurmser. Then he deserted from this army to avoid being hanged for dueling. In a rush he joined Bonaparte's French army in Milan under the name of Carlo

Hossondo. They became suspicious of him, thinking him a spy, which made his life very miserable. One night, while he was under guard, he determined to escape the French army and got his guarding, yet unsuspecting Frenchman, to drink a deadly portion of opium. He escaped to a southern village in Switzerland. It's here that he became known as Johan Eugene Leitensdorfer. His family found out his situation and sent him a purse full of money. Eugene bought watches and fine jewelry and traveled Spain and France, selling as he went.

"Finding himself in Toulon, Leitensdorfer took a ship to Egypt where the French General Menou was in charge. He worked in agriculture for Napoleon's French Government. When the English army arrived, he slipped in with them and ran a coffee house for their officers. He did very well, bought a house, and ran a theater for the gentlemen of England. Another marriage here to a Coptic woman.

"When the British left Egypt, so did Eugene, leaving behind his wife and child and all his property. He disembarked in Messina, Sicily and finding himself without means, joined, as a novice, a monastery of Capuchin friars. Here he was fed and housed as Padre Anselmo until the wondering footloose urge struck him again, and he took a sail for Smyrna. It was at the port of Constantinople that he was put off by the captain, and for the next three days he lived without food or shelter. A Capuchin priest was talked into lending him a pistol and a deck of cards. Using what he had, he amused the locals with various tricks and stunts, and the silver mites that was tossed in his hat sustained him.

"The French General Brune who had served in Egypt came to Constantinople as Ambassador. On hearing this news, Eugene, afraid that he might be recognized and arrested for desertion, joined the Turkish army. His division was sent to fight in Egypt against the Dey Elfy and was defeated. To avoid capture, Eugene shaved his head and traveled into the desert. He solicited protection from the Bedouin tribes. By some means he returned to Constantinople and sought out the Ambassador from Moscow. He wanted a passport to travel to that country. Eugene was refused that passport, so tried to enter the Turkish army again. He was rejected.

"Renouncing his Christianity, professing faith in Mohammedanism, after circumcising himself, he asked to join the Dervish community. He entered that religious order under the name of Murat Aga. Soon he was traveling with a group of Mohammedans to Trebizoud. The local Bashaw was sick and presumed dying and was also suffering loss of sight. After being admitted to the Bashaw's presence, Eugene perceived that he would live, had them wash his eyes with milk and water, ordered sweating to be accomplished by warm drinks and blankets. The Bashaw gave him a well filled purse, and Eugene departed. Well, many days later the word of the Bashaw's recovery swept across the desert and, upon landing in Eugene's ear, caused him to return to Trebizoud. Again he was presented with many gifts. This is only a small part of the saga of Eugene Leitensdorfer's life. However, I think this gives you the flavor of this unusual renegade that my father calls Dorf. It wasn't until he met our General Eaton that he found a home and now he is going to become an outstanding citizen of this, our great country.

"Colonel Leitensdorfer is in our country after having worked his way here on an American merchant ship from the shores of Barbary. General Eaton has sent him to Washington City where I have frequently met him working as a map maker in the War Department and not very happy with this type of work. He has just come here to Boston to consult with the General. They both now think it would suit the Colonel if the Government gave him some land in the West. Eaton had told him about his Miami adventure in Ohio and the good farming land he had seen when he acted as a scout for General Wayne. I think the War Department has plans to give him back pay for a year as a Captain for his service in Barbary. General Eaton has sent several letters to influential congressmen asking them to grant such land to the Colonel. I will also do my part with my father-in-law, Secretary Smith. I 'm sure he will also act for the man who did more than his part in the capture of Derne.

"Now I'd just to like tell you what I saw on the field of battle on the day we captured Derne. First we had a Council of War, but it was pretty obvious that we had better get the fighting underway before the relief army from Tripoli arrived. Our scouts said they were about two days from Derne. So, knowing that the Navy was ready to do its job, the General ordered us to our assignments. I went with our twenty Greek cannoneers and foots. At the General's order Lt. O'Bannon fired the first shot to signal the land attack. We worked our small field pieces as the three warships fired their twenty-four pounders, leveling Derne's sea defensive positions. We did quite well, for we had practiced nearly every evening on our long march across the deserts of Barbary. Then in the excitement of the fight one of our cannon blew up and damaged the other. Oh! And the next thing I knew the ramrod on the naval gun was mistakenly shot into the enemy's defences. Our artillery attack was over, done with, extinct. That's when the General came to take a look at the situation. Seeing that the cannon were useless, he turned, twirled his scimitar over his head, and we all charged into a hail of Barbary pirates' lead.

"We all were shootin' our personal weapons and racin' toward the wall where we quickly drove those sons of Allah from their defences. Soon the Marines under O'Bannon were chasin' the beaten Turks down the streets of the city. The Captains of the naval ships changed their fire on seeing the wall breached and started pelting the Arab army as it fled into the western part of the city.

"Lieutenant O'Bannon soon had a red, white, and blue flag flying in place of the green one. We all cheered and cheered again. Then the General sent an order for Hamet to sweep the west side of the city's defences, and his cavalry did — but without Hamet Bashaw. I think he fell off his horse with fright. By four that afternoon we had the city in our hands. The ruling Governor had not allowed the General to sever his head even though he had said, 'Your head or mine' — He was a damned bloody coward and more."

"Eli, I think it's time to end this epic story. I say, let's go back to our cousin's home and see if he has a bed he can put up in my rooms for you," the General suggested. Eli nodded.

"A round then for all those whose ears I've stuffed with words to overflowing. Waiter, be quick and bring me the charges for those drinks."

This was a great night for our formerly missing B. Smart. He just had to tell the patrons of the Bunch of Grapes what he knew about that man Dorf.

"I met the man called Dorf when I was in Africa many years ago. Had finished that Lion hunt and was down at the quay to meet a shipment of pirated goods when this man came off the ship and ask me, the only white man around, where he could find a place to bathe and some food . He looked like he needed both pretty bad. He smelt like someone had mopped the slops with him. But looking at his size, I doubt that. Now I told him the place for I had been in Tangiers about three months and was pretty well acquainted with the port area. ..."

With the flamboyancy of actors, the two old friends swaggered to their chairs at the Bunch of Grapes, drank, ate, and talked. Colonel Leitensdorfer was in Boston to see his General and to request another letter of commendation to the Honorable U.S. Senator Stephen R. Bradley from Vermont, Eaton's mentor, and a second request for the U.S. Congress. The Colonel expected some reward for his services in the Barbary War. That agreed to, the night's reminiscing took precedence.

The General, as usual, appropriated center stage and began,

"I want all you old war veterans and any others of my dear royal — no, just plain loyal — listeners to meet my comrade-in-arms, Colonel Leitensdorfer, who will be with us for a few nights before he marches off to Washington City to receive his rightful reward. Now I'll go back to my journal and take up where I left off. I'm not gonna read but use my journal to keep the events in order. The next date is the sixteenth of April,1805 and THIS is a day the Colonel and I both well remember, don't we Dorf? For this was the day we had run out of both food and water. Then came the clear glorious dawn, and we were euphoric that morning. For the sun illuminated ships — United States of America

Naval ships. Our long cold vigil on the mountain top was rewarded, for I could tell, with my glass, that one of them was the *Argus*, and it came sailing right into the small harbor of Bomba. We raced to the shore. There was no jetty— no landing pier — but soon boatload after boatload of life giving food and water came ashore. Finally, Captain Isaac Hull himself came ashore.

He hardly knew me in my Arab robes with my face as black as some of our light skinned slaves here in America.

"After I had eaten and quenched my thirst, I did consult with Captain Hull. Looking up from my empty plate, I saw the *Hornet* sailing into the harbor. Hull said she was laden with supplies and that there were also a ketch and five or six...hmmm, yes six gunboats waiting to help me capture Derne. Hull was most amazed that I had crossed the sand of Barbary and had ended up at Bomba. He asked me what I laid my navigational ability to. I said, 'Not my guides, for they were lost after the first fifty miles.' I pondered and answered Hull thus, 'General Eaton relied in part on his instincts but called upon Divine Providence, knowing he needed the help of the Lord. He did not fail his humble servant, and the corps arrived less than five miles from the appointed place.'

"My army was tired, thirsty, and hungry. After they had thanked Allah for their General Eaton's ability to command the sea and send food and water to save them from certain death, they all drank, ate, and slept. Then I moved my army down the coast. We covered twenty miles in three days. There we found a cistern that Captain Hull had told me about, a bountiful supply of water for my dehydrated legions. MY army — one that had grown mightily in the last week, swelled by hordes of Tripolitans ready to throw off the oppressive yoke of their bloodthirsty Bashaw Yusef. They had their own arms and were mounted on good horses.

"The ships sailed and anchored near to our camp, and

I see that we spent three days bringing from the ships my military provisions and then organizing them. Hull had sent the ketch off to search for more food. My force was much larger than he had been informed. I received several thousand dollars from Commodore Barron, but he had refused me the hundred Marines that I had requested.

"Also Barron, who was very ill, had dictated to Colonel Lear a letter for me. They castigated me for collecting an army to put the rightful ruler back on the Tripolitan throne. Yet a few lines later Barron gave me his word that the Navy would render active and vigorous support to my land movements. I think Lear was assuming he might settle the Barbary problem by bribing Yusef and thus capture all the glory to leave me hanging in the wrong place.

"I never thought that General Eaton would be hanging in the wrong place, and soon I was more determined than ever to capture Derne. Then I would sweep up the coast with a mighty army, capture Tripoli, and send the false Bashaw in chains to the capital of the United States of America, Washington City. So when my spies sent me word that Derne was being reinforced by Yusef, I started toward that city but made sure the news concerning his buttressing was kept a secret by us Americans.

"We would need the help of the U.S. Navy to level their bastion. Captain Hull had made all the arrangements for them to be ready to attack Derne at the same time my army of the desert was ready to overwhelm it. Plunder the city was the promise. My Greek artillerymen had been dry shooting their cannon most every evening of our long march, and they were ready, able, and sure that they could make good use of the powder that Hull had handed over. Now we had also powder left from the dry shooting. We marched off in a cold rain and high wind, over steep mountains, into and out of rough ravines, and then through fertile cultivated fields. On the 25th of April, the Arab cavalry, headed by that damned unreliable Chiek il Taiib and Mahamet began a retrograde marching. I offered the Chieks two thousand dollars. Oh! ...I had been given a strong box of money by Captain Hull. I offered this amount to be shared among them if they would but advance...another rebellion overcome with gold. We camped that afternoon on the Green Mountains overlooking Derne. I quickly sent out a patrol to reconnoiter the area. NOW! I was looking at the city toward which I had marched for over five hundred miles, contending with hot shifting sand and sharp dangerous rock. Suffering under the intense hot midday searing sun and shivering every night in the freezing cold and wind. Sun and cold rain, yet I had been at home all the journey. A mighty trek to capture a Barbary city and to bring about the release of our brave men in prisons at Tripoli.

"General, I tell some of the perils of journey to this, your audience? General, I'm sure you wery much too modest vith your past and present tale." Colonel Leitensdorfer interjected in his Germanic accent.

"You may, Colonel, relate a story or two to these parched veterans, but only after I have given the waiters time to fill their mugs with Vilas' ale and bring us a couple bottles of Madeira for our table. Hans, did you hear me? Now be quick!" The waiter answered, and Leitensdorfer began,

"I tell a few quick actions he take vich saved Christians lives. First happen vhen ve vere only small not disciplined army scattered in long thin column. Some of dem vild Arab tribesman travel on horse in high ground behind de rocks along side us und shoot muskets at us. Dey vere God damn poor shot, never hitting any our troops. Das ist wery annoyin'! Damn annoyin'!"

(*Because this story would be to difficult for most readers, the author has translated Dorf's Lingua Franca into near English.*)

"General Eaton select several good riflemen from company. Trained the men and sent them after the brigands.

They chased those murdering thieves but never caught a single man. After many of these fruitless charges the General decide to lead them...so he mount his big strong black Arabian horse and race straight at a gathering of them bandits. His Arab robes was flying in the wind, his scimitar waving as he gallop amongst them. All the while he was wildly shouting in Arabic. Shouting 'Kill! Off with heads', and many other cussin' words that only should be spoken in private. He stunned and surprised those damn sneaky raiders and spurrin' his horse he swings a mighty blow with his scimitar. Four turbaned heads rolled down onto the sand. Then the rest of his cavalry came up to help him. Soon they wipe out all them corsairs, fifteen, maybe more. Our Arab troops took their horses, weapons, clothes and left those dead naked white bodies for circlin' vultures to eat.

"My General repeat that for next few days with very good results. Soon those murderous pillagin' Arab get the message. All pot shotting cease.

"Now once when we had to go on short rations," the Colonel continued, "our Arab cavalry mutiny and faced us Christians with load rifles and drawn sabers. And more than one Arab officer shouted , 'Kill them Christians.' Then my hero, General Eaton, walk out and join that millin' mob of ugly, murder-in-de-eye Moslems. He yelled, 'Attention,' and in very good Arabic he ordered them to stop in their tracks. He quell the riot, and when he discovered the two worst ring leaders, he had 'em brought to his big tent , his markee. After he question them, he found them guilty, so he ordered their death. General Eaton whipped out his scimitar, and in one swift sure stroke two traitorous bloody black turbaned heads rolled down the sand hill that early mornin' in front of the assembled army, Christian and Moslem.

"That's not quite the way my journal records it, but I did have two Moslems dispatched for mutiny." The General added, "I acted as judge, jury, and executioner because the laws of Western civilization are and are NOT applicable in the wild lawless Arab desert. Hans, bring me a large cut of apple pie and a cup of coffee. Thank you."

"I tell more, General?"

"Yes, Dorf, but don't overdo it."

"I doubt de General tell dis on him man, Aletti," Dorf replied. (*The author's reconstruction follows:*)

"Aletti was thirsty, starved for sex. My General was very firm from the start, 'no wives, no whores, no women.' But when we near Derne many big tribes join us. When fifty fightin' men, mounted and armed, come with wives and children, bring their own food and supplies, well, our General relented. So soon normal t'ings happen. Aletti see a very good lookin' young girl, and he wanted her. He made a bargain with her father...her weight in dates to father, and she would be his.

"So Aletti stole the dates, took them to the father, and carried the girl off to his nightly abode under the palm trees. In the mornin' the father discover dates are old and rotten. A battle of strong words breaks out. The fighting soon includes our General. He listen to facts and then ordered new dates be bought, also fifty dollar. I think that too damn much for one night with such a young and inexperienced girl and also the girl was to be given back to the father. I'm sure that Aletti thought he had bought the girl. Ya! Aletti's pay was kept until the debt was paid. And believe me Eaton's servant, Aletti, paid willingly.

"Vun more, General, den I'll valk you to your billet. Vell, I don't vant get ahead of de story, so I'll go back to vhen ve vere in Alexandria." (*The author retells this story in modern English.*)

"My General, with his own money, bought cloth, knives, boots, trade jewelry, and great many cookin' dish. When we camped at some small oasis, General Eaton would ride ahead and greet the headman in Arabic, askin' if we might share grass and water. He made sure no member of our army drew a weapon or insulted any of them people. He always took time to greet and talk with all the elders and chiek. When we were ready to depart, he left presents for each family. Most of the time he gave something to every man, woman, and child. That was one of the reasons we had many large tribes joinin' us. Word had spread across the desert, faster'n any wind, that our American General was a good, wise, and generous man — a friend of righteous Arabs. And he was also led by his God, for without maps or good scouts he had brought the corps to Derne. A most remarkable feat in the eyes of most Arabs." Leitsendorfer turned to Eaton.

"Now, my General, drink, and we will leave. We go to the French place tonight. You said girls there made you feel young again, eh General? God! when I say those words — wasn't they said about you by traitor Burr in Richmond. I wasn't there but the newspaper reported him asayin'—"

"Vila's broadsheet has the date — same time — right here," Eaton said loudly, cutting short the Colonel's last remark. "I'll tell about the first capture of a foreign city by the armed forces of the United States of America. With six, or was it seven, very good Marines?"

Mr. Smart, being just a little hard of hearing, had found it difficult to understand the broken English that Dorf had used but he wanted some attention, so to that end he took the vacated center table and started a long monologue about the religion of Barbary and some of their rather unusual customs. Beau was heard to say,

"They do some dang thing to females, I think I can say it right. I know a lot more Arabic than I do German. I lived in Tunis for some time in my youth. Yes, I mean its what Jews do to men. Circumcision, that's the word they use, but they do it to very young girls. Damndest thing to do!"

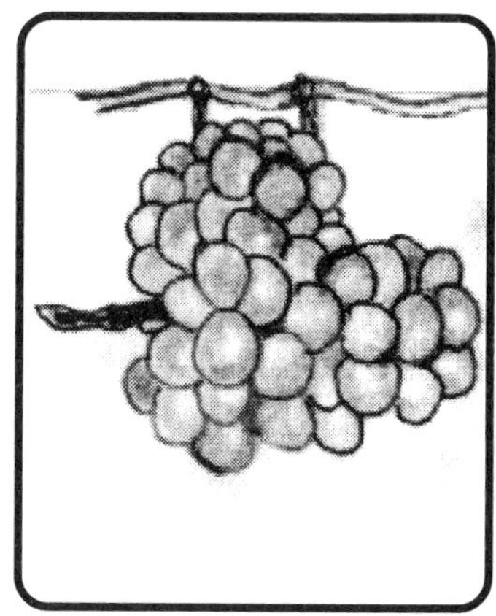

The story was being told by our hero of Derne, and the Bunch of Grapes common room was packed full with many of his regular listeners and also a goodly number of first timers whom Vila hoped to convert into regular customers. Many old-timers had come early just to hear this part of the story.

General Eaton was at his reserved table and his words came out in torrents.

"In the Green Mountains and the hills that overlooked the ancient Roman seaport city of Derne my army of adventurers, mercenaries, thieves, and the pride of Araby, Bashaw Hamet, our horses and camels and almost-warriors milled about passing the NEWS, for it had been told by the local Arabs that Bashaw Yusef's forces in the city already had been strengthened by large numbers of well trained loyal Tripolitan troops.

"Courage was replaced with panicky stomachs, and Bashaw Hamet had it — the worst case of the ailment. He searched for General Eaton and said, 'I am going to seek my brother Yusef's protection and beg to be allowed to remain in some part of Tripoli, for my forces will not prevail.' Many other weak-kneed sheiks started preparation for a move to their former oases. General Eaton and the Marines and my Greeks were the only ones to pitch their tents and sleep soundly that night. However, I, General Eaton, had made it very clear by sending one of my Lieutenants, Rocco and Selim... " He paused, searching his memory.

"Yes — I said to Selim the Janissary and Lieutenant Rocco, 'Go into the camp and pass my strong words to all that, if anyone is caught leaving he would be treated as a deserter. And that Pashaw Eaton would himself remove their traitorous heads.' The word was passed. Then General Eaton ordered his loyal guards to surround Hamet's tent to make sure HE stayed for the coming capture of Derne. Money and strong threats with promise of lots of booty in the city kept them all from running away. I ,General Eaton, was determined to meet my destiny right there on the plains of Derne.

"Most of the milling army spent the night eating and drinking water or juice, for the area is a fertile garden. Fruits and vegetables are in great abundance in this part of Tripoli. The plains of Derne contained lots of water and grass for our animals.

"That afternoon the need for knowing the defensive posture of one's enemy led me to mount my black stallion, not the one I bought in Tunis. With my best and brightest Arabic robes flying behind me I, with a few men on their horses, did a very thorough reconnaissance of Derne. I found an eastern gate was open, and the guards were inattentive, so spurring my steed into a faster canter, I entered the city. I discovered that Derne was defended by eight nine-pounders and a howitzer all pointing at the harbor. The city seemed to be divided into three parts. Two parts were the people who were for my Hamet and one for the bloody usurper, Yusef. His people had nine-pounders and howitzers and also the greatest amount of military supplies. I observed that most of the houses had blank walls with many loopholes for musket fire. They had also thrown up temporary parapets in positions that weren't covered by the battery. The usurper's appointed Governor, the Dey Mustafa, lived in this department.

I dismounted my horse and, after testing my lingua at the friendly market, I bargained for presents for Dorf, Aletti, and my stepson Eli. On leaving I compelled two of the enemy defenders to accompany me to my markee where I questioned them for information. I soon had their cooperation. Dorf knew the art of extracting truth from those two.

"They told us the Governor had about eight hundred fighting men and that Yusef's reinforcements had not yet arrived. I compared their confession with what a small party of sheiks who had come out to join us had told us that same day. Yusef's forces are not phantoms! They are reported to be a few days march to the west.

"As is the custom I sent the following letter in my own Arabic hand, with terms of amity, under truce to the Governor. I'll just read it from my journal.

April 26th, 1805.
To His Excellency, the Governor of Derne.
Sir:

I want no territory. With me is advancing the legitimate sovereign of your country. Give us passage through your city, and offer us your hand in friendship. For the supplies of which we shall need, you shall receive fair compensation.

No difference of policy or religion induce us to shed the blood of harmless men who think little and do nothing . If you are a man of liberal mind you will not balance on the proposition I offer.

Hamet Bashaw pledges himself to me that you will be established in your government.

I shall see you tomorrow, in a way of your choice.

William Eaton

Commanding, the Armies of the Bey Hamet Karamanli Pasha

"And as I have told you he replied, ' My head or yours.' What a great exchange of pleasantries. Oh! I must admit an error... I was on the Christian calendar not the Muslim.

"The city had a small harbor with enough fire power to defend itself against ancient raiders but not enough to defend against our modern naval ships with their long range and high powered cannon. Derne had a high rock wall in a semicircle on the land side facing us. I had found the streets paved with stone and many of the houses also made of stone. Maybe I need to tell you that when I entered that city one of my companions was Colonel Leitensdorfer ... and two Greeks. My! When Dorf did a final extraction with hot coals to the bare soles of those two captives' feet, I learned that the seafront was commanded by one of the best officers in the pay of Yusef, the well trained Sheik Muhammed el Layyas. He was also known to be very courageous.

"My reconnaissance informed us that the best attack would be from the southeast since the southwest had narrow and very steep ravines; only a few foot soldiers could engage the defenders there. The southeast, with the breastworks inside the stonewall, appeared well planned. It was the very place I had seen the city's strongest defenses. This was where we had to breach their wall and overrun them—overrun them before the strong reinforcement I knew was only a few days away would swarm onto the plains of Derne and trap us against that very wall we had to breach. That stonewall would have to be split asunder for me to capture Derne.

"General Eaton called a Council of War for I was ready with a plan. I had signaled with smoke the *Nautilus* in the harbor and had, with my glass, read her flagged code reporting the *Argus* and *Hornet* would arrive late that very evening. I had already sent the smoke into the air that told Hull, 'the attack will start at dawn next day.' This brings me to Milton who said , 'Hail, holy light of spring of Heav'n first-born, Or of the 'Eternal Coeternal beam....May I express thee unblam'd? since God is light...' Book three. Now back to the fight...

"At the Council of War I allowed everyone to put in their words, and when they had finished, I presented my plan. They all agreed and I made the assignments. It was evening, time for eating and resting for the coming battle. I ate a very good meal of goat stew and drank a mug of ale, a small gift from Hull. I did this in my own tent with no Arabs present. I had a very good restful sleep and was dressed and ready for the coming engagement shortly after four in the morning. I ate the leftover goat stew and made the rounds of all the detachments.

"The day before, the sailors of the *Hornet* had brought to shore two of their cannon, and we pulled them from the shore partway up the heights, but, they being so very steep, we left one and then readied the other for use in the fight. I had, furthermore, sent off two men in separate ways to deliver my sketch of the city and the information that had been burned out of our two prisoners. Well, Isaac Hull did need to know the size of the Arabs' cannon.

"MY plan was simple and easy for my untrained troops to carry out with dispatch. First I divided them into four commands. To command Group One was my Lieutenant O'Bannon, whom I gave his six Marines, twenty -four of my Greek cannoneers plus twenty-six foot Greeks to help support them and about a hundred of the most ferocious looking nomads, some mounted. On the maps I had just made, I showed them where to place our cannon, and pointed out the southeast wall that they must overrun — breach it quickly. This was to be the key to our winning. I was very emphatic, 'O'Bannon, all will be for naught if you don't do the job forthwith and without delay.' Group Two was Hamet with his mob of foot and mounted Tripolitans.

They were put in the care of Selim the Janissary with Farquhar as his second. Hamet was to appear the commander, but I gave my order to Selim, 'Your force is to penetrate the southern plain, carefully since the terrain is quite rough, and hold it.'

"Group Three — The better part of the Arab cavalry I sent off west to prevent the city's garrison from escaping and to drive off any advance parties of Yusef's army that might be coming from the east. Also they were to be ready to act as my fast flying reserves.

"I put all the remaining troops and cavalry under my personal command. They numbered over a thousand, and I planned on using them to fully exercise my taste for combat. That was Group Four.

"I've talked and talked and have had not a drop to drink. And I am starved! This story is too compelling to stop, but I need the food and drink. I'll have two Flips plus two bottles of Madeira and for food — I think I smell pork roast. The pork plus some vegetables with a large cut of mince pie. Hans! On your feet NOW!"

A "Ya" was directed at the General. Hans was quick for he liked being near the General.

As had happened before, General Eaton was asking for Mrs. Vila, to leave her kitchen. The mince pie was what had reminded him of the need to offer praise when it was due. Made for taste buds, the brown flaky crust was filled with well blended spices and meats. And so, the General raised his voice and commanded,

"Mr. Vila, would you ask your lovely loved wife to come take a bow. Now all you patrons that have eaten Vilas' victuals stand and give a cheer on my command."

As the middle-aged wife came into the common room, red-faced and wiping her hands on a linen towel, the tavern erupted with a mighty cheer,

"Hurrah, Hurrah for Mrs. Vila, the cook of Boston!"

"Thank you, Mrs. Vila, for the many times you have enticed my palette and now my eyes again." The General gave her a courtly bow. Verna did a quick bow in return and then a wave to all the paying customers as she left the room.

The patrons of the room fell into private conversation. The General had used up his reserve of energy and so he left the tavern and made his way home. Soon after, Beauregard Smart did get some of the patrons' attention and gave them the geology and meteorology of the states of Barbary.

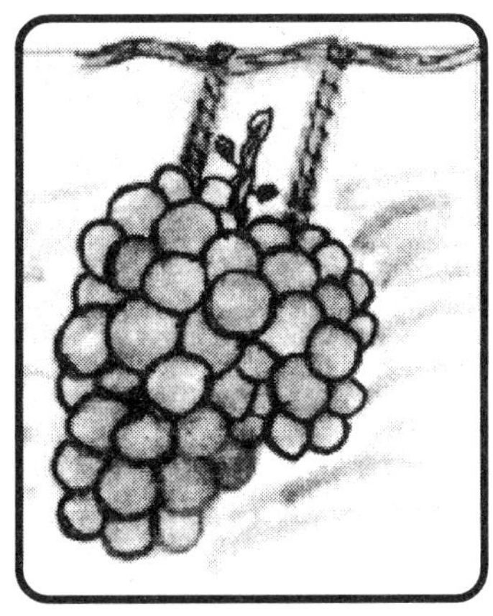

The sign swinging in the evening breeze off the ocean at the head of Boston's Long Wharf rattled over a mob of people entering earlier than normal. The word and the broadsheet had spread it all around the city that Eaton had arrived at the Battle of Derne in his story. The common room was well over its capacity when the hero of Derne swaggered into the tavern. A pathway was pushed clear by his old time followers so the General could walk to his familiar table. He had ridden his much admired white and black stallion, and the day had warmed, so Eaton was giving off the fine odor of horse. Mr. Vila came to his table and said,

"Genr'l, for this one night I'll buy your food and drinks."

"Then," Eaton replied, "I'll buy this nice respectful crowd one round of ale."

" Y'r order, Sir?" Vila asked as he counted the house and reflected on his good fortune.

"Two Flips to start with and a bottle of Madeira for now. Have them bring me a helping of the venison that my nose says is cooking. Potatoes and corn and squash. Make sure they are all hot."

Entering the tavern, Colonel Pat Patrick marched his way to the General's table and took a chair. Upon Vila's return with two Flips, Colonel Pat said,

"I'll have one of those, and now, my good man, bring us two more Flips. Mr. Vila, you make them so tasty that a person can't stop at two of 'em."

Vila wasn't sure that he had included free drinks and food for the Colonel, but for this once...well the General was buying a round. That was not his habit...so a few Flips and supper....Better get the waiters pouring that ale.

The table was loaded with victuals for that night's repast, and the two old friends talked and ate slowly, enjoying one another. Before the mince pie came, the proprietor approached and discreetly asked,

"General, are you going to finish the story about the battle of Derne tonight? I would very much like you to tell this crowd. My waiters have heard a rumor that you might not do it tonight, for sure. Some of these patrons came very early to get seats, and some have been standing here for an hour or more. I fear they might cause a rumpus if they find they came for naught."

"I'm gonna tell it all right, so I'll tell 'em right now." Eaton struggled to his feet, for his gout was acting up.

"Patrons of the Bunch of Grapes, this is the night that you all have been waiting for, and you will not be disappointed. I am going to relate the amazing capture of a Barbary city by only seven good United States Marines and this Hero of Barbary, General Eaton. So, I'll start the story." Eaton started the drama.

"Helped by a landward breeze, the warships *Nautilus* and *Hornet* sailed to their assigned positions. It was just a little after midnight when Lieutenants Evans and Dant dropped their anchors within one hundred yards of the city's battery. Captain Hull on the *Argus* anchored a little to the south of the Nautilus and was so close that his 24 pounder easily struck the heart of the town. I had directed O'Bannon, with 24 cannoneers, 26 Greeks, 6 American

Marines and a few foot Arabs, to set up their guns in the southeast quarter in a sheltering ravine opposite the enemy's strongest defensive spot. I had told Hamet Bashaw to take his cavalry and seize an old castle which dominated the plains on the land side of the city. All his foot partisans were to stand in the rear of his cavalry.

"The action started when the Derne gunners at the shore batteries opened their firing at 5:20 that morning, the 27th of April,1805. The Navy responded by firing on the city. Because Lieutenant Evans was anchored within 100 yards of the battery, his fire was very effective, and Lieutenant Dant's cannons broadsided directly into the enemy battery. Under Captain Hull, the *Argus* was throwing her 24 pound shot into the center of town, causing great confusion. Smoke and thunder from the guns rolled onto the Derne plain. I used my glass and saw the local populace running toward the west trying to avoid our naval gun fire.

We advanced to our positions, and I ordered Lieutenant O'Bannon to put the plan into action. He pushed his troops forward with great vigor, but the southeast wall defenders lay down a very heavy hail of lead. O'Bannon's men ran forward, fired, and then crawled from cover to cover, still sending hot lead toward the infidels. But I could see that O'Bannon had gotten his troops pinned down. They were too far from the wall to use the grenades they had ready for this action. I had carried out a simulated attack on the trek by using powderless grenades. They could not run over the stonewall defense.

"Word came that Hamet's forces had captured the old castle on the heights directly south of the city. Selim the Janissary had ordered them to dig trenches so their field of fire would keep the Derne defence forces from sallying forth to attack our flanks. The Greek cannoneers had been firing slowly and carefully over O'Bannon's troops with little success in breaking a hole in the defenders' rock wall. Then I saw the ramrod flying toward the enemy. The Greeks had put our only usable cannon out of commission!

"Just before that mishap another cannon had blown up, damaging the remaining nearby field piece. Only a few minor cuts and bruises for the Greek cannoneers.

"I had taken a close visual inspection of the carnage of cannons. It was my awareness that a large force from Tripoli could be soon upon us that caused me to send a message to O'Bannon, 'Since your field guns are of no more use, CHARGE, ATTACK! ' And then I ordered all troops who had the means to continue the fight. We were nearly at a stalemate then. Yet the roar of exploding powder rolled back and forth across the plains of Derne.

"Around three in the afternoon Dey Mustafa's sea batteries were totally demolished by our naval guns. I observed that he was moving these idled men to his outer stonewall so they might fire on O'Bannon's Marines with their personal weapons. Now I determined that those men were in a precarious position lying in the open plain. The Dey surely must have reasoned that the stone wall and its enclosed trenches were sufficiently strong to keep us from overrunning him. Well, I had to do something.

"I did have my reserve cavalry which might have penetrated the western wall, or I could take my small force and come to O'Bannon's aid. I chose to take charge by bringing my men to the aid of O'Bannon.

"That's when Dorf came forward with the idea of having the Greeks issued grenades. They had only seen my Marines practising with them so we could not expect very much from these inexperienced troops. We gave every Greek cannoneer five grenades and told them to join the attack on the rock wall.

"Waving my scimitar over my head and yelling, 'Follow me!' I ran with all my troops of Group Four right at the very part of the stone wall where the heaviest firing was. Right to where the billowing smoke from the bursting powder created the largest black cloud. I knew now was the time, for, with my army, tomorrow would never do. The Arab nature was 'Do it now or not at all', so I took the chance of failure and came sweeping down onto the firing enemy with my scimitar flashing in the waning sun even though I had not a steed under me. I had handed my good stallion over to Private X of the Marines. He had been watching the show because, well I don't know. He was a strange one. I got to see him so seldom, but I'm sure he was called Private X, rather dark in coloring, might have been part Indian or part Negro. We rushed forward against a host of savages numbering more than ten to our one and fired when any head with a dirty turban looked over the wall. The Greeks stopped to light the grenades. Then they rushed and threw their missiles over the wall. The black smoke billowed up and many sharp grenade reports assaulted our ears. I could see that the defenders had never before been charged with grenades. I yelled at the Marines as I rushed by them, 'Stop shooting and use your grenades.'

"The rear ranks were mighty slow coming up to help carry the wall. I led the Marines and those Greek cannoneers right into the heated fire of the Dey's reinforced troops. As the Marines mounted the wall, tossing lighted hand grenades, and I stood swinging my scimitar, the turbaned sons of Allah started to run away. We soon drove them out of their hastily prepared battlements. As they fled from their coverts irregularly, firing in retreat from every palm tree and partition wall in their way, we kept up our hot pursuit. I saw an angry face looking down from the roof of a stone house. I pulled up my rifle, took aim, and fired. The dead man rolled off the roof. Yelling for the Greeks, I went to pursue a small number of enemy troops down an alley to the right. I was pointing my scimitar to show the Greeks the right direction when I received a ball through my left wrist. I was now deprived use of my hand and ,sadly, of my rifle, but with the help of a few Greeks I, and my scimitar, wiped out that small band of turbaned Tripolitans. Their blood flowed in the street.

"Mr. O'Bannon, accompanied by Mr. Mann of Annapolis, raced forward with his Marines and a few Greeks. Mr. Mann ...Oh, he had helped bring the cannon off the ship and stayed to fight with my Marines. As they all ran through a shower of musketry from the walls of the houses toward the now deserted batteries, Private John Wilton, U.S Marines, was shot in the head. The bullet entered near his ear and came out his neck on the opposite side. John kept right on running with the others for several steps, his momentum propelling him. Then he fell to the stone street. Soon his blood turned the stones red. Our first hero of the day but not our last. For as our Marines followed O'Bannon and Mr. Mann to the tower, the firing dwindled, but some of the defenders kept up a small amount of well aimed lead which, entering the pathway of our troops, struck the bodies of Marines Edward Stewart and David Thomas. Two Greeks took charge of these wounded Marines, and the rest ran with greater vigor toward their goal— the enemy's flag flying atop the tower at the battery. Ordering the few sons of Allah that were there to drop their weapons, the Marines took possession of the enemy battery. Then they ripped down that green rag and hoisted an American flag upon the ramparts of the city of Derne in the country of Tripoli. The Greek cannoneers continued shooting at the Tripolitans. The forces of Yusef were ducking into alleys and running pell-mell toward the West. A few still fired occasionally from their houses from whence they were quickly dislodged by the heavy fire of our naval vessels. Hamet had gotten possession of the Governor's Palace (the city hall where Bey Mustafa was the Governor under Yusef of Tripoli) because his cavalry soon out-flanked the flying enemy. By four in the afternoon we had completed our possession of the city. The damned Governor took refuge in Hiram, which is the most sacred of sanctuaries in a mosque among the Turks. I want to tell you he didn't have my head, but I sure wish that his had been cut off. I suggested several times to the naval men that we might use this Governor in exchange for Captain Bainbridge and his crew. " The General stopped to check his pocket watch.

"My God, look at the time, and I've not had a drink. Patrick, Patrick, will you find a waiter so we at least can quench our thirst?" After drinking the ale that the waiter had placed on the table, the General said to the assembled listeners and in particular to Leitensdorfer.

"The night is not over yet, and if Dorf is willin' to go on to the Turk's Tavern with me we can drink and have a delightful romp with some of the gels that will be there awaiting us — I'm ready, let's go!"

True-blue Beau was present and told the nearest drinkers from the General's purse,

"I think the General had most of his facts right tonight. The other night when I was here at the 'Grapes', and Mr. Mann was too, it all came together. Yes, it did. That I knowed Mr. Mann when I worked in Washington City. Yes, he was Midshipman on Captain Hull's *Argus*, maybe he still is. Mann told me that Eaton as Governor of that Barbary city stayed dead sober and without a female in his bed all during his stay in Derne. That sure wasn't true of most of 'em. Why I heard for sure them Greeks they each had two or three young girls a sleepin' in their quarters. Well you know'd they did more than sleep. Eaton didn't seem to care because Mann said the General had a big drive to get the protectin' rockwalls up. Eaton knew Yusef's forces was about to march on Derne. Now I know they fixed a fort which them Arabs called Eaton's Fort, and I've heerd tell it's now called the American fort. Yes that's what I ... ."

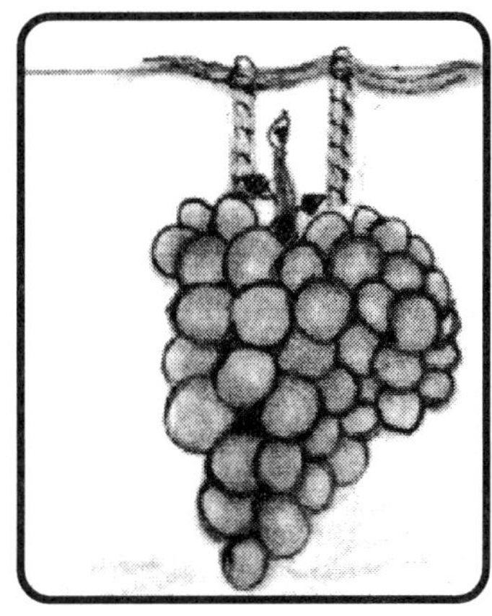

The table where the General usually held forth was empty. Vila would be out the cost of the broadsheet. Yet word had spread that Eaton had come down sick and was indisposed. Dorf and some of the other regulars were at the Red String. B. Smart was out of town and thus it was that a total stranger, Rocco, was spinning his story.

"I was a Lieutenant in Eaton's army, and I have been here in Boston a few days. I was at the tavern called The Orange Tree, over on Hanover street, when I heard that General Eaton has been spendin' his evenin's here at the Bunch of Grapes. I thought I'd come by and meet up with him again, but Mr. Vila told me he wasn't comin' tonight. I was there the day we captured Derne, and I did a bit of collectin'. I specialized in gold coins. They can help you in many ways.

"It was a night-long affair. Eaton was alettin' his victorious army ransack the department that he said was loyal to Yusef. The General sent the word to each group commander no, absolutely no, looting of the areas that had been loyal to Hamet. By noon the next day most of the valuables had been carried off by the mob what had been an army the day before.

"I was in shared quarters with Eli and Dorf. I saw they

had found their share and had bundled them for the expected land trip to Tripoli. O'Bannon and his Marines had carried out burial duties before they could join the looters.

"It was a race to the best homes and then a seek and find routine. Those that had done it before found the most booty. I had been in a few booty-findin' forays. I looked where other rich money-men had squirreled away their gold.

"After the plunder collecting was nearly over, we were all together in our rooms when Eli and Dorf offered to share a prize or two with Eaton from their collection. Eaton had been occupied with his duties and had not joined in the fun. Eli showed him their pile of confiscated goods. I saw among the loot was a John Arnold chronometer. Havin' been impressed into the British navy, I recognized this valuable time keeper which had, without doubt, been lifted from an English warship. Most naval people knew that John Arnold of London was England's top watchmaker. His store on The Strand was the holy of holies for watchmakers. The British Navy used his time mechanism to navigate the world. And to top it off there was a Breguet. I had picked up one of those once when I had been in Bonaparte's army. It was the *creme de la creme,* the very best French watch. The Breguet was a gold carriage clock, a watch shaped thermometer, and a boxed chronometer.

"General Eaton's response to their offer was, 'I can see that you know valuable things but did you come on a scimitar? That would be more to my taste then these valuable mechanisms.'

" 'Yes, we went by a maker of sword, that's what I think his sign said. We didn't go in as I wanted to find these time keepers. Dorf was sure that we would find such valuable instruments. I — we both knew more about them than scimitars or swords. If you want, General, we could go take a look and see if that place has any.' Eli responded.

" ' Let's do that later today after I have written the needed proclamation for Hamet to sign. Come by around two. I should be available then.'

"I joined General Eaton and Eli at the metal working shop, and we found that the shop had a great variety of swords and scimitars. We picked out the best of both, then returned to our quarters with several valuable additions to General Eaton's growing scimitar collection." Rocco ended his story and turned to the waiter.

"Could I order a small meal and a bottle of wine? I have a gold coin in my purse to pay." Hans brought it and Rocco ate and drank and left.

The evening was short. The tavern soon emptied of patrons, so Mr. Vila started to close with the hope that General Eaton would recover from his illness before the next agreed-upon date. To make sure of that he better send — no, go — and visit Eaton before he spent his money on the broadsheet. Oh no, he had to go back to Maine to finish the land deal. That sure would help put his Bunch of Grapes in top-notch condition. Yes it would. Verna was able to go and check on his health. I'll tell her tonight. Then he locked the front door of the tavern and went home to sleep in his single bed at the top of the stairway's small room.

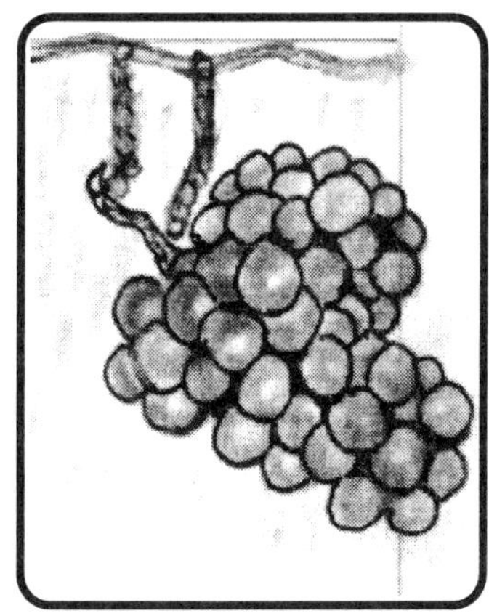

"Ya,Ya, de Generals not here. Vot ve do den is you buy me a round, and I vill tell you about General's Punch Bowl visit, Ya. Punch that be why he goes." The audience had been awaiting the General, but only Colonel Leitsendorfer was there. The rumor was late in reaching the Boston dock area that General Eaton had gone abrawling and would not be at the Bunch of Grapes. He was home and in bed recovering. The broadsheet had been sent out by Verna after she had checked on Eaton's condition. He said he'd be up and at his usual place as agreed.

On that visit she was invited to the General's bed. She had accepted and they had spent the whole morning. That was when Verna had confided to the General that James had been a good sexual partner when he was young but now at middle age why...why, she said....well...it didn't stay hard — no, it didn't *get* hard — the way it used to. God it was great to have a real good — in the General's bed. She was sure they could arrange for another time. He liked removing her garters. The effect was...oh...just a thrill going up your legs and it made you wanta —

Back to the tavern... as Colonel Leitensdorfer's mug was being filled for the tenth time at this early hour, he addressed the pub patrons in a commanding but alcohol-slurred accent. (*The author will now translate the Colonel's lingua franca into something approaching English*).

"Vhen my General gets into a bad dark mood, he sometimes goes vhere some heads can be banged. Ya! Banged. Heads. Liken he did in Barbary to some of his troopers as punishment. But here in Boston he has no army vhere he can bang some heads. This just be funnin' that's vhat our General thinks.

"His man Aletti tells me that the General mounted his big white and black stallion one evening last week and galloped down Ann Street. Yes, and Aletti said the General's mood and stallion vere much the same. Yes. Now, vhen the General kicks his horse in ribs with spur, that black stallion rear up and scare the street people. Yes. He rides at full gallop into Dock Square makin' sparks fly and people fly. Vhen the General comes to a livery place in the back of the Sign of the Punch Bowl, which is not such a quiet place as Bunch of Rapes— no, Grapes, Eaton spurred the horse and it rears up and makes big horse snort and expel at rear. Vhat a commotion. Ya. Herr Eaton jumped off and give stallion to the groom just like his horse is a soft old milk cow. Ya. He handed the stable boy a good solid half dollar and said, 'Put my horse in a good clean stall and feed him a full quart of your best oats.'

"I heard the General hardly limped as he swaggered up path from stable, flings the pub door open, Bang, showin' he is the Big United States General. Ya, Herr Eaton says in big and commandin' voice, I remember it well, 'You popeye waiter - you stinkin' scum from the sewer. You no good fart of a woman, clear me, Eaton, a path to best table in this den of snakes.'

"Herr Eaton marched with waiter to center stage and sat down, and to waiter said , 'Now, bring me , double quick, first a large whisky and then a hot Flip. Do it! Run, Run before I kickin' your black ass to the kitchen. Go, Run!'

"In a very short time, even before he got to drink his Flip, a big fight broke out. Just vhat he vent for, Ya. Lots of bad rowdy men be swingin' fists and some chairs. Two men came right at General. One hit him from behind, the other kicked a table into Eaton's face. Soon many bodies were all rollin' on the floor. Eaton vere havin' lots of fun, but one bad man had his fingers into General's purse. That made the General so mad — angry. Even vhen two strong thugs get on top of Eaton, he call up his great strength, pushed them off, swung a table at one and then another till they be bloodied. General was doing good until the other friends of them thieves take on the General. They banged him up pretty damn good , but then the Boston Irish Coppers come into Punch Bowl with sticks and made... make order. Was General Eaton clever? He run out the back door and found his horse and quickly mount before the Coppers could swing on his head. He spurs and gallops that big stallion down the street, back through Dock Square going to Ann Street. Aletti had sent friends to the Punch Bowl to warn if they seen the coppers coming and to help the General stay alive. They told Aletti and Aletti told me the whole story I just told you. Ja.

"Tongue not so good this night so if you want more vait 'til Herr General comes to Bunch of Rath— no, NO, Grapes, Ja." Colonel Leitensdorfer didn't leave early but found a few old friends, and they played cards until the wee hours of the morning in one of Vila's small private rooms. He felt lucky since the U.S. Congress had just voted him a bonus of a large tract of land out near the Ohio River. And it was his night, for when morning came, he had won a pocket full of U.S. greenbacks. His communicating skills improved with each winning hand.

"Yes, it was old mentor, Senator Bradley of Vermont, who put a bill into the hopper and got it passed into the law that gave Colonel Leitensdorfer 320 acres of land and the pay of an army captain. The House of Representatives upped the land grant to 640 acres (a square mile) in the wild lands East of the Mississippi River. But, the Senate prevailed, so he got only the 320 acres."

Beauregard Smart informed the regular patrons of all these events the next night Eaton was absent. He dropped a small hint that Eaton had been visited by a middle-aged lady who had spent the morning at 16 Ann Street.

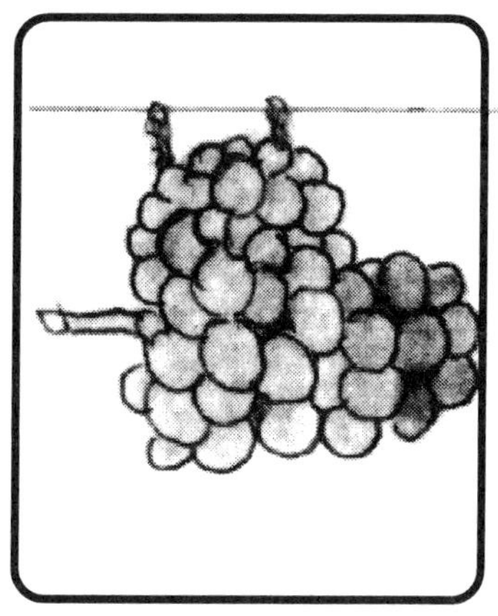

"**Welcome to the first production** of my play called MUGWUMPERY — all in one act. Playing tonight only, at the Bunch O' Grapes. No admittance charge, and the drinks are on the author. Now, since the day has been long and I have been sober— much to my dismay— I will have a small glass of whisky. Hans, you will fetch it now. Then you can bring me some of that roast beef that I can smell, some vegetables, and two bottles of Madeira, then you can offer these old lost and forgotten heroes some of your ale while I have my supper." The food eaten, the General moves on to his drama, as is right and fitting for a Dartmouth alumnus.

"MUGWUMPERY will have these distinguished *Dramatis Personae*: Commodore Barron, Colonel Lear, Captain Preble, Marine Lieutenant O'Bannon, the other warship captains, and General Eaton, U.S. Naval Agent. 1804 is the time. The location is the Commodore's cabin the on warship *Constitution*. Barron is having a Council of War:

Barron: I will ask each of you the same simple question. Please be brief in your replies and to the point. The question is this. Will we bring about the release of our prisoners in a reasonable time if we, with all our present warships, bombard the city of Tripoli?

Eaton: Commodore, I say that we shall never force the Turks of Tripoli or any of these Barbary pirates to yield by means of bombardments, even if we place hard bombardments one upon another. And for how long shall we sit in their harbor and leave our good sailors as slave to these corsairs? To extirpate the evil heads of piracy, we will need to invest their lands with a large army made up of Arabs who support Hamet Bashaw. President Jefferson is of this persuasion since he gave me gold, Marines, and rifles for Hamet. Mr. O'Brien, who was a slave of these pirates, is of the same mind. If we should level this city of Tripoli, the inhabitants would move to some other seaport such as Derne. And from there they would continue to capture our merchant ships and enslave the seamen.

Colonel Lear: While I'm new to the situation, I do have some thoughts. I have been in several wars, and now the President has deemed that my intellect might be useful in solving this very touchy problem. As a diplomat, I think that I should accompany Eaton under a flag of truce and confront the Bashaw Yusef with the present situation. Now that he has seen all the mighty warships in his harbor, he may have considered the consequences of demanding outrageous sums as ransom for the good seamen he now holds. I say that before we bombard, we ask for a meeting.

Captain Preble: My warship did some damage, and so did the *Intrepid* when she blew up amongst their fleet. I say we should get in battle formation and give them an afternoon of heavy bombardment.

Captain of a lesser rank: I, Sir, agree with the word of Captain Preble, Sir.

Captain of yet lesser rank: Sir, might I say, that we could fire our guns all afternoon, I say, and give them no rest all night by firing our biggest cannon during the night every once in a while, Sir!

Lieutenant O'Bannon: I, Sir, am ever ready to do the

Commodore's bidding. I have no strategy for defeating these pirates. All I can say, Sir, is let's get on with it.

Captain Preble: Commodore, Sir, I think Bashaw Yusef must realize as he looks out into his harbor and views his present destruction and the many warships ready for action that his days of making us pay tribute to a pirate are over, done with ,and no longer a valid conclusion.

Commodore Barron: I see we have a near agreement that the Navy has the situation well in hand. However, I will send Eaton and Colonel Lear under a flag of truce to present this renegade with a means of handing back our sailors and still let him save face. That is the proper thing to do, for I think this Yusef must be a sensible ruler and would not want us to level his city. I am sure you diplomats can find a way for him to look strong and yet hand back to us the *Philadelphia*'s crew.

Eaton: Commodore, I have known this dog. He killed his own brother, and would have killed the rightful ruler if he could have. He is not in the western mode of thinking. Our fleet may bombard him, but he will have all the land of Tripoli to feed and succor him while we must soon go for supplies and possibly combat a devastating north blowing storm which may sweep down on all our ships and drive them on the shoals of the harbor.

Commodore Barron: Then it is agreed that Eaton and Lear will be put ashore ... "

At this point in his 'play', Eaton was interrupted by a very dark-colored man who had been at several other of Eaton's recitations. He had been overlooked as his garb was much the same as that worn by the heroes and hangers-on at the Bunch of Grapes.

"Sir, General Eaton, may I have the right to speak?" Eaton stood to get a close look and replied,

"Yes, and I do think I know you! If my eyes do not deceive me, you are Selim the Janissary who took the old ruined castle on the heights of Derne. Come join me, and, yes, I'll give the night over to you if you wish to address these, my loyal heroes and friends. That MUGWUMPERY thing was mostly for my amusement. Hans! Bring my fellow soldier a bottle of your best wine. Or would you prefer something else, Selim?"

Standing at Eaton's table, Selim shook his head and looked over the roomful of fellow travelers.

"I am honored to be here and doubly honored to be allowed to speak to this noble gathering. I was at Derne with the General, and I wish to tell the story about how this good American treated the people of Derne. As soon as the battle was won, Eaton wrote and handed out rules to live by. This he did in the name of Hamet. They were signed by Hamet and posted on the palace doors. He put a firm price on the farmers' produce, which they didn't like at all. His Arab troops , after the victory, were pressed into rebuilding the city's defences. And I took to rebuilding the old castle into a fort. We called it 'Eaton's Fort'. We built it like he showed us.

"Many days, Eaton walked the city streets in the morning and held court in the afternoon. He was much dismayed at the natives seeking justice posturing themselves on the floor and trying to kiss his shoes. Eaton Pasha did all this even when the surrounding army's general offered twenty-five thousand dollars for Eaton's head and thirty -five thousand dollars for Eaton alive. Our General never stopped walking without body guards in the lanes and byways of Derne. He was fearless. Just as Robert Treat Paine said in his poem;

"Eaton all danger braves,
Fierce while the battle raves,
Columbia's Standard waves
On Derne's proud wall.

"We got rid of the Governor Mustafa. He escaped and

joined General Hassan Aga the next day, I think it was May 13th. Did you bring your journal, General? Will you check that date, while I take sip of wine?" (*A Moslem away from home-ground quite often drinks alcohol.*) Eaton flipped through his journal, and said,

"It was May 13,1805 when Hassan Aga's entire army, all those still under the influence of Yusef, came down out of the Green Mountains and the hills onto the plain of Derne with the expectation of recapturing the city."

"Yes, General, they came on horse and on foot, thousands upon thousands, and that's when we all thanked your forceful orders that caused the defenses of Derne to hold. At the fort, we had a clear field of fire as they all paraded past our guns. Not one of our men was even nicked by an enemy's bullet. The stone walls and the captured cannon, yes, and the naval ships in the harbor threw up a wall of hot lead that Hassan Aga's troops could not withstand. Some of his cavalry breached the defenses and entered the city. Cannon fire from the warships splattered horses and riders against the palace walls. Hassan's ferocious warriors stampeded out of the city right past our hail of lead.

"I remember that after the battle we counted their dead, piled in the field, as thirty-nine, fifty-seven severely wounded, and we had just a dozen with minor cuts. And if we could have seen the enemy's tents that night, I think we could have counted hundreds with more than minor cut and bruises.

"Hassan Aga did come back for a second try, the fool. Eaton Pasha had proved that ... he was a master at offense and also a master at defense. Hassan Aga was too thick of head to know it."

"Selim, you've forgotten that little battle I had with a small force of cavalry which came to smell out our defenses. I on my black stallion led about ten other mounted troops into the ravine where Yusef's men had retreated after our naval guns had peppered them with hot shot. I caught up with them, and together we all took a few separated heads for trophies. They were to replace the head that Governor Mustafa had offered but cheated me of."

"Oh, I also forgot," Selim interjected, "General Eaton talked with an Italian from Hassan's forces, and this escapee said that Hassan was planning on capturing Hamet and dragging him in chains all the way to Tripoli. So the General had Hamet put aboard an American warship." He stopped to have a drink of the good red wine Hans had brought him.

After a small pause, Eaton stood and said to no one in particular,

"The damned Navy. Now, if they had pressed the attack on Tripoli as soon as they had received the news that I had captured Derne, war would have been over and done with. Damned old women. No fight in their bellies. Damn again, for the next sorry event should never have happened to me or my good and loyal heroes of Derne."

To set the record straight — we know John Rodgers had put the hot shot to Tripoli and a white flag had been hung out by the Dey Yusef. Eaton was this night still angry at the Navy for the many problems in this Barbary affair. His mind and body both were in disrepair.

Eaton left by way of the rear door near the toilet and, struggling, he had to ask for help before he could get his worn body and mind to coordinate his entry into the waiting hack. His man servant Aletti was at his abode to take charge of the body, and put it to rest.

Beau had heard it all and said, when there was a small letdown in the usual banter,

"Well now, I can quote poetry too. For I just finished John Pierpont's *Ode to the General,* and it goes like this,

'And Eaton trod in triumph o'er his foe,
Where once fought Hannibal and Scipo...' "

Author's historical insertion:

Some people of Africa's northern shores are inclined to earn their living by piracy. If Eaton could speak from this page, he would tell you of the many times other peoples or tribes attacked them to reduce their pirates' dens to rubble. These raids have continued. We allies sent our armies to drive out a pirate of a different sort. Adolf Hitler and his cohorts were plunderers in an exponentially greater way than any previous Barbary pirates.

To remind my reader of those events, I present the following information. From London, *V for Victory* was played over and over — Dah Daaaah — by the British Broadcasting Corporation to all its warriors fighting the forces of evil. Stirring and majestic notes of L. van Beethoven's Fifth Symphony circled around the earth at the speed of light. Courage was the message — we will be victorious!

On the northern rim of Africa, a war was raging to prevent the Germans from capturing Egypt. In 1943 we heard the English cannon roaring out a victory — **Boom - Boom - Boom - Booooom** - in answer to the deeper roar of German 88's in defeat.

The English General Montgomery was driving the German General Rommel's forces west — west over the very terrain that both these Generals fully understood from studying the details in the journal of America's Barbary General — General William Eaton. They each had a copy.

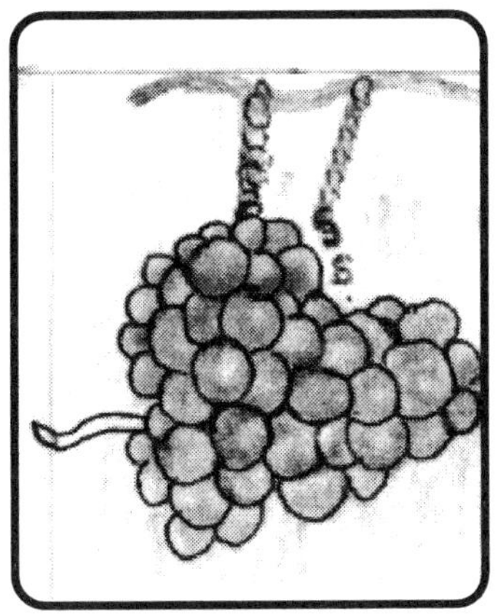

General Eaton was alone at the center table where he had eaten, drunk his Flip and wine and was into his discourse of the evening. Again, just an average-size crowd was drinking and eating in the tavern at the head of the Long Wharf.

"I'm going to paraphrase a small part of the six-page letter I sent to Commodore Samuel Barron, Commander in Chief of the Mediterranean Fleet, a letter I started on the 15th of May 1805 and sent off in the *Nautilus* the night of the 17th. I'll leave out most of the many flowery words one uses to address a Commodore." General Eaton had an audience whose attention was on the wane. The battle was over, and some were heard saying,

"I've had enough of that pompous ass, plenty of I AM GENERAL EATON — enough for a good long time."

Some of Eaton's words were overpowered by the small chatter of those patrons who were more interested in the latest news — news that another merchant ship had been boarded by a French Man O' War and several men had been pressed into their navy. Eaton continued,

"The letter now begins, 'Since my last letters to you, we have been occupied with movements of the enemy's troops; contrary to what we expected, they advanced and gave us battle on the 13th. They had discovered our numbers from the former Governor who had escaped and told all. He had informed them that the local inhabitants would turn upon we Christians. We were out-gunned and they came into the city proper, right up to the castle. Fortune was with us because a nine-pounder from either the *Argus* or the *Nautilus* smashed into the mounted enemy. That bloody mess soon caused the rest of those infidels to make a very hasty retreat. Hamet's cavalry chased them sorely in their flight, killing a large number of them. So we continued the battle, but never at night. Now we are too weak (here at Derne) to force their lines. Without the needed powder and other provisions. Furthermore, we will soon run out of food because the enemy is in the surrounding hills, cutting off all land approaches.'

"I wrote, 'I ought not to conceal my apprehensions about the many days without (military) supplies. If, Sir, your naval ships would offer a heavy blow at Tripoli, it would cause Yusef's forces here (Derne) to capitulate or retrograde to Tripoli. Now, Sir, if our navy were to destroy Yusef's Tripolitans, word would travel quickly over the desert to Derna, Mustafa's men would surrender, and my path to Tripoli City would free of all hindrances.'

"My next letter had these words to the Commodore, 'If the burden of expense which must accrue from pursuing the cooperation (with Hamet) seems an insurmountable obstacle, I am apprehensive that the ultimate expense of maintaining a peace with Joseph (Yusef) Bashaw will be more burdensome to the United States than that accruing from this cooperation (with Hamet); besides it is calculated that this expense will be reimbursed by Hamet once he is on his throne. It is insinuated to me that the Consul Lear is opposed to this measure (helping Hamet).' That ended the letter to the Commodore.

"Now before Barron stepped down, he sent me the word,

dated May 27. He wrote 'If the Dey Hamet, after having been put in possession of Derne, (where he had been Governor), his former government and the district in which his interest is said to be the most powerful, has not in himself energy and talent, and is so devastated of means and resources, as not to be able to move on with successful progress, seconded by our naval forces acting on the coast, he must be held unworthy of further support, and the co-operation as a measure too expensive and too little pregnant with hope and advantage to justify its further protection."

"That, my loyal listeners, is a direct quote from my journal, and it was a real blow. All the money he sent me was two thousand dollars. I needed three times two thousand just to settle local bills. The good news which came to us at Derne was that John Rodgers was no old woman. He was unlimbering his warships' guns in preparation of levelin' Tripoli.

"On June 4, Captain Isaac Hull came ashore and told me the bad news. He was ordered to take me, my Marines, and the Christian members of my force to Syracuse, Sicily. I firmly said I would not go. Then I wrote a letter of explanation to John Rodgers and sent it off on the *Nautilus*.

"Now I wasn't there, but in the days to come I was told that John Rodgers really did put the shot to that bloody Yusef from all the ships in the harbor, and they pounded Tripoli until that thick-headed scoundrel finally ran up a white flag and asked for terms. On June 3rd — a white flag! And stupid Lear had him sign a preliminary treaty which I later found very poorly done.

"It was June 11th. We had just finished killing over a hundred of Hassan Aga and Dey Mustafa forces, and they had surrendered all their units to me. The word had indeed traveled. Now I would have no opposition by land until I came to Tripoli. The road was clear and I would have a mighty army eager to crush the usurper, because hordes of booty seekers would unite with me on the march. We would put the rightful ruler on his throne and make a treaty that required no tribute.

"Then as night fell, the *Constellation* came into the harbor, and I had a letter from John Rodgers. It was a damned cold day in Hell that day because he addressed me as a master does his slave. God, it was just stomach turning; it still is. I was told, 'Get your men on board the *Constellation* or suffer a bombardment.'

"The second letter I was handed was the Treaty that the weak-kneed Lear had written. God, it was just ... I was in a rage. They were to pay more ransom to that goddamned Yusef. Yes, payment for our sailors to that bloody pirate who had run up a white flag of surrender.

"I was in my rooms at the palace when Captain Campbell came ashore. I admit I was still mad as hell, and I told the Captain to tell John Rodgers where he could go. And I think maybe he did, for the *Hornet* left for Tripoli, and Campbell's ship sat in the harbor while I continued my job as Governor of the province of Cyrenaica, of course in Hamet's name. In ten days the *Hornet* was back, anchored along side the *Constellation*. Campbell came ashore. By now I had cooled my temper, and we talked most of the night. We had enough goat meat and fruits to last the whole time. Letters and talk. By morning we had reached an amicable solution to our problem. I said to the Captain, 'Sir, I cannot dishonor the men who have achieved America's greatest victory since our nation won her independence. It would be a disgrace beyond my ability to endure if our friends in the Navy were to bombard my American heroes. Therefore, Captain Campbell, we will accompany you.'

"In the morning, I told Hamet all the facts. I invited him to come with us. That is all I could do for him. I told him Yusef would be recognized by my government but that

I would try to find a home for him and his retainers. I was relieved when he was the first to go aboard. Then with my own money I paid all my debts, Tripolitans, Greeks, and other mercenaries. I entered the cabin on the *Constellation* with damn few coins left.

"I led my Marines down out of the city of Derne with sadness in my heart and tears in my eyes. As the gig was rowed out to the ship, I never looked back. Only ahead to my duty of telling those in the Senate and House what a fool, Lear, State had sent to deal with the wily Barbary pirate named Yusef. The treaty had no provision for Hamet, but when I got to Tripoli, I made Lear change it. Yusef made the promise that Hamet could live, with his wives and children, wherever they pleased if Hamet promised that he would make no further attempt to regain the throne. They were reconciled and Hamet disembarked." The General was interrupted by a small dark-skinned man in some old military clothing.

"Gen'r'l —", With a southern lilt, the man repeated, "General, Suh?"

"Yes." The Gen'l turned and studied this semi-militarily dressed man.

"Sir, I was the Marine who led your stallion off to be sold at Derne, and, Suh, I was here when you told about the battle, and, Suh, you didn't say then a thing about them caps you made us wear. Wear so we'd know who to shoot at. Why, my French cap sure put some lice in my head and I'm still scratchin' and ascratchin'..." General Eaton interrupted the speaker of the lice with,

"You're Private X, for sure — one of O'Bannon's Marines! And yes, I did buy those Napoleonic caps in Egypt. They were inexpensive because no good Egyptian wanted to wear a French cap. Now back to the story — Hans! take a beer to Private X and put it on my bill.

"I was cheered by all the men on our American warships in the harbor at Tripoli, and even in the city many large crowds came out to see me when I, General Eaton, walked their streets.

"John Rodgers got around to inviting me for dinner and called me General, which swept some of my bitterness away. Commodore Rodgers also admired my neat and detailed financial report. He was amazed that the total expenditures from leaving the United States until my arrival at Tripoli had cost only $59,108.58 and $20,000 of that from my own purse. Rogers told me Tobias Lear had paid the token $60,000 (?TOKEN?!) for the release of the *Philadelphia*'s crew. More to come Yusef's way later! Well, John Rodgers gave me my State Department pay just as I was going back to my accommodations on shore in Tripoli. We then took a naval ship to Tunis, where we had a much better reception from the Dey of Tunis, now that he understood we could and would fight. I had some time to look around in the city of Tunis, and so I visited with some locals I had known when I was there before. Now one of these friends was a breeder of Arabian horses. Ali Vardi Khan was a rich dignitary and a very interesting man. I spent three days at his palace and, when I was ready to leave, he gave me the choice from a dozen high-strung beautiful Arabian stallions. There was one which was marked in a most unusual way, his front-quarters were black and hind-quarters were snow white. He held his head high and danced on his toes. And can you believe it? He pranced right over and nuzzled me. Me, who must have smelled different. Well...maybe not, for I had eaten like an Arab and was dressed in Arab clothes. So I would say it was also my Arabic speech which charmed my white and black stallion. I found a merchant ship and paid the Captain to bring my unique horse to Boston.

"My army had disembarked at Tripoli and would seek their fortunes in Barbary and other Arab climes. We sailed for Syracuse, reaching that port on July 16, 1805. And there

I saw a wonder of wonders, for in the Roads sat six mighty frigates, four well made brigs, two sleek schooners, three fast ketches, and one sloop! And even more, fifteen well built gun boats. All under Commodore John Rodgers' command ... a naval man who knew what to do with this mighty armada.

"And now, my good loyal friends, I must leave, since I have an appointment with President Adams at nine tomorrow."

Eaton stopped to see Mr. Vila on the way out, but as he was again visiting in Maine, the General was met by the overheated Verna who said,

"General, my garter is in great need of removal.... You'll take it off my leg, I'm sure, so I'll be ready in your bed later tonight just as soon as I lock up."

Beauregard Smart had taken it all in, and after the General had warmly kissed Verna and exited the door, he started to tell more than he knew about the breed of horse called Arabian.

"I was a groom back in my youth for that Kahn man Eaton were talkin' about. Now I was also his horse doctor, for my father had been schooled in that art. You see we were all talented in my ...." Beauregard stopped talking when he finally noticed that patrons were leaving.

Mr. Vila had escorted the two veterans to the center table. Hans, seeing Eaton, offered ,

"Ya, mine General, vant meal now?"

"Do I smell pork roast? If I do, then, Herr Hans, bring the Colonel and me a large serving with a side order of potatoes and string beans, for it must be that time of the year. And bring us two servings of ale now. And with the food my usual two bottles of Madeira. Pat, if you want to change your order, you may."

"I'll eat the pork with you , but I'd like your permission to leave then, Sir."

"Well, then let's enjoy ourselves, Pat. The story can wait." They ate and talked and then Colonel Pat left. The main room at the tavern by the Long Wharf was nearly full of fallen heroes and more of the same, when the General gave his wine glass a sharp blow which caused the chatter to almost cease. Then most of their eyes and ears were ready for the next episode in the life of General William H. Eaton.

"We boarded the *Constellation* at Tripoli for home on July 6, 1805. I was so wrought up about the $60,000 Lear had given Yusef for our sailors' release that I cannot tell you if it was a good passage or not. We ate with Captain Campbell and some of the ransomed sailors from the *Phila-*

delphia. They sang my praise all the way home.

"As soon as the Constellation docked on November 5 at Baltimore, Eli and I left for Washington City. Oh yes! We did buy ourselves some suitable clothing in Baltimore before hiring a conveyance. If clothes don't make the man, then new clothing makes the man smell like an American not like an unwashed Arab.

"I had spent the whole crossing writing and polishing my report for the Secretaries of War and State, Mr. Smith and Mr. Madison. I had made copies for the Senate and the House. In this report I made it very plain that Tobias Lear was solely to blame for the inadequate treaty that would perpetuate the very situation whose oblivion my capture of Derne had made possible. The outcome should have been no more ransom, only fair treatment for the United States. And Commodore Barron was not to blame for this betrayal by Lear. Eli had spent the time eagerly anticipating reunion with his sweetheart, Secretary Smith's daughter. Long distant letters had made this union a number one priority for my handsome son. I was looking forward to a Washington wedding, one to which I could invite some of my best friends from the hallowed halls of Congress — and yes, some in the executive branch.

"Secretary Smith said to me after reading my report, 'General, you deserve the thanks and gratitude of the whole nation.' And even better was James Madison over at State. He verbally awarded me, the Barbary General, The Hero of Derne, with laurel wreaths. Smith praised me in the halls of Congress and in public. Commodore Preble sent me a lavish letter of congratulation and had copies made for the press. Preble wrote, 'The arduous and dangerous services you have performed justly immortalized your name, and astonished not only your own country but the world. If pecuniary resources and naval strength had been at your command, what would you not have done?' Those were some of his words of praise.

"And he continued with: 'As one familiar with every aspect of the multitudinous problems you faced in Barbary, I salute you, Sir! You have acquired immortal honors and established the fame of your country in the East! It gives me great pride to be your compatriot!'

"The newspapers were delighted — sales way up and profits way up — as they vied to make me even a greater hero. I have to admit some of their published yarns were hardly recognized by me. Many children were named William, and streets in over forty towns were named the General Eaton Street. Right here in Boston the street near the capital has been named Derne Street in my honor.

"The freed men of the *Philadelphia* were telling my story all over the towns and cities of America. They said the capture of Derne had caused the usurper Yusef to look on America in a different light. Some of the old women in the Navy came by and said they were glad to have been a part of my grand design. Then banquet after banquet, public dinners after public dinners, all to recognize me, the General who had, with a few good Marines, beaten the ransom — really tribute-demanding whores — yes, that is what those demanding pirates of Barbary are in the eyes of world. All citizens of the United States wanted no more blackmail from any damned bloody pirates. I said at every one of the gatherings, 'I don't want your kind words of welcome, your rich food, and your fine wines! I demand justice! Let there be an inquiry into the sorry state of this nation!' And Lear was then and now the cause of our shame! That treaty of Lear's should not be ratified. Never, no never, ratified.

"Both houses of Congress were preparing to give me a special commendation and a gold medal, but as you all know that didn't happen. Yes, the head of the politicos in Washington City sent the word out, 'Eaton may be right, but let's not let him push us into a corner.' They did have a joint hearing which I think started in January 1806. My good friend Tim Pickering, the same as I had named that mud fort in Georgia after, was now the Honorable Senator from Massachusetts. He and John Randolph both became my strongest supporters. I spent day after day giving my testimony. The one Senator that I would have liked a duel with — and I would have really cut him up — was the sardonic, talkative Henry Clay. He made a derogatory point of my taking the title General. He was, in my eyes, the one who put my gold medal in limbo. Now, I was the person who led the army, and that made me a General. I told Clay that I was General Eaton by right of my capture of the enemy city, Derne.

"I was made aware of this stalemate by Tim Pickering, and that is why I took matters into my own hands and carried my case to all the country. I addressed audiences from one town to another, city after city. While I was in Boston, I thought it might be proper to see my wife Eliza."

"General, Sir," the queerest sailor present interrupted, "I've been to most of your evenin' talks, and I've yet to find out if your wife Eliza had any children. Yes, I know about Eli Danielson, but are there any more yours and hers and just hers in Brimfield?"

"Well now there's a question! I think I'll have to take a look in the journal where I have the birth dates. So since I've been interrupted, I'll order everyone a drink of rum, and I'll have a large one too. Now let's see.

"Yes, Eliza and I did have children even if it was difficult to have any sexual intercourse with that cold blooded woman. Now — Ah! Here 'tis. Eliza, born Feb. 22, '95; Charlotte, Oct. 24, '97; Almira, July 20, '99; William, Aug. 30, 1804. Strange that you should ask at this time, for on almost every visit to Eliza's home we had a total disagreement about something or other, and her bed performance was as cold as the first night of our marriage.

"Well, and so it was on this trip to Brimfield. I left for Boston after ten days of squabbles. My belly was full. I left gladly, for I was invited to address the legislative body in Boston, and after they had finished cheering me, they gave me my land grant of 10,000 timber rich acres in the District of Maine. That summer I traveled to Washington City with my bill for the twenty thousand I had personally put into the capture of Derne. I made a presentation to State , Navy, and the Treasury. It was while I was in the Capital that I received a letter from Hamet. He was living in Sicily and was without any means. Yusef had, of course, threatened him again, so Hamet had taken his wives and small children to safe haven. From Nashville and Pittsburgh and all cities between I received invitations to make addresses. I read Hamet's letter to all of them with my demand that we, the great country of America, do the right thing and save this destitute hero of Derne. On these travels I had to go alone because my Eli had married the Secretary of War's daughter. What a party we had at that wedding, it cost the Secretary a pile, I'll say. Eli is now a Lieutenant in the Navy. I was alone. Aletti had begged off this trip. He was a good and faithful servant, so I left him in Boston with a purse of money. Even so, I dressed well, with perfectly tailored clothes and my gold-headed cane. I had my now white hair arranged...I looked like a very distinguished gentleman but just slightly elderly." He stopped and looked for Hans.

"Hans! Hans! " Hans came to the center table and was again addressed, "Hans! I don't want those other waiters; you have become my waiter, and so I called for you. So, please bring me two bottles of Madeira. Quickly.

"I returned to Washington City in the fall, and soon was given my medal. But those same men ratified Lear's unholy treaty! And my $20,000 was in the hands of these same people — not in my purse.

"Then in short order they all...well nearly all but not

Clay...but most of them signed and got me my money, got Hamet his money, and signed a report that made me look better than I had ever dreamed . Now I had climbed to the very top of the mountain. I was The General. I was The Hero of Derne. I WAS THE MAN WHO HAD LIBERATED OVER THREE HUNDRED AMERICAN CREW MEMBERS FROM SLAVERY... "

The General's white maned head hung heavily, then slowly sank to the table, and he fell asleep.

Mr. Vila called for a conveyance, and he and Verna helped the overtired General into the coach. Eaton slumped over in the seat, and so the unknowing Mr. Vila sent his wife along in the coach to the home on Ann Street. Verna thought that unsatisfying performance hardly worth the effort of helping Eaton to his bed. He really needed Aletti who was in a different bed not too far away.

As Beau was leaving he had watched the tucking in of the General by the Vilas and had seen Verna climb into the coach. He mused that might have been a mistake by James Vila...those previous encounters ... Beau had seen. He was on his way to the Sign of the Turk, for he had found a job there of sweeping and cleaning up after the pub had closed for the evening. His pay would be a place to sleep and breakfast. Heavy work was not in his line any more. Old age was creeping up on him just as the General was drawing closer to his end. Beau was thinking that the General's life surely had been a ride up, but, my God, he sure took a big dip down — no, a total fall — a fall into nothingness.

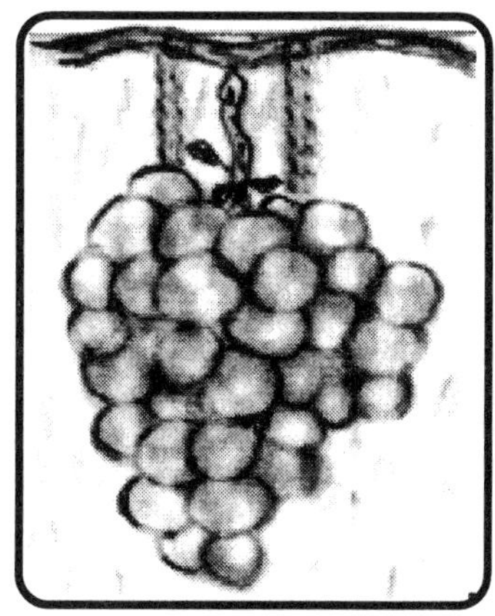

The rains had come down with such fury that the General had delayed his arrival at the Bunch of Grapes. James Vila was entertaining the hangers-on and was about to tell a political joke when the dripping wet and hungry General came into the great room. Beckoning to the proprietor, he was helped to take off his wet cloak.

Vila took his cloak and hung it to dry. Then he and Hans helped the old and forgotten hero of Barbary to his table. Eaton said,

"One of your good Flips, and thanks." Hans came with the flip and said,

"May I bring Herr General his meal? First venison und potatoes and carrots. Ya, und raspberry pie?" After Eaton had been warmed by the drink and food, Hans brought him his usual bottle of Madeira wine. The General greeted some of the nearby listeners and began the night's recitation.

"I had been elected to the Massachusetts General Court as an independent legislator. I was strongly against party affiliation, nor had I sought this seat of honor. I was not a party to the New England Federalist faction which was for running Jefferson out of office and even worse, to dismember the very country that I and many other heroes had fought for. A horrible nightmare was my thought on that. They were counting on Aaron Burr to help them and New York to become a part of the New England newborn country. So, because Burr lost the governorship of New York in 1804 and then because of hot and scandalous words spoken by Alexander Hamilton in Albany (not his territory), Burr called him out. The duel resulted in Hamilton's murder. His son also had been killed a few years before in a duel. Both lost — Hamilton his life and Burr his honor as he started his downward path to being a spy for hire.

"A letter was found that had been given to Anthony Merry, the British consul, which plainly put Burr up for the highest bidder. Then to top things off, the damn fool met and met over and over with General Wilkerson of the Western Army. As was soon evident to most anyone with a tittle of brains, the General was fully in the pay of Spain. No wonder *The Gazette of the United States* headlined: 'How long will it be before we shall hear of Colonel Burr being at the head of a revolution party on the Western Waters?' It was also known by some of us that Burr had joined Wilkerson in taking pay from Spain. They gave him $2,500 to help his cause. In the end, Wilkerson, when he was to start the revolt, got cold feet and sent Jefferson a letter blaming it all on Burr. He said it was a deep, dark and widespread conspiracy and sent a letter he had received from Burr with incriminating evidence, but with all the evidence against himself blacked out. Well, you can see why I was not reluctant to testify against this enemy of my Country. Enough about those traitors — on with my story.

Early that summer I was subpoenaed to a trial for treason of our former Vice President, Aaron Burr. The trip to Richmond took some time. I did stop to visit in the halls of Congress because I was seeking an active commission in the Army, Diplomatic Corps, or any other full time position commensurate with my ability. I was without Eli because he had joined the Navy. Sarah, the youngest daughter of General Danielson and Eliza, nearly twenty and desirous of finding a mate, accompanied me to Richmond.

"I think I was very much the most effective government witness. I told them of the many times Aaron Burr had tried to get me to join him in establishing a new country in the Texas and New Orleans area. And I read into the record the letter penned by Burr which Colonel George Danielson had come by, and I had taken to President Jefferson. That letter indicated Burr was intent on forming his own country in the West. The Chief Justice was the highly praised John Marshall but in this case not too judicial. I was a very effective witness, but the government lawyers were a bunch of incompetents, and Burr won. You must remember that Burr had been Vice President under Jefferson. I had once been to a party given by Jefferson when Burr made a fool of himself over that young widow who, as I remember was, or soon became, engaged to Mr. Madison. He was overt in his flirting - to everyone's embarrassment. I had talked many times with him while I was seeking the Barbary funds from Jefferson. But, damn him, I knew he was guilty as he could be, so I bet large sums of money that they would convict him. But luck was not in the cards for me, I lost and lost. The cost of living in Richmond was all too high, and I thought that a few trips to the gaming table would make me solvent. Lady luck was not with me and my debts grew.

"Sarah was often asked to many of the best balls, and it was soon evident that she had found a mate — the handsome Doctor Asa Lincoln of Taunton, Massachusetts. They got married on the 14th of September 1809.

"The greatest pleasure I had in Richmond was that of bedding a very attractive redhead that I had called Raska Ahmar. And a few others, to tell the truth. The same Inger Van der Mey that I had cavorted with in Barbary. Together in our flowing Arabic robes, we did the local taverns, and then we shared the remainder of the nights under my sheets. God! She was what old men have night-dreams about! She was the same Dutch girl that could cause an erection in the oldest male alive. You must remember that I had bought Raska Ahmar in Tunis and set her free. The Redhead had left for her homeland, but when she arrived she found that you have trouble being reunited with those who have not seen you for many years. None of her family wanted a daily reminder of their past sin in not sending money for her ransom. They had been sent the request for that ransom and had not seen the need to relinquish the small sum, for she was only a young girl. Together we spent the summer eating, drinking, and making our bodies happy with that pleasure of copulating whenever we felt like doing so. The trial came to an end and, on leaving, I furnished Raska Ahmar with a small sum of money I won at cards the last night of playing. I ended up returning to Brimfield in time for the second session of the General Court in Boston that December." Eaton paused and sat back.

"My God, if my frock is dry and if one of you will call a cab, I'll be off to my abode. I am weary of the many pains from my winter's stay in the North Country and from my war wounds." Again the Vilas helped the General into a coach, but when James asked Verna if she would see that the General got home, she said she had a headache and needed her rest.

After the General's commotion in leaving had subsided, those drinkers remaining looked at Beauregard for his usual comment. Beau got up and moved to the table vacated by General Eaton and ordered a mug of ale. After his throat was lubricated, he began his critique of the General's recitation.

"He has given you some of the facts in this case, but this time I must tell the facts as I saw them, for I, too, was in Richmond when Burr won his acquittal. The city was in a great uproar all that summer long. General Eaton was received as the hero of Derne.

"All vied for the chance to buy him a drink or to sup with him. None of the many females he consorted with were of good reputation. Yes, as he said, the Redhead was with him most of the time, but whenever she took leave there was another to take up the frolic. Frolic! Did I use such a mild word, for indeed the General did more than frolic with these trollops. God, yes! For one night at the very inn where I and many others were eating and drinking, the General arrived with the Redhead — both in their barbaric robes. After having more to drink than they should, suddenly they were on the floor, and he was on her. Robes off and the whole assembly watching as they finished. The two of them fully exposed to our eyes. Now that...uh... uh...*frolic* was reported in all the newspapers far and wide. General Eaton was, from then on, not the Hero of Derne but the rake and reprobate of Richmond. They say that he came with a most attractive stepdaughter, but on the return trip she disdained his companionship and left with a Doctor Lincoln.

"Now you see why he comes to this Tavern and no longer is invited to sup at the homes of his former friends with the exception of the mighty Adams family."

The patrons, with James Vila's tenor leading, all took to singing a rollicking song that had just found its way to Boston from the British Isles.

"Sing the song the maidens sing
Sing the song the maidens sing
in the Spring
in the Spring
Dance with the maidens
Dance with the maidens
in the Spring
in the Spring!"

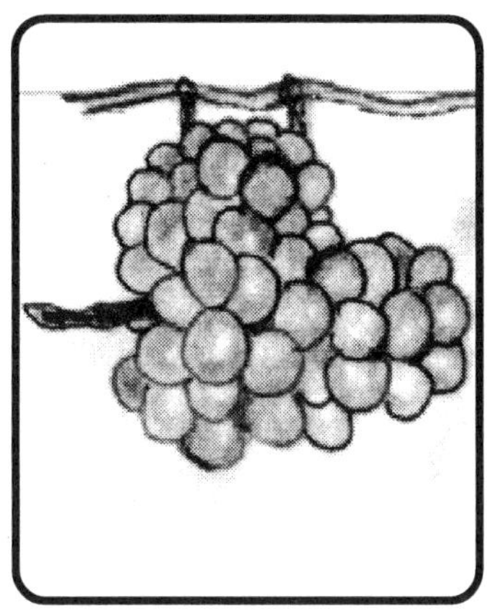

It was nearing the later part of summer 1809. Because the day's heat had carried into the evening, Eaton's vassals had straggled in later than usual. He had come by gig and was being helped into the main room of the Bunch of Grapes by Hans and another waiter. Having seated himself at his reserved table, Eaton ordered two Flips and bantered with the next table. The Flips arrived and he drank one in a hurry, then before starting the second, ordered a meal. Colonel Pat had not yet arrived. Eaton was nearly finished with his eating when the tardy Colonel came to his table.

"General, I'm sorry I'm late. It's this oppressive heat. I don't sleep well at night and end up taking a nap late in the day.

"Pat, this heat? My God man, it's like a cold north blow compared to the blistering heat of the sands at midday on the march to Derne. I find this weather just perfect — well, a lot more to my liking than weather in the Province of Maine. There the mercury froze at the bottom of the glass."

"General, I think it's time you gave us that story, but do it after I have some substance in my stomach." And so the stage was set for this night's tale. Colonel Pat finished, stood, and said,

"Now the General will tell us about his sojourn to the

big north woods which are in the wilderness and the biggest part of our Province of Maine — his royal grant of 10,000 acres of trees." Eaton took over with,

"Enough Pat, I'll do the rest of the tale. So, here is another story! Going to the District of Maine is as strange as going to the coast of Barbary. First, I took passage on a sailboat from Boston to St. John City (N.B.). This was the easy part. Next, I took a sailboat to Fredericton, a military post for the British on the St John River. Then I rode a barge pulled by mules farther up the river. We took to the woods trail at Perth and struck the Aroostook River after some ten miles. We continued walking for about seven or more miles until my surveyor, Charles Turner, said, 'We need a shelter. Let's build it near that brook coming in from the south.' We built it in a hurry near a large flat area which extended to the west. (*On what is now Goughan's Strawberry Farm, Caribou*) The soil was very favorable looking. It was late autumn, and even with the small crew of men, we soon had passable temporary living quarters. For the next thirty or so days we were busy building a substantial log house. Then we divided the work — some went hunting for meat, caribou being plentiful. Others cut wood for our fireplace. Mr. Turner continued his work of marking the boundaries of my land grant. I visited some of the local woods camps and practised my French.

"The heavy snow came before the end of November and never melted as it does here in Boston, and the temperature fell and fell. The mud plastered vent was not too well done, and so smoke filled the rooms frequently. I soon found walking on the river ice was the easiest way to go from one place to another. That was the longest winter and coldest place on earth, I think, that man has ever found. The sun spent very little time warming us due to our northern location. Yet my French timber harvesters never stopped cutting pine trees — the biggest trees I had ever seen. And it was an eyeful to see oxen pull them to the river. There, men with axes cut them square.

"When the sun did shine and the river melted, these squared timbers floated to Saint John City where they were loaded on large ships for the King's navy. When I heard the going price of the finished tree at Saint John City, I wondered if the King of England had found a Midas touch. We got to that port in late spring and saw the harbor full of ships taking on this pine for England. Some of the trees were whole length and not squared. These I thought were for masts.

"I made plans to establish an estate to rival the one our first Secretary of War, Henry Knox, built on a hill on an arm of the Atlantic Ocean. I sent money and men to build a manor house and out-buildings. Eliza could have cared a little about this but was totally uninterested. I assumed that when Eli retired from the Navy he would need a place like my Maine manor — " Pat cut him off with,

"General, now I'd like to have the privilege of addressing these loyal listeners. For I've just heard that the "Eaton" plan in Barbary was tried again by our Navy. They had sought out Hamet and took him to Derne, which they had recaptured. Hamet was then made Governor of Derne. Yet, because they didn't give him enough military supplies and cash it failed. Now Hamet is back in Egypt in permanent exile."

After this news, the tavern fell into many conversations about that turn of events. That story over, the General reverted to the one incident he couldn't forget, for he was aware that his actions in Richmond had sullied his good reputation. He was further depressed over the government's refusal to give him an active role, in military work or any meaningful endeavor. All they offered was the pay of a inactive Brigadier General which he had refused. So, once again he retold of his Richmond trip to an audience who was still enthralled.

"You all must know that I was called to testify against Burr in that infamous trial. Maybe I've said this all before, but it's worth repeating. So bear with me.

"As you may remember, I had sent and given various letters which implied Burr's sedition to President Jefferson. My solution for these unseeming acts by Burr was that the President should send him abroad in some capacity which would keep him out of touch with General Wilkerson. Now, my wife's brother-in-law, old Colonel George Danielson, had received a letter from Aaron Burr. It truly had the seeds of sedition in it. President Jefferson added it to his collection of evidence against Aaron Burr.

"The newspapers had one story after another concerning Burr's purchase of large blocks of land in Louisiana. He admitted that he was going to settle there and had asked army veterans to come join him — to make up an army to invade Spanish possessions. Some said for his own private nation. Rumors flew up and down the country."

A limping, tired General was then helped to the head by Colonel Pat and Hans. Returning and taking a sip of ale, Eaton took up the tale.

"Now, I had in years past dined often with Aaron Burr while I was in Washington City. I found him to have a brilliant mind, and he was a joy to converse with. However, I was sure, by the spring of 1807, that he was a traitor. General Eaton received a summons for the trial in Richmond Virginia.

"That letter which Wilkerson had written to Burr said, 'I'll give you a war with Spain when you give me the signal.' Then when Burr did send the go-ahead signal to Wilkerson, that rat turned the letters over to the government lawyers. He had erased and written over the contents in an effort to point the finger at Burr. There were reasons to believe that Wilkerson was the traitor. I believed the same of Burr.

"The trial in Richmond was a disaster. The city was mad. Rumors of foreign powers which would come to Burr's aid with a military force sped around the city. People of all persuasions filled every lodging and pub and spilled their convictions that another war was about to fall on our shores.

"It is true that Justice Marshall did keep the peace in the court room, but outside, the mood of the populace was for lynching Burr and all his cohorts. I was thankful to have Aletti with me when we arrived in June for it was a hard journey. Yet, it might have been better if he had stayed in Boston because Burr's lawyers made him take the stand in an effort to destroy my testimony. They got him to say that I had enjoyed many mistresses. The Government lawyers left Burr's reputation intact. Yet you and I have heard that he bedded every available woman, single and married, young and old. He had no taste.

"I was invited to eat and drink... Drink! My God, Hans ,where is my Madeira? Yes, to dine with a great number of the local gentry. I had been vindicated by Congress, so I wore my gold medal on my new and stylish clothing. I was admired by the street people and all the fair women who swooned at my presence — I was seduced. For over four months I was without a battle to fight, and so I relaxed and did what most of you would have done. I found me companions for the day and bed partners for the evenings."

"Ya, mine General." Hans put the bottle and two glasses on the table. After taking a drink, Eaton continued,

"Back to the trial. It took some time to pick a jury because the potential men were all sure that Burr was guilty. He was clever in that he said to them, 'I am of the opinion that you all are fair minded men and will weigh the evidence with blind eyes.' Yes, he was brilliant. That won him some converts right then. Burr implied that the government had paid me and the Morgan family to testify against him. This was in no way true.

"Chief Justice Marshall, in his instruction to the jury , said, 'It is not the intention of the court to say that no individual can be guilty of this crime who has not appeared in arms against his country. On the contrary, if war be actually leveed, that is, if a body of men be actually assembled for purpose of effecting, by force, a treasonable object, all those who perform any part, however minute, or however remote from the scene of action, and who are actually leagued in the general conspiracy, are to be considered as traitors.'

"When I heard those words, I was sure Burr would be pronounced guilty, but the jury came back with the fence-straddler — 'not proved to be guilty under this indictment by any evidence submitted to us.' Was I wrong! A very costly summer. On Marshall's words I had bet 5,000 dollars and lost.

"I did make it back to Boston and to the job for which Brimfield citizens had elected me. When I entered the chamber, they were having a debate over whether one by the name of William Eaton was worthy to sit in that august body which had been the home of John Adams, Samuel Adams, and Hamilton. When they finished, I marched to the podium and stated my worth. I reminded them I had received the thunderous cheers of that House and that they had not so long ago done me the honor of a gift of 10,000 acres in the District of Maine. When I, Representative Eaton, left the lectern I had no seat, for I was of no party. The Sergeant-at-Arms found me an empty cubbyhole and brought me a chair. That treatment is beyond the pale, and the next time my name came up for a seat, I wrote to all my friends and said, 'Please vote the opposition.'

"Now, General William Eaton has filled your ears with his last episode. I'm leaving for Brimfield, whence I have sent my faithful Arabian stallion, who will be my close and very good companion for my brief remaining time on this terrestrial ball."

The audience was stunned, for they had not seen that the General's health had deteriorated greatly during his many recitations. Eaton was helped into a coach by Hans and Colonel Pat. Pat, seeing Eaton's struggle, decided to accompany him home in case Aletti was out courting his future wife.

As the coach wheels slowly ground over the cobblestoned street, Eaton, who was overly tired and just a bit overwhelmed by alcohol, began a confession of his life to his dear and close companion Colonel Pat.

"Pat, it seems I was born under a bad sign, starting with my early upbringing in a strict schoolmaster household where you were called out for saying 'pissmire.' God! Father was tough on us and on me. He had me reading and writing from very early on. And I had to memorize long pieces every day. I never knew about the flowers and bees. God, Pat, I was as innocent as a new born baby when Sophie Appleby played with...and then while I was sick and in bed she taught me. Sophie...yes, I was a teenage lover, in love with love all my life. Obsessed. Yes, obsessed, Pat, with my unrequited love for Sophie Appleby. Pat, I've never been able to resist an invitation to bed... no, I sought them. Pat, I even bedded Vilas' wife: not that I wanted to but she kept presenting herself. And, Pat, dearest friend, that Richmond thing! God, I wish that redheaded devil had stayed in Arabia or at least Holland. Damn it, but Pat dear old companion... yes, I was the one who pulled her to the damn floor.

"Now I'm a sick old man, Pat, and I'm going off to my fate to live with my cold, uncaring wife Eliza. We preserve each other — You know I mean deserve. I hope you will come by Brimfield and visit me in my last days. I am in my last days; that is why I sent my stallion off to Brimfield. We're going to be buried together. You'll see to it for me — won't you, Pat...?"

Colonel Pat, after being the father confessor all the way to 16 Ann Street, helped the slobbering General to his bed and left him fully clothed to sleep off his night of overindulging.

Meanwhile, back at the great room, the groit Mr. Beauregard Smart had been quiet for about as long as any man could be with all that knowledge in his head. Beauregard stood on his table and yelled out,

"Gentlemen, Gentlemen, I have not the means to buy you a drink, but if you will remain quiet for a few minutes, I will tell about the Burr trial and about William Eaton's monstrous acts in Richmond.

"I read the papers in Richmond, for I had found employment there. They had all this in their reports. First, when Eaton's servant Aletti took the stand, he blurted out the very names of the trollops that Great General Eaton had consorted with when he was in the service of our glorious country. Secondly, the papers also reported that the Barbary General had wagered large sums of money on the outcome of the trial. Thirdly, he was reported to be intoxicated most of his stay in Richmond. Fourthly, in great detail they all told of the sexual intercourse which Eaton had with one of his old whores. They said she was the very one he freed in Barbary by the name of Henna, a real bright redhead. And lastly, the newspapers said that he carried out this act on the barroom floor." This late in the evening most of the patrons had left, and so did Beauregard.

The Brimfield Inn was close enough to his home for the old and forgotten hero, General William Eaton — if time were not a factor — to struggle there on gouty feet. The diners were few at this early hour. When he entered, the first person he laid eyes on was the local Congregational minister.

"So! We Eatons aren't good enough for your church, Reverend. Well! I've known some of your sanctimonious members, and I could, if I wanted, tell a tale or two about their adventures at the Red String in Boston."

"General, I took the matter to the whole congregation and with much searching for God's will they voted not to allow you and yours membership in our church. I could remind the General that if the newspapers of the day are even remotely correct, than the General must look to his conduct as to the reason my congregation turned down his request."

"Well, thanks for your self-righteous assertion that only the very pure can join. When I was taught the Bible verses, I found that Christ invited all. But I see you Congos have your own cliques so ...." The Reverend Minister said,

"Good Night," and left for a church meeting which would not reconsider a request to have the Eaton family entered on the rolls of the Brimfield Congregational Church.

Eaton took a table in the center of the room, and after he had ordered a small meal with only one glass of wine, began, as was his custom, a soliloquy on his life.

"When I took the stage to Brimfield in July of 1809, it was carrying too many passengers and their mountainous luggage. The four weary horses had a hard time pulling the stagecoach through many spring rain-induced deep mud holes. Sometimes we had to get out and help by pushing. I was bored by the uninteresting company, and my gout was acting up. I was in a state of mental depression. I was, however, guarding my collected copies of letters to and correspondence from people in high places. I had spent the wee hours of many long nights in Boston sorting, organizing my Journal, and writing my *"Life of General Eaton,"* for I was intent on having my heroic deeds known by posterity. After a month of Eliza's plain food and drink here at home, I am quite fit, and have been amazed at Eliza's love makin'. We are making the old Danielson's bed squeak and groan under our nightly cavorting. We did have the essence of some apple blossoms in the room. My overdeveloped sexual appetite, which I have blamed on Sophie Appleby, is now satiated by Eliza.

"During late September, I traveled to Connecticut to visit relatives and friends. I found that my oldest sister had traced the Eatons back to England. My father Nathaniel's father was also Nathaniel. He was the son of Thomas, who was the son of John, whose father was also named John. This I wrote down for my children— Eliza and her husband Eli Goodwin, Charlotte, Almira, Billy and Nathaniel. I did that as soon as I got home. I sent a copy to Woodstock.

"The next week, I went to visit my publisher, E. Merriam and Company, in Brookfield, Massachusetts where I spent several days with an editor named Charles Prentiss. This was my last story, and I was desirous of setting the record straight — but only after my death. I visited my brother Eb (Ebenezer) and his wife Dolly — maybe she is named Polly. Well — they have two boys and a girl and live in Danville, Vermont. I'd been there when I was quite young. Remember the green horse I rode years ago in Bennington?

"Now, I've been told to drink no more spirits , but one ale will wet my vocal cords so that this audience of fellow citizens can hear the rest of my monologue. I find that my creditors have cleaned my purse, so those expecting a free drink can leave now. God! I might have now a fuller pocket if I had not turned down the General's retirement pay Jefferson's party had offered me. That's over and done with. Get on with the tale. Yes. But! That book of mine will make me be remembered as one who knew what glory and honor was due a heroic General— General William H. Eaton.

"My most loyal promoters could not secure for me those positions in which I would have done a great service for my country. Some of them like Military Attaché for France or England, even Prussia. And yes, for State — I'd already proved my ability as a diplomat.

"I had sent letters of entreaty to all those who had helped me in the past, and I really think most every one of them did his best to award me my rightful dues.

"Well, I did make Eliza's house into a pretty respectable home, with the commodious addition I had built onto the east side this summer. I had time to do that and also finish organizing my book. Eli helped me with the writing of my book as did my brother-in-law, Major Amos Paine of Woodstock, Connecticut. My brother Calvin said he might, but it was never convenient for him."

Many local and distant friends who had been on the receiving end of the General's hospitality would long remember the generous entertainment at William and Eliza's home on the major stagecoach route between Boston and Springfield.

The Eaton residence in Brimfield, Massachusetts.

Courtesy Brimfield Public Library

"It was Christmas, and I was with Eliza again. That's when I received the shock of my life. The letter, addressed to General William H. Eaton, Brimfield, Massachusetts, informed me that Eli, my son, was dead from a duel. I got it from Lieutenant Fitz H. Babbit. That night I wrote him a letter in which I said, 'I lament more the absence of his prudence than I should the loss we feel had he fallen in the legitimate field of glory. For you remember the manner of Hamilton's death added nothing to the luster of his fame; and the circumstance of Burr's killing him gave no man the more confidence in Burr's honesty nor patriotism: the catastrophe satisfied no one on the merits of the cause which produced it.'

"I wrote letters and letters of distress and complaint, and many high officials, including President Madison, sent their regrets. The regrets found me sick in heart and in bed. Sick and in my bed, a wonder of wonders happened. Eliza became my most loving nurse."

Just as Eaton paused in his oration, the Frisbees, Ginger

and Percy, arrived at the Brimfield Inn with the Ellinwoods, Tertius and Nancy, and took the table next to the General. They introduced themselves, and since the topic of the day was how the British were taking American sailors off our ships and forcing them to be their cannon fodder in their war against France, Eaton gave the diners his interpretation of the current dilemma.

"Before I left Boston I had a long evening's talk with our Senator Pickering and President Adams. The President and the former Secretary of War are for the Federalist theory. They maintain we don't have enough war materials, men trained for soldiering, nor enough seamen to fight a war with England. And our few warships...well we can't get into a war. Yes, I've seen slaves made of our seamen. I hate it! Yet those are few compared to the number of sailors who would be killed in a small war with the ruler of the seas."

"General, that isn't in line with your past ideas. For I recall you sought to devastate the thieving Barbary pirates." Percy interrupted Eaton's spate of words.

"You're right, young man, but then I did have enough manpower and war material to lick them bloody scoundrels. Yet a few cargoes confiscated and a few seamen forced to man England's war machine, well, that is a small price in the world of commerce. France is also boarding our ships and forcing our men to sail their cruisers. Should we take them both on with our minuscule Navy?"

"I read that we had some of the best naval men in the world, men like Preble, Rodgers, Somers, and Hull. We have read about them and their victories in the papers." Ginger Frisbee stated with some force since she was the only literate person in that party.

"Yes, it's true we have some in our navy that can win a battle but we don't have anywhere near enough warships to scratch the naval might of Great Britain. And really, as it is now, we find that all the ports in our New England are really prospering with the trade. The few losses incurred are totally acceptable."

As his political speech wound down from fatigue, the General left for the welcoming and loving arms now found at home.

After the General had gone, the Ellinwoods and the Frisbees had another round of cider and talked about the mortician's tale circulating around the village. It was said that the General had visited his law friend and then the casket seller. All of Brimfield knew the General was extremely sick and probably would die in a short time.

Tertius put on his best performing voice for the story so that everyone in the room could hear,

"I was at the store, and the two men, one his lawyer, the other the casket maker, were asayin', 'Eaton is leavin' all his worldly goods and chattels to his beloved wife Eliza.'

"And then the lawyer snickered as he continued, 'whom he has always cherished and whose love he has cherished all the long days of their marriage.'

"Then the mortician said, 'The General didn't take to a pine coffin. Hero Eaton said he hated the smell of pine.'

"And then we all snorted as the good mortician continued with, 'Eaton implored me not to place him on his back in the casket since he had found that position resulted in his having terrible nightmares.' "

All four had a good laugh, and then Tertius said in a very sober voice,

"I was at the town office when the General came in and asked the clerk, 'Is there plenty of room in my cemetery plot for me and my black and white stallion?'

"You should have see Sarah Jane's face! I nearly haw-hawed myself. Well, Sary Jane did keep almost a straight face as she said to the General, 'General, you know that there is a cemetery for horses right here in Brimfield. I'd sell you a plot right now. Don't you want your good old

Arabian to be buried amongst his kind just as you would like to be buried next to your wife Eliza?' The General chortled out loud and said in his pompous voice, 'Now Sary, you know how me and Eliza have been for many years. My horse is my truest, longest friend. And I put it in my will that I want the horse shot and buried next to me. That's why I'm asking the question.' "

"I don't believe you men. I think you've made up the whole story," Nancy said. "Now I find that last bit too revolting for my good Christian ears. Let's change the subject." Ginger responded with,

"I'd have that old fool taken to the nut house if he was mine. The housekeeper says that the General calls the damn horse when in his cups, and he mounts him and rides the Arabian up the indoor stairway. You could expect that of some lively young child with his pony. But a grown man? R e a l l y!"

"Well no damn man better try that at my house, boy or man. But did you hear about the goings-on at Mr. Brown's Tavern the other night? I heard that one uv them high strung Foot boys and one uv John Durkee's sons had a real set to."

"Now ladies, that wasn't no fight at all— just the two younguns a testin' their strength," interjected Tertius.

The two men were excused from the table and left to relieve themselves behind the stable in the rear of the inn.

"How are your two older boys doin' in Boston, Ginger?" asked Nancy in the hopes of changing the subject to one more pleasant.

Ginger responded with a thought that she had been mulling over in her mind all evening.

"Nancy, I was wantin' the men to leave so I could tell you what Martha Danielson said to my Sue. Martha is a big girl now, and she says to my Sue that Eliza and the General are hittin' it off like newlyweds. And Eliza up and told her that she had finally realized that although General Eaton would never be a replacement for her saintly first husband, she should show him affection in these last few days of his life. Then Martha says to Sue that Eliza and the General were acting like well... people in love and young ones at that. Ain't that somethin' after all them years of them a fightin' like cats and dogs? Martha said they all could hear 'em in that old bed of Danielson's a bouncin' and squeakin'. Oh! Nancy, here come our life mates, so we can't talk about that anymore. Shh!"

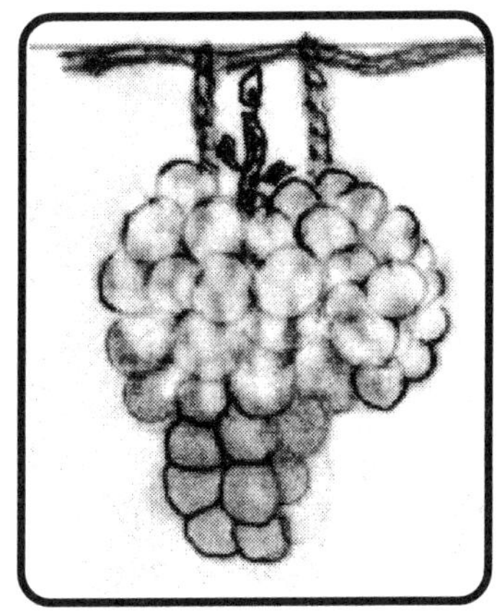

The Bunch of Grapes was quiet. The main attraction had left Boston, but his shadow had not. As the lost and forgotten heroes gathered, they still heard many reports about the deeds of General Eaton conqueror of Derne. The night's discussion was already under way, led by a veteran of that expedition.

"I was on the *Constellation* when our General Eaton left Derne. Lieutenant Wederstrandt took the orders from Captain Campbell to General Eaton. I was a bunk mate of the Lieutenant's, and after we had got underway from the port, he told me that the General had cried, raged and swore that he would tell the world about the meddling of that Consul Lear. Eaton knew their hardships of crossing the desert and capturing the Arabian city had all been in vain. The country that he loved was now ready to pay more ransom for years to come. The shipping trade in that part of the world would still be subject to the Barbary pirates. My God! I remember reading about this in an old history book. Old Christopher Columbus' early experience as a sailor was on an expedition to beat up on them damnable pirates. Now we, all of us recipients of the General's generosity, should remember what it was that drove him to the rash things he done because of his heavy disappointment with our government's continued payment of tribute.

"That drunken and public mounting of the trollop at Aaron Burr's trial was caused by the heavy burden he carries concerning the uselessness of his heroic deeds. Sarah Danielson, his wife's daughter, was in Richmond with him at the Burr trial. I saw her there, and I say she was a mighty good looking twenty-year old. Sarah met Asa Lincoln and much of her time in Richmond was with that young whippersnapper. If I hadn't been married, I think I'd have chased Sarah. Well, that wasn't to be, but I can see why Eaton married Eliza despite her rumored cold and hard ways. Sarah was turning heads all the time she was in Richmond...."

Beauregard was also at the Bunch of Grapes that night and could not keep silent any longer. He stood and forcefully interrupted Lieutenant Thomas Turner of the Marines. He told the hangers-on this unrecorded episode.

"It was when the General was seeking the rightful ruler of Tripoli in the bowels of Egypt. Just the other night when I was at the sign of the Turk, I met Paul de Chamillard, Captain of Marines. He told me this:

" 'I had been assigned by the Navy to watch over this maverick of a man, Eaton. I was told not to interfere nor do anything but watch and report his actions to Captain Hull of the *Argus*. So I was watching Eaton when he recruited those two murderers, Juse and Bubaa El Kady, in Alexandria. They were on the run from the law, for they had murdered their master, a Turk of high bearing, and run off with his two best horses. Eaton promised them protection and a chance to plunder Derne. Now these two cut-throats were a part of the close personal guard that Eaton surrounded himself with.' I heard from the General some many nights ago about the heads he severed with his scimitar. Believe it or not, those heads were the very ones he sliced — the two that he had brought closest into his inner family, but they had become greedy and sought to lead an uprising against the Christians so that they would have more loot at the city of Derne.

"This is my last night in Boston. I have Smart relatives in Springfield, and I plan on visiting them and finding employment there."

The evening coach came into Brimfield and stopped at the Inn. The worn and famished passengers all went quickly to the dining area. Beauregard Smart had to share a table already occupied by three men of various stations. When the meal had been placed on the table, the best dressed man started out with,

"Today, June 4,1811, the village of Brimfield buried one of its most unusual citizens, Lieutenant General William Eaton. He died June first, and we had Colonels Sessions, Morgan, Lyon, and Patrick for his pallbearers. The Good Reverend Doctor Welch of Mansfield came over to Brimfield to lead us in the honors for this man. If you look to that table over next to the window , you'll see all four of them still in their uniforms."

"I've met Colonel Patrick, and I've known General Eaton in Boston. He came to the Bunch of Grapes Tavern at the head of the Long Wharf— the same one that was a meeting place for the Sons of Liberty." Beau had taken advantage of a break as the storyteller stopped to sip his ale. But then lost it to another stranger's interruption.

"I'll explain why they had to have the Reverend Doctor from out of town. First, the local Congregational minister had snubbed Eaton, and the family would not have had him even if he had been willin'. That Congo crowd is very self-righteous. I'm a farmer, and I left that church to join the Methodist Episcopal, and we ain't athinkin' you're pure of sin as long as you join. We say we are on the way to perfection, and we mean that ...despite our human failin's we can be forgiven and get on the straight path, the one that leads to heaven ...."

The best educated man at the table interrupted the Methodist layman and started a sermon on the Goodness of God. He had attended the Harvard University School of Religion and was a confirmed Unitarian. Smart was not able to find a space in time to present his story, and so he took leave of the erudite discourse.

William Eaton's headstone reads: "This is erected as a faint expression of filial respect and to mark the spot where repose the remains of Gen. Wm. Eaton who died June 1, 1811. Æ 47."
The dapple-gray Arabian stallion was not buried with Eaton but was interred in the famous Brimfield horse cemetery.

Courtesy Brimfield Public Library

It was a late June night at the Bunch of Grapes. A small number of patrons had gathered around a dark-colored man in his late twenties. He had a southern accent and was reading aloud from a newspaper. Some of the patrons were ignoring him, but a few, probably those who couldn't read, were attentive.

"Now Ah've heerd tha Gen'l, he was here most every night. Ah woulda ben if Ah'd aben in town, but Ah was on a naval ship what run away as fast as she could from a big British Man o' War. It fo' sho' was big. So now Ah'll jest read this here about our big Gen'l Eaton. Yeah, Ah was with him when we captured the city o' Derne. Yeah, Ah was there 'cause you see Ah was ahelpin' O'Bannon with his geah off tha ship *Argus*. When Ah was ashoah, the ship lef, and O'Bannon had ta keep me. But most a the time Ah'se he'pin' them men in Eaton's army who was bringin' the supplies. Yeah, now the Marines learnt me how ta read after I'se left mah old home way down in Gawgia. I'm never goin' back there ag'in 'cause some— well Ah'd be a pickin' cotton fo sho'. Now Ah'se better read this here notice 'bout tha Gen'l's passin'."

"Who are you?" asked one of the nearest men.

"Ah'm called Private X 'cause that how Ah first signed mah name. Now Ah sign it Private Axe Marine 'cause y'all see Ah can write now. Now ya need ta hear this, so Ah' ll read it loud-like so y'all can heah 'bout our hero Gen'l Eaton..."

The nearest man had had enough southern talk. He had attended Harvard, so to stop the atrocious English of Private Axe he said,

"My dear fellow, if I may, I think I can read that newspaper article so that these listeners will completely understand the words." And he reached and took the paper from Private Axe Marine's hand and started to read.

"June the 5th day in this newspaper called *The Boston Gazette*, General William Eaton passed on..."

Interviews after Eaton's Death

The questioners are insensitive reporters from local newspapers.

Aaron Burr in New York City

Question: "Mr. Burr, you had a brief encounter with General Eaton before he led his army across the North African desert, and then he testified at your sedition trial in Richmond. Tell me, do you think this man was as great a leader as the papers portrayed him before your trial?"

Burr: "I rather thought General Eaton had pulled off one of the greatest tactical maneuvers — one which should place him in the company of a great many military leaders. Later, I found him to be easily led astray. You, of course, know about his dressing up as an Arab while his so-called friends had some whore from a house of ill repute in like attire at the tavern — and in public he mounted her — to the cheers of the onlooking scum. He was drunk when he testified against me, and his gaming was the talk of the court. He was a first class rake, having all types of female company, mostly trollops, and when he left Richmond that autumn of 1807, he had no reputation left."

Question: "How was he on the witness stand?"

Burr: "My lawyers took him apart. They brought up his court-martial. Most of the country had not been aware of this blemish on the hero of Derna. We also cited his unhappy relationship with his wife and proved that he had taken many mistresses throughout his life. We had his manservant Aletti on the stand also. What a day for the newspapers — made a fortune. The whole country snickered. And I won."

"Thank you, Mr. Burr."

President Jefferson at Monticello

Question: "Thank you, President Jefferson, for taking some of your valuable time to sit with me, and thank you also for the serving of this most unusual frozen cream. You said 'ice cream', didn't you?"

Jefferson: "Yes, and I predict that we Americans will make it one of our favorite desserts, just like apple pie. Just as firmly I also predict that human bondage will be removed from this Great Nation. What a stain on our morals."

Question: "I agree with your slavery views. Mr. President, you and General Eaton had several meetings alone. I wonder if you would care to tell the American people what you talked about?"

Jefferson: "We talked, of course, about many things not in the public domain, but let me tell you about one on which we agreed wholeheartedly — slavery. It was when he came asking for guns, Marines, and gold that one of my black butlers dropped Eaton's cloak on the muddied floor. Washington City was a quagmire then and still is in the spring and fall. I may have said more to the good man than I should have. After all I did have red hair then. When the meal was over and Eaton could see that I was no longer in a pet, he told me about seeing American sailors and others, white and otherwise, being used as slaves by the Barbary pirates and how it made him wish that the civilized world would recognize the evils of slavery. He said bondage was abhorrent to him, and that if most good men could see it in North Africa, they would never own slaves. I certainly agreed and said that it was the one point I was forced to remove from the Constitution which, if I could, I would put back into the document. We both said we thought that in time man would see the evilness of slavery and change his ways."

Question: "Did this slave discussion help you in your decision to give General Eaton the means to defeat the Barbary pirates?"

Jefferson: " Yes and no. I had already made up my mind before I invited Eaton to dinner. The yes was that I gave him just a little more encouragement than I had intended."

Question: "You know that Eaton later asked the government for money that he claimed he spent out of his own pockets?"

Jefferson: "Yes ,I do , and I'm pleased that Congress approved his old bills and that I signed the enabling act."

"Thank you for this delightful time, and I surely would appreciate the recipe for that frozen cream!

The Reverend Mr. Fay, the Congregational Minister in the town of Brimfield, was the next to be interviewed by a local news publisher.

Question: "May I ask the length of your acquaintance with the General?"

Rev. Fay: "I have met and conversed with Mr. Eaton over a period of nearly twenty years. His long absences from Brimfield, of course, should be taken into account."

Question: "Could you give me your truthful judgement of the man?"

Rev. Fay: "Yes, I will do that, for I am sure you must have discovered that I refused to baptize him and his family. I did this after I had met with my deacons, and we had prayerful discussion on the General's request. There was unanimous agreement that this man was not, nor his family, fit for the rolls of our Lord's Church. He had once been a confirmed Congregationalist but had become a drunk, an adulterer, and had not received communion for years on end. We were firm, and I wrote the General a letter putting our refusal in the proper light.

"I know this man was generous to a fault. He gave away things that might better have been sold to feed and clothe his children. He was a wastrel, and his property was at the threat of being sold by the bailiff. Yet he was a man whom God had endowed with knowledge and leadership ability. But this General Eaton was not one to bow down and ask for his sins to be forgiven. No. He was proud and very headstrong. So the letter I wrote him was God's way of telling him that he needed to ask to be forgiven and then to accept the Lord's forgiveness."

Question: "Did Eaton ever give any sign that he would change his mode of living and seek the love of his Lord?"

Rev. Fay: "As far as I know, Mr. Eaton continued his drunkenness and never asked for the washing away of his multitude of sins by the Saving Grace of the Lord Jesus Christ."

"Thank you, Reverend, for your frank appraisal of General Eaton."

The Barbary General

by H.C. (Mike) Lamoreau

Hark ye, look now——
Nine score years and know ,
To the days of Washington, Jefferson,
Adams, Hamilton and Monroe.

Lived then a man named William. Eaton,
Patriot and soldier of the Revolution,
Dartmouth College, Honors , class of '90
Tried Vermont politics — not a solution,

Joined he then the Army regulars
Known to them as the American Legion.
Commissioned a Captain of Infantry,
And training officer of the Bennington region.

Eccentric, Brilliant, and opportunistic
Courted friendships in high -places,
Excellent horseman and rifle marksman,
Truly a man of many faces.

Transferred west to the Ohio Valley
Learned the tongue and many ways
of the ferocious Indian tribe Miami,
Scouted and lived among them thirty days.

Eaton's next assignment was in Georgia,
Met the Creek tribe at the border
Spoke their tongue and counseled wisely,
Prevented war and maintained order.

Studied Islam and Eastern religions,
Speculated on western land expansion

Quit the Army to protest slow promotion
Visited Adams at his presidential mansion.

Espionage assignments were successful,
And debts of gratitude were owed him,
Thus he gained his life long ambition
Named the U.S. Counselor Agent to Tunis.

Muslim nations—Morocco, Tunis, Tripoli, and Algeria,
The Barbary Coast was a pirates lair
Blackmailing nations, stealing cargo,
"Send your ships here , if you dare."

Eaton revolted at paying tribute or ransom
To the Deys as a contribution.
Advised we should take a course of action
That would result in retribution.

Obtained a vague and suspect authorization
To replace one Dey with his brother
Raised an army of many tongues and orders
Kept them separate , one from the other.

Now he's known as General Eaton,
Commission thus by Allah or some other God,
Marched he this motley crew or army
Using his scimitar to rule and prod.

Over six hundred miles of Libyan desert
From Alexandria to Derne, deposed shore,
Traveled Eaton as an Arabian chieftain
Captured Derne, deposed the Dey, and asked for more.

Eaton planned on further conquests
But the Navy had other plans.

They had agreed to further ransom,
And Dey Yusef had the upper hand.

Eaton was ordered back to his beloved country ,
To a hero's welcome and presidential acclaim
But Eaton chafed at the official actions
Of paying tribute to those he held in such disdain.

He gained some measure of revenge
When his actions were officially supported
And his feat of the incredible saga,
Was soon made public and widely reported.

Fame is fleeting and soon forgotten,
And rum did blur fact and fiction.
High positions were not forth coming,
And he did retreat into his addiction.

A land grant in Maine of many acres
Had been given him by a grateful nation.
Eaton built a cabin by the river,
But found the wilderness below his station.

Bitter in mind and sore in body
He returned to his Brimfield home,
Wrote his will and suffered badly,
Died and buried swiftly in an unmarked tomb.

So ends the life of William H. Eaton.
A great man in the early history of our nation,
Seldom mentioned by studies of that era
A sorry comment on early public relations.

Mike Lamoreau was a classmate of mine at Mapleton High and a friend for life. He lives now in Hudson, Maine.

Grace Notes

Boom - Boom - Boom - Booooom - The English cannons roared in answer to the German 88's. Thus the Morse code . . . V for victory was playing out on the Barbary desert as Montgomery was driving the Rommel forces west — west over the very terrain that both these Generals fully understood from studying the tactics of America's Barbary General, William Eaton. Both modern Generals were well aware of the Beethoven score with its heroic implication. It resonated out from the B.B.C. in London to the waiting world. In the Battle of Dernah in World War II, both sides used Eaton's journal to find water and valleys.

Eliza (Sikes) Danielson already had a houseful when Eaton came courting. She had five children by her deceased first husband, General Timothy Danielson — Sarah, b. Aug. 17,1786; Timothy, b.1787, d. in Army Dec. 21, 1812; Martha, b. Dec. 24,1788; Eli, b.1789, d. Brooklyn, N.Y., Aug. 5, 1808; Sarah, b.1790, m. Sept. 4,1809 Dr. Asa Lincoln Jr., b. Taunton, Mass., June 1782, she d. Aug.10,1830. Eliza's children by William Eaton added to the number with Eliza, 1795; Charlotte, 1797; Almira, 1799; William, 1804, and Nathaniel, 1807. The widow, Eliza Danielson Eaton, buried two Brigadier Generals and a son, Eli. In 1828 she buried their son William, a graduate of West Point. He served on the frontier of Iowa in the 6th U.S.Infantry. The penciled-in name (in the records) was for their son Lieut. Nathaniel Johnson Eaton, who was born June 28, 1807.

Derne Street near the capital in Boston was named in honor of General Eaton. The poem "Derne" was written by Charles Greenleaf Whittier after the General's victory.

Some books use these titles for the Barbary pirates — Dey of Algiers, Bey of Tunis, and Bashaw of Tripoli. I chose to give them all the title of Dey because there is little difference in meaning in our present-day dictionaries.

It was not until Charles X of France sent a naval task force against Algiers in 1830 that the Barbary pirates came under a measure of reasonable control!

Aletti became a butler for the widow of Eli Danielson in Boston, and Aletti's son became a professor of Latin at Harvard College.

History records the names of the eight Marines who accompanied General Eaton to Derne as: Corporal Arthur Campbell, Private Bernard O'Brien, Private James Owens, Private John Wilton (killed in action), Private Edward Stewart (died of wounds), and Private David Thomas (wounded in action), plus the unknown Marine (X) — all commanded by Lieutenant Presley O'Bannon. Afterwards, Lt. O'Bannon went off to Kentucky and became such a distinguished citizen that the U.S. Navy named a warship after him. The *U.S.S. O'Bannon* had a very active role in W.W. II. She took on the biggest and best of the Japanese fleet and remained unscratched. A monument to his honor was erected in Frankfort, Kentucky. In April,1992 the Governor of Alabama, Guy Hunt, signed a proclamation honoring the ship and the man.

To Jacques Offenbach's music, an unknown Marine (another Pvt. X?) wrote the words to *The Marine Hymn* "From the halls of Montezuma to the shores of Tripoli...."

BIBLIOGRAPHY

Boston Directory - 1789. At the Maine Historical Society, Portland, Me.

Eaton Family Records and Eaton-Hayden Genealogy, Woodstock, Conn. at the Woodstock Library.

Edwards, Samuel, *Barbary General - The Life of William H. Eaton,* Englewood Cliffs, N.J., Prentice-Hall, Inc., 1968.

Fieldhouse , D.K., *The Colonial Empires from the Eighteen Century,* Delacourte Press, New York, 1965.

Fisher, David Hackett, *Paul Revere's Ride,* Oxford University Press, New York, 1994.

Fleming, Thomas, *The Man from Monticello -An Intimate Life of Thomas Jefferson,* William Morrow and Company Inc., New York, 1969.

Forbes, Esther, *Paul Revere - The World He Lived In,* Boston, Ma., Houghton Mifflin Company, 1942.

Hardison, Grover M., *The Romance of the Eaton Grant,* Caribou Library, Caribou, Me.

Minnigerode, Meade, *Lives and Times - Four Informal Americans,* G.P. Putnam & Son's, New York, 1925.

Powell, Alexander E., *Gentlemen Rovers,* Charles Scribner's Sons, New York, 1913.

Prentiss, Charles, *Comp. Life of the Late General William Eaton, Principally Collected from His Correspondence and Other Manu-*

scripts, E. Merriam and Company, Brookfield, Mass., 1813.

Sparks, Jared, *The Library of American Biography,* Harper & Brothers, New York, 1837.

Whipple A.B.C., *To the Shores of Tripoli,* William Morrow and Company, New York, 1991.

Vidal, Gore, *Burr*, Random House, New York N.Y., 1973.